# Restitution

# Restitution

*Maureen Duffy*

FOURTH ESTATE · *London*

First published in Great Britain in 1998 by
Fourth Estate Limited
6 Salem Road
London W2 4BU

Copyright © 1998 Maureen Duffy

1 3 5 7 9 10 8 6 4 2

A catalogue record of this book is available from the
British Library

ISBN 1-85702-466-4

Typeset by Rowland Phototypesetting Ltd.,
Bury St Edmunds, Suffolk
Printed in Great Britain by
Clays Ltd, St Ives plc

*For Brie Burkeman with my thanks and love*

Lead us from hence where we may leisurely
Each one demand and answer to his part
Perform'd in this wide gap of time since first
We were dissever'd. Hastily lead away.

*The Winter's Tale*

# Part I

I

Chill spring, still unsprung as if the year couldn't get going: the tumblers of warm rain and light that should fall and unlock the gate for the girl with her basket of buds and leaves to come strewing, had rusted fast in the raw dark air. Late March and snowdrops wintered the hedge bottoms whose unclothed stems were still a bristly wickerwork against the grey road beyond. Betony, staring down from the long window of the bedroom that was hers in her grandmother's house, knew, though she couldn't make out this far away, how each frilled and frozen teardrop trembled on its grey-green stalk.

The girl with the basket had hung over the dining-room mantelpiece in sepia engraving all Betony's life, colourless yet still somehow flushed with promise. She herself had never felt like that, especially at thirteen, the age she'd decided the spring girl must be. Later at the art school, she'd identified the figure of her adolescence as Botticelli's *Primavera*. Now she turned away from the window to finish putting her few things in the overnight bag before going down to lunch so that she could make a quick getaway after, ahead of the rest of the London-bound Sunday traffic, and caught an echoing glimpse in the long cheval mirror of the detritus of her childhood, of every settled childhood, a commonplace collage of scuffed toys, fisted books that she'd once, when she was seventeen, thought of clearing out but been unable to let go. She was old enough now to know they would enjoy their reprieve at least as long as her grandmother was alive.

3

'Bet darling, lunch!' her grandmother's voice scaled up the staircase with its basket banister to ease a hooped skirt. Betony drew the zip abruptly across the canvas bag with a sound of tearing sheets. At art school, when her fellow students asked her in fresher week, she'd said her name was Tony, trying to escape her namesake grandmother who was now Gran Bet but had once been, when the century was in its twenties and she in her late teens, Betty of the bob and chiffon scarf, single-strap shoes and waistless georgette shifts, who danced the night away at the Swalecliffe while her vicar father waited up, fob watch heavy in his plump hand. After her marriage to John Falk she signed herself formally *Betony Falk* in a bold and beautiful hand that was still as firm.

'Must you go tonight? I so hate you being on the road in all this traffic.' She had been born into a world of horse carriages as yet only interspersed with snorting combustion engines. The Great War had changed all that.

'I've got a job tomorrow with an early start. And then I hope my answering machine will be full of messages from the ad I put in this week, with amazing people who want to share the flat with me.'

'It's definitely over with Mark then? He isn't coming back? Could you pass me the pepper-mill, darling.'

'Yep. I'm afraid so.' Betony prepared herself for her grandmother's sigh and to be calm and patient where once she would have been coldly cutting, or earlier raged and then cried guilty tears.

'He sounded such an interesting chap. Oh dear, it's so different now. We didn't live together until we were married.'

But there was still adultery and separation, bastardy, wife-beating, drunkenness and almost unendurable misery, loneliness that had to be papered over to pretend it didn't exist, except among the very rich where it was titillating or the very poor where it was disgusting, Betony wanted to say and would have once. Instead she picked up the wooden pepper-mill, with its

4

brown patina from so many passing hands, and said, 'It's all right, Gran. It had come to the end.'

'I don't like the idea of your sharing with a stranger.'

'Everyone's a stranger at first. Except you.' She forked up a crusted orange roast potato and some flaccidly pink cauliflower, prodding them onto a piece of the cardboard quiche her grandmother conceded to Betony's vegetarianism, overdone to a turn above her own withered breast of chicken.

'No grandchildren for me yet then?'

'Not yet, Gran.'

Sometimes, in her worst moments, she wondered whether it was love or just duty that brought her here every month or oftener, when flu or arthritis took her grandmother down into fear and self-pity. Or compassion, that queasy compound of them both. 'You're all I've got,' she would hear then: the flattering, shackling cry the old and alone impose on us until it's our turn to cry out in pain. And sometimes she saw herself in the next stage, trailing up the drive of some detached villa on the outskirts of London, leafily discreet, with its chirpy nurses and grasping matron.

'One day this house will be yours. You'll have to decide what to do with it. I can't.' They had reached the apple crumble's glutinous sweetness.

Glebe House was Regency in smouldering brick. Her grandfather had bought it early in the Second World War. Gran Bet had come there with her own baby, Harry, Betony's father. Family portraits of the Falk family stared down proprietorially from walls they had never known. When she was nine Betony had longed for them to step out of the heavy gilt frames as they did in the favourite storybooks on her bedroom bookshelves and whisk her away into other lives. That was before her father died.

'Gran,' she had once asked in her phase of fiercest feminism at sixteen, 'why do you have all your husband's family on the walls and not yours?'

'They weren't very interesting, darling, the Thorpes, except

5

that they probably came over with the Vikings. By the time anyone thought of a picture of my ancestors the camera had been invented, or at least the daguerreotype.' There was one of these on the stairs: an all-black profile of her grandmother's grandfather as a boy before he went on to become professor of English at a London college and publish the delicate Thorpe reprints on tissue-thin paper in gold-tooled bindings. The name Thorpe Gran Bet had told her, just meant someone who lived in a hamlet. Or on an outlying dairy farm and no doubt drank a potent fermented milk. Whereas the Falks went back to Domesday. The first Falco had come over with William of Normandy, with the Duke's tercel digging its cruel claws into his gauntlet, to be let fly at the Saxon hawks, tear out their plumage and bloody their breasts. For this he was given a chunk of Kent to pacify. His son, Hugh de Falco, followed Coeur de Lion in his crusade of rape and pillage. Betony had admired Hugh at first but later, when she was doing the Plantagenets for 'A' level, she had been seduced by the elegant Saladin in his silken turban, urbane among his fountain courts and silver basins of rosewater where velvet petal skiffs swam. Hugh now seemed merely an upper-class thug stinking of sweat, his own and his charger's, and of his rank leather breeches sodden with piss from days in the saddle. She felt sorry for his wife Matilda, who had brought him Havering-athe-Bower and parts of Surrey, so when he came back after Saladin had brokered a truce, leaving their only son dead on the battlefield of Azotus, he boasted that he could ride from the sea to the king's court at Westminster without quitting his own domain. He had been succeeded by his grandson as she would one day succeed Gran Bet.

'But what about our own name?' she had asked another time. 'Betony?'

'Yes. What does it mean? Where does it come from?'

'It's a plant, a very old plant. *Stachys* something, depending on the kind. It was used for medicine and dyeing. My father liked it. He was interested in old herbals. I expect if he'd had more children he'd have worked through the whole of Culpeper.'

'Cooper?'

'Spelt Culpeper. You know, like the shop.'

There was one in their nearest city, close to the beached whale of the cathedral, beside the National Trust shop. It sold clove-spiked oranges, pomanders sovereign against plague and car-farts, packets of spiced pot-pourri, aromatic soaps and herb pillows that might have been concocted in a Tudor still-room or that a crusader might have brought back from Saladin's garden palace.

'My father thought we might be related to the Culpepers.' He had been vicar of a poor parish in Cambridge which had helped Gran Bet to her place at the university.

There were no pictures of the first Falco or indeed of Hugh but once when she was even younger, about seven she thought, her father had taken Betony on a train to the village that had once been the family seat, though the house itself had a habit of burning down and finally wasn't rebuilt, and shown her the elongated stiff figures, reclining in stone mail with their swords and lions, of those early Falks. Three years later he was dead and now that too was twenty years ago. Sometimes she thought that she didn't remember him at all but only reinvented him each time she thought of her father. Yet she saw him in dreams and so knew that his image was still there imprinted on her memory. Somehow she had just lost the switch she had to press to call him up. She thought she remembered those stone Falks too but perhaps they were figures she had seen later when stopping off at some other country church.

The Falks had picked the wrong side in the time of Edward II, leading the revolt against the king's favourite, Piers Gaveston, and being compelled to surrender their lands but had bounced back in subsequent reigns, wisely becoming gentlemen of the bed chamber to three Tudor monarchs and following their masters into Protestantism and the wool trade. These Falks, Betony thought she remembered, had elaborate tombs of lacy stone fretwork with a frieze of dead children below and their wives beside. It was with the great Virgin Elizabeth that the real portraits began. By this time they were rich enough for Ralph Falk to lend the queen money and name his eldest son after her father. The baronetcy and knighthood flowed inevitably. Sir Ralph celebrated with a commission to the sergeant painter. Sober in black stuff gown under the kind of black cap judges used to put on to pronounce sentence of death, Ralph sat in his dark oak chair with modest fluted ruffs at neck and wrists. Only his gold buttons glinted with his riches. Beside him hung his wife Rebecca, allowed gold-embroidered sleeves to her black gown and gold chain round her spread stomach, dangling her keys of office, with a bunch of cherries ripe in one boneless hand.

It wasn't these two that Betony had hoped might step out of their frames when she was a child. She knew they would have been prescriptive, forbidding her to run or climb trees. She had to wait another hundred years for the red velvet boy at the harpsichord who turned towards her, resting his hand on the ivory jacks in order to smile directly into her eyes. She knew he would have been happy to run out into the garden and be taken to all her favourite hiding places. That boy had come to no good in spite of his velvet coat or perhaps because of it. His grandfather had disapproved of the king's assumed right divine to govern wrong, said so in Parliament, was sent to the Tower and when released, forced to accompany Lord Chelmsford into Germany at his own charge. It had begun a downward spiral in the family fortunes.

The velvet boy had gone up to Cambridge and become a vicar about whom there were dubious whisperings. The family had previously been awarded five thousand pounds in compensation by the Commonwealth Parliament for their sufferings but that was soon swallowed up. When the Stuart king returned, though they were still baronets there were no more knighthoods or royal jobs. Their earlier aptitude for managing their lands, sheep and trading seemed to have deserted them too. By the end of the eighteenth century the then impecunious baronet was given a benefit concert by his friends to raise money by subscription for the support of himself and his family.

Not of course that they were really poor as Gran Bet pointed out. Compared with the poor thronging the London alleyways, that is. They still managed to get one son to Oxford or Cambridge in each generation, followed by a useful living in some country parsonage, though several of these in Burke's *Extinct Baronetcies* 'died. unm.'. The other sons had enough money scraped up for them to buy a commission in the army or navy, while suitable not too demeaning marriages were usually found for the girls. When Betony first read Jane Austen for exams she was easily able to slot the novels into their proper and familiar historical place.

Their time had provided another portrait she wished might come to life: a self-portrait by a girl in her teens.

'It's so good, Gran. She could have become a real artist.'

'Not in those days; not and stay respectable.'

Instead she had lived out her life in her brother's parsonage, drawing charming family pictures of his successive, excessive children and taking over their upbringing when his exhausted wife died in her late thirties.

'And that one? Betony had asked of a stocky figure, displaying the last kneebreeches and hose in the collection.

'That's German Herman, a distant cousin who came to be the final steward before the family lost the estate. You're lucky to be named after me. You could have been called Adelbrit like Henry's mother, after Herman's wife.'

The next fashion move had been into pantaloons and for the girls pantalettes below their skirts: showing their knickers Betony had secretly called it. A gaggle, or was it a giggle, of girls and little boys were sketched into someone's commonplace book, busy at their toys and pastimes while rain occluded the windows with its delicate hatching from the pen of another lost female artist.

Only in Betony's imagination, her longing, had the children in the pictures ever stepped down and now they never would. She was too old. She had never told anyone about this fantasy, fancy. Gran Bet would have prescribed fresh air, a ride or a game of tennis. Her father, when she remembered him or tried to, in spite of their expedition into the past to the family home, had been a quiet reserved man with nothing exotic, or outlandish as the family would have thought imaginary friends, about him. Betony supposed such ideas must be part of her mother's genetic bequest but she had died within days of Betony being born, leaving a silence, an emptiness even more profound than her father's later absence.

Betony got up from the table. 'I must go Gran or it'll take me twice as long. I'll just wash up.'

'No, leave it, darling. It'll pass the time, give me something to do when you've gone. You'll ring me.'

'Of course.'

She backed the little Volkswagen out of the garage, wound down the window to wave to the thin figure stooped under its dowager's hump waving back from the steps, and let in the clutch, still waving herself as she went down the drive and onto the tarmacked lane that led up to the motorway. Betony pushed the button on *Hits of the Sixties* and eased into the London-bound traffic, singing aloud as she kept her place in the three lanes that moved in parallel like beads on an abacus, to hold off the pain and loneliness she knew were waiting in her empty flat.

She had bought it with the money left by her father and held in trust until she was twenty-one. Now its value had dropped by a quarter but at least it was all hers. Her father's bequest had been enough to buy it outright but she still needed someone to share the expenses. While Mark was there he had chipped in. It had been three months before she accepted that he wasn't coming back and forced herself to advertise. Filtering left over the river Betony drove across the dark common fringed with swan-neck sodium lamps and into the grid of late nineteenth-century development that lay around it. When she came back on a summer evening, birds chortled from the weeping pears and private hedges of the patchwork gardens and when she opened the hall door she stepped into a wash of reflected colours puddling the tiled floor from the fan-light behind her and slopping over her sandalled feet with an illusion of warmth.

Now as she backed into the kerb, she saw she had forgotten to leave a light on. An already grey day had darkened early. The house looked deserted, forlorn. The psychiatrist who had the downstairs flat with every window barred against intruders must be weekending in her North Essex cottage. Betony opened the front door, feeling for the light switch before she closed it behind her. While Mark was there she hadn't worried about coming home to a dark house. Not that he was always in when she got back from Gran Bet's but the knowledge that he would be returning, his things, his presence about the flat, was like a nightlight fending off shadows.

If she had even had a cat, a curled breathing body that would wake to wind itself about her legs with a couple of dried-up saucers of half-eaten food in the kitchen, it would have been some comfort, but Betony had always felt that living on the first floor and so often away made her an unsuitable pet owner. Perhaps she should try keeping a bird or fish that wouldn't mind being left and didn't expect to go out.

She had met Mark first at the art school where he had taught photography. Nothing had happened then. 'You were a student,' he teased her later, 'loco parentis and all that, abuse of a dominant position, or at least a position of trust.'

'Not everyone feels like that. Bowser was always having it off with his students.'

'Comes into the staff common-room with his assessment of the new talent at the beginning of every year. He's so up front about it no one really believes he does anything.'

'You never even noticed me.'

'Well, I bet he did. Cradle snatcher.'

They had met again in the queue for the Cézannes at the Tate. 'Mr Aird?' Betony had recognised his back. She had seen at once that he didn't remember her. 'You used to teach me at Haverhall.'

'I hope I taught you something useful.'

'I use it all the time for all sorts of projects.'

'Projects?' His tone was satirical as it always had been. A way of keeping his students at arm's length.

'Jobs, shoots, for designs. Anyway, I wanted to say thank you just in case people don't. You're going to the Cézannes?' She was stumbling now, wishing she hadn't spoken to him, had kept her place silently behind him in the knowledge that if he did turn round he wouldn't recognise her. As he hadn't.

'I'm in this queue so I must be.' He was teasing again. 'Are you interested in his pictures or just part of the fashionable throng?'

'I don't really know them, apart from the ones they always put on postcards. So I thought I'd see for myself.'

They had cruised the exhibition, Betony forced to stand on tiptoe to see over heads and shoulders. 'Why don't you shove your way to the front like everyone else?' He wasn't tall himself. About five feet ten, Betony judged. But he was tall enough to see easily and pronounce Cézanne a painter's painter. Betony's bobbing and craning seemed to irritate him. He moved ahead of her, coming to swift judgements about each picture that left her straggling behind or hurrying to catch up and missing something she might have lingered over.

Afterwards, though, he'd asked her if she'd fancy a pizza and they'd strolled to Victoria where he knew a good little Italian place. Then he'd asked her if she liked music. What sort of music? Early music. There was a programme from the courts of Elizabeth and James I by the Tudor Consort in St John's, Smith Square on Friday if she'd be interested. Betony remembered madrigals from her schooldays and anyway she wanted to see him again, knowing where that might lead and noting that he must be at least ten years older than she was and had probably been through a wife or two already.

'Only one,' he said when they were lying in bed after their first love-making. 'Once bitten. I've learnt that my way of life isn't what women want. I could tell Father Freud that much.' It was too soon for Betony to know what she might want of him except that already she wanted him there all the time. When he had to go off to Haverhall to teach and she hadn't a job of her own to go to she felt hollowed out, sickish in his absence. After a couple of weeks he was staying at her flat most of the time, using his own bleak place as studio and darkroom. At first she had imagined they would lie deliciously long in bed on Sunday mornings but she soon found that once they had made love he was restless to be up, into a shared bath and out to look at churches, pictures, artefacts from any age or place or just people, always with his hands reaching for his camera when it wasn't forbidden.

Betony had been enjoying a run of work that had briefly filled up her bank account and when her last lodger had left to tour Australia in a minibus she hadn't bothered to fill the room at once. When she had met Mark her string of jobs had suddenly petered out. She could indulge herself in the pleasure of Mark about the place, walking naked to the bathroom, without having to worry about work or what anyone else might think or want. Only his own restlessness could take him away from her.

She would try to keep him in the bath by cupping his heavy hairy scrotum in her hand and gently massaging the balls in their skin bag against each other until the small pink egg that looked as if the soft stem had just extruded it began to swell and lift. Then he would laugh and grab at Betony's breasts.

'Sexy bitch. Who can't get enough? Well you've had my all for this morning.' And the moment would pass.

'Have you ever had a circumcised one?' he'd asked her quite early on while they were still exploring each other's bodies and histories.

No she hadn't. Why was he circumcised? Betony carefully pinched shut the little eye at the top of the smooth red plum until it wept a clear viscous droplet.

'My parents weren't really orthodox but they thought it was the right thing to do. It seems pretty barbarous to me.'

Another time he asked: 'Do you always go for older men?'

'Not that I've noticed.' She wasn't prepared to tell him that although her temporary lovers had all been about her own age it was older men she looked at and wondered about. She also avoided any precise narrative of her upbringing. It was in such contrast to his own, 'dragged up in Poplar' where his parents had a small tailoring business that had prospered after the war, when a bespoke suit in lovat green was still every man's aspiration, before the ubiquitous machine-washable jeans knocked the suits off their hangers. By then his parents had made enough to move to South-gate and take tea at Garfunkels but Mark still felt himself an East End boy.

He had been excited by the students' radical demands of the late sixties and that had pushed him towards art school and pho-tography but by the time he got there four years later the protests were all over. Life including art, and especially photography as his tutor was keen to point out, was all about surface not substance: the image not the ideal. He advised his students to concentrate on film: the moving not the still picture that merely echoed painting. Mark had noticed though that his mentor didn't follow his own advice. He decided to adopt the practice rather than the precept: Bill Brandt was his template.

Mark's great-grandparents had come to London from Riga at the end of the nineteenth century in flight from prejudice and pogrom. 'The natives here might not have been very friendly, "four by two", "saucepan lid", that sort of stuff, but at least my great-grandparents weren't murdered.' They too had prospered in a modest way, apprenticing their son to a fellow immigrant, a tailor, and so beginning the line of business that had ended with Mark's father. 'And what were your lot doing all this time?'

'Oh, they were soldiers,' Betony had said vaguely.

'Obeying orders, keeping up the Empire, keeping down the nig-nogs.' Betony hadn't contradicted him.

'And Betony? What sort of a name is that?'

'It's some sort of herb. Something to do with my great-grandfather. I was lucky not to be called Rosemary or Laurel or even Parsley or Chicory.'

He had complained when she had first said she would have to spend the next weekend with Gran Bet. 'Why do you have to go? Where?'

'Near Reading. She brought me up after my parents died and she's all alone.'

'And expects a lifetime of gratitude. You don't owe her. It gave her pleasure having you, kept her from being lonely. Family ties are just chains.' Mark had a sister, married in Finchley with two small children, who took care of his parents' septuagenarian needs. 'Why can't I come with you?'

'You'd be bored. There's nothing to do there and I have to give her all my attention.' She could just hear his comments as they turned into the drive.

'I could take pictures of nature: cows and sheep.'

'There aren't any. It's horse country.'

Gran Bet herself was curious too. 'Who was the young man who answered the telephone when I rang the other day?'

'He's not that young, Gran: fortyish. His name's Mark Aird. He used to teach me at Haverhall. I bumped into him again at the Tate.'

'The art school? Perhaps you'd like to bring him down one weekend.'

'Oh I don't think he'd be very good at the country. He's a city guy.'

'Is that the in word: "guy"? It's been around a long time then. I remember it before the war in American movies.'

'It's taken a turn,' Betony said, 'you can use it for women as well as men now.' Gran Bet liked to be told these things. Betony imagined her at drinks in the village where she picked up tips from the local racehorse owners, prefacing the words with: 'My granddaughter says . . .' and letting them fly like the magician's doves across some drawing-room, stopping the conversation.

Over the next months Gran Bet made several attempts to meet Mark on her own ground but Betony managed to keep them apart, a strategy made easier because her grandmother no longer came to London as she had once done to shop, and lunch at Fortnum's before catching the train back to Reading.

Betony climbed the stairs and let herself into her own flat, switching on the light and dumping her overnight bag on the carpet and her mobile phone on the hall table. She had forgotten to water the tall irisine before she left and it was near to collapse: the spindly stems sagging, the floorboards underneath it spotted with the red splashes of fallen round leaves that gave it its common name of bloodsteak plant. The little green slot of the answering machine flashed her its luminous seductive beckon. She pressed the button, heard the tape wind back and the voices, some urgent or faintly aggressive, some cajoling or self-consciously cheery, let out of the box. There was a message from Sadie, who worked with her as an assistant stylist and had seen her through Mark, arranging to meet on the job in the morning. Then came the short string of strange voices pulled in by her advertisement whose telephone numbers and names she wrote down, listlessly but methodically.

11

Soon as I heard the name I knew, didn't I? 'Tweren't possible for there to be two of them unless they was connected. Not two Betony Falks. Course, I didn't answer like this when I heard the voice, light and high. A girl's voice. I answered posh as I always do, as almost everyone I know now does. This here is the voice for in me head. That comes out of Nana's voice. The voice I grewed up with at home and in the playground. I uses it to keep a hold of things when they move as fast as they do: a rope thrown down the well to haul us up. It was her encouraged me to learn the other language of outside and up there. Said as how she'd had to in service. Not that she'd ever quite lost the burr and she'd slipped back fast enough once she'd married and gone to her own place. But then she went back into service again during the war to help out, taking Margaret with her, and it were only after that she settled down into the old ways with words, when she come back to our village for good and Margaret went away to Australia. Only then that old way of speaking was dying out and it was as if she was clinging to a life-raft of a language cobbled together out of bits of broken memory while everyone else drifted away from her.

She used to write at first, did Margaret. Then a letter come that said she were marrying a chap out there, a window cleaner who dangled over the side of tall office blocks like a caterpillar on a silk string, Nana said. Gradually the letter dwindled to a card at Christmas and for Nana's birthday but nothing for the baby she'd left behind, our mother June. Then even the cards stopped, though Nana went on sending for years, dropping them into a void as she said, keeping her up with the family news. Last she wrote to tell her our mother had died but even that didn't get an answer.

'What does she care? She hasn't clapped eyes on her since she were a babby.' Nana's contempt were the sizzle and spit of a saucepan boiling over.

But I didn't write after Nana's death either though I found the address in her little buff address book, and neither did Laura as far as I know. Perhaps if I ever get to Australia I'll look her up. 'Hallo, Grannie,' I'll say and watch her face. Margaret would be old now if she's still alive. Sometimes I wonder if she did come back, perhaps for a visit or even for good, and lives somewhere on a leafy estate in a semi. She might be sitting on a bus or train next to me and I'd never know.

Like our father, who might be in heaven but more likely hell, who took one look at me and was off. Took a powder, did a runner, legged it, vamoosed, scarpered. Pinched out of our lives like a candle flame. Ray Idbury, jack of all trades. Could turn his hand to anything, and anyone. Divorced for desertion after five years by our mother June. Nana, who was nearly seventy, had to turn to again, take in her granddaughter and two squalling babbies and while June got the bus into Reading and the biscuit factory every day, Nana washed and shopped, and cleaned and cooked, just as she'd always done.

Our mother had pretty dark tight curls and a translucent olive skin. I'd watch her smoothing on her liquid make-up and reddening her mouth with a neon pencil of lipstick. That must have been when I were about eight and Laura were nine. Three evenings a week she worked behind the bar at the Jolly Brewers. On Saturday night she went out with her mates, usually to another pub or the dance-hall in Reading. She'd put on her face downstairs because she said the light were better. She'd stand in front of the kidney-shaped mirror with the bevelled edge, that hung on its heavy silver chain above the fireplace, balance a neat court shoe on the wooden fender with its black fingerprint charrings, and dip into her pink plastic make-up bag that smelt muskily and faintly greasy from her jumble of little pots and sticks. Some days when I got home from school and Laura were talking to Nana in the kitchen I'd slink upstairs, slide open the top drawer of her dressing-table, take out her make-up bag and put my nose into it. Sweetish it smelled, like those heartshaped Love Hearts that tasted just of grit and cheap scent.

Sometimes she would go out for a few months with some guy she'd a met in the pub and we would know, me and Laura, that June was carrying on by Nana's set face and quick temper. It were a time for keeping quiet, eating your cabbage, getting out from under her feet. I would hear them rowing in the kitchen after June came in. Laura and me never spoke of it to one another although we still slept in the same room. We knew it were the edge of danger, of possible change, and once for a bit June and Laura went to live somewhere else, leaving Nana and me alone together. I missed my pretty mother but Nana made up for it, calling me a good boy, teaching me to talk proper from the telly and finding money for dancing lessons.

What first set me off dancing were seeing it on telly in old films with male soloists, elegant ice dancers on the news, and

New Rave. Those proud entrances, one hand held out, the head pricked, erect or slightly thrown back, the other hand at the invisible left nipple, the arching insteps lifting the muscled columns of the legs right up to the two hard cheeks of buttocks. Entrancing, prancing entrances.

'Nana, can I go to dance classes?'

'And why would 'ee want to do that?'

'I seen it on telly. On the ice as well.'

'There ent no ice rink near here as I know of.'

'You don't have to have ice. You can just dance like that Russian.'

'That New Rave? Listen, 'tis different over there. There they'm got all sorts of schools where children can go and learn to dance about, even if they'm poor, not got two ha'pennies to rub together even. Here you have to pay.'

'Oh Nan!'

'Oh all right, boy, don't whine. I'll look in the *Journal* and see what I can find. Mind, there mayn't be anything so don't set your hopes too high. Now don't go soppy on me. You know I'm not a great one for all this kissing just because you've got your own way or think you have.'

She did find something, though it meant going on the bus to Reading like mother June. The first time she took me herself. 'Now 'ee must take note of the way cause I can't be bringing 'ee every time and hanging about to fetch 'ee home again. I haven't the time or the money.'

'Later,' Mrs Alys Rockwell, ARAD, said, 'he'll need ballet shoes but I like to start them off in bare feet first. Well, he has the build for it if he doesn't shoot up too quickly. Of course, he should have had at least two years already at his age. We'll just have to see what we can do. He'll have to work very hard and be regular in attendance. He'll be the only boy in his class and if there's any trouble with the girls or their parents you'll have to take him away at once, Mrs Marsham.'

There wasn't any trouble that I knew of. We were all as serious as eight- and nine-year-olds can be. The girls were younger than me and had been at it a year at least but they didn't have time to tease me. Only Vera Levinsky questioned me at first. She was Mrs Rockwell's eldest and favourite pupil, and trying for a place in a real school. When I said I wanted to be like New Rave she didn't laugh but just nodded her head gravely. We were holding onto the practice bar at the time. Vera rose on her points and lifted a dropping wing of white arm before sinking down in a graceful gesture of acceptance.

Mrs Alys Rockwell, ARAD, had herself been a professional dancer before her marriage to an accountant, which had ended in divorce though he still did her books. She had the sinews of an old horse and kept herself in training by teaching, not just children during the day but adults as well in the evening.

At the end of every year her pupils put on a show so that their parents could see they were getting their money's worth. As the only boy I was thrust into the limelight at once. Apart from Vera's solo and a couple of pas de deux it was all ensemble with me centre-stage as the prince in Mrs Rockwell's adaptation of *Swan Lake*. Years later, when I went to see if she was still in business after Nana died, she confessed: 'I know it was corny dear but it was what the parents wanted. A nice clean sad story they could understand. Even the dumpiest daughter could be a cygnet.'

By the end of the first year Mrs Rockwell had decided I weren't going to be a New Rave. I were too old already at ten. Nana was proud as punch though, when she came to see me in the show. Afterwards Alys Rockwell sought her out.

'Well Mrs Marsham, what did you think of Gill's performance?'

'I never expected nothing like it. I'd never have thought he had it in him. He looked so, so . . .'

'Like a prince.'

'Well yes, if you say so. He'll be getting a swelled head. I hope he's been no trouble.'

Alys Rockwell patted my hair lightly. 'No trouble at all. I've

got a very soft spot for your young man. There's just one thing . . .'
What were she going to say? Were I about to be cast out of that
little Eden after only a year? 'I think we should try him on other
kinds of dance, not just ballet. Jazz and tap, for example.'

'Like Fred Astaire?' Nana said.

'Exactly. It will give him more options.'

'Options?'

'If he ever wanted to turn professional. Unlike in Russia, there
are very few chances in this country for boys to train and become
classical ballet dancers.'

'You mean he might do dancing as a job later on? Well, I
don't know, it seems such an uncertain sort of way of earning a
living.'

'Yes, but I think he's got talent, real talent. We just have to
find the best outlet for it. After all, if he keeps up his ordinary
school work nothing's lost.'

'You wait till I tell our June,' Nana said as we jolted home on
the bus. 'That'll make some people sit up.'

Nobody at my ordinary school knew how I spent Saturday
mornings and, later, afternoons as well. If they had they would
have made life a misery. As it were I got plenty of stick.

'Why'm you black and your sister's white? You got two different dads?'

'Shut your face. I'm not black. Anyway you got a face like a
squashed tomato.' But at home I asked: 'Why am I black and
Laura's white, Nana?'

'You'm not black. Just got a little touch of the tarbrush that's
all. 'Tis nature.'

'But how, Nana? They asked me at school if we had different
dads. We didn't, did we?'

'Goodness boy, questions, questions. You want to know the
ins and outs of a mag's arse.'

I knew then I wouldn't get no more answers. Nana didn't hold
with 'effin and blindin' so if she were roused enough to say 'arse'
it were time to back off. Course, I had to fuck this and cunt that

at school with the other boys or they'd have laughed at us rotten, specially now we were in top class and would soon be going on to the town comprehensive.

'You'm like my black prince,' Nana said relenting. 'Only not so dark. 'Er come to stay when I were in my first place. Said I were a dear girl and give I a tanner. He had a sapphire in his turban big as a whelk. That were before the Great War but I've never forgot him.' Nana was the same age as the century. 'Me and the Queen Mum. But there the resemblance ends.'

She had gone into service as a nurserymaid just before the outbreak of that war when she was thirteen. She'd been taken to another house when she was only twelve but at the gates her mother had turned back.

' 'Er said 'tweren't big enough for I, not enough staff. I'd never get nowhere, just be at everyone's beck and call. But Gisborne Hall were big enough even for her. To I it seemed like a palace I'd never know me way about. And so dark in winter til the lamps was lit, with all the trees pressing up against the windows. But in summer when the king and queen came visiting then it were all sunshine and everything had to be done up to the nines. That were King George with his little goatee and sad eyes, and hoity-toity Mary with a back like a ramrod who wore a toque as if it were a crown. Even the stones in the courtyard had to be whitewashed and us servants scrubbed til we shone, the bath taken down from the scullery wall and carried upstairs with jugs of water. Us maids had to share of course. We were all lined up on the steps to bow and curtsey when they arrived. Not that we thought that much to them but it all went with the job, bowing and scraping. I seen cook spit in the soup before she sent it up and then laugh. "They'll enjoy that," she said winking. "What the eye don't see the heart don't grieve over." '

Nana had a whole clutch of sayings about food itself. 'Eat a peck of dirt before you die' were a real puzzle. Were it a command, something you had to do? Or just a statement of fact, meaning you wouldn't die til you had? And how much was a peck? I remembered it turned up in the Bible, measuring corn. 'What's a peck, Nana?'

'Don't they teach you nothing at that school? Four pecks, one bushel. That's how they used to measure the horse's feed.'

When a caterpillar showed up in greens or salad and I pulled a face she'd say 'twere only a skinful of cabbage or lettuce and couldn't do no harm. She lived to see a Chinese takeaway in town, pizza houses in Reading and curry with chips everywhere but stuck to her meat and two veg with an occasional daring lapse into fish and chips, the jellyfish translucent ribbing of skate or the milky whorl of rock salmon, not put off by her sailor husband's tales that dogfish feasted on drowned eyes. 'I can't be doing with all them bones in plaice and cod. That skate slips down like a piece of silk. As for that trout that's bummed up to be so fine I had some once when a whole half fish come down untouched from the dining-room. "Try that, Lilian," cook said, "and you can say you've dined off the fat of the land like a lord." But 'twere nothing but bones and that dry I could only get down a mouthful or two without choking.'

'Tell us about the black prince, Nana.'

'Her were beautiful my dear. His fingers, such slim fingers like a girl, were covered in gold rings with stones in them like carbuncles.' I didn't dare ask what a carbuncle was. 'You'm got nice hands for a boy too, but I can't see them ever doing any proper work.' She meant clinging to the rigging like long dead great-grandfather or hefting the blacksmith's hammer and tongs of her farrier father and brothers.

Since June and Laura had gone away I had a room to myself and I'd secretly practise arm and hand movements in front of the spotted dressing-table mirror. There wasn't room for practising steps, feet tangled in furniture legs but my arms were free to float. I'd look along my outstretched arm and flex my fingers, loading them in my mind with jewels. The only machine in our house for music making was a broken-down Dansette that had once played a whole stack of our mother's forty-fives, dropping them

23

onto the turntable one after the other so the dancing could go on for half an hour without a stop. I'd sometimes wonder about those days before me and Laura, or I should say Laura and me since she were the eldest by a year, and whether our parents, June and Ray, ever danced together to that record player and where. But you couldn't ask Nana too much at once. Suddenly she would lose patience and accuse me of 'blacking your nose'. So the stories came to me piecemeal to be strung together later.

Our mother had no time for telling stories, out all day and most evenings, and no time for it in the other sense anyway. The tales I heard then were of long ago and stopped with the Second World War. Laura had no interest in Nana's memories either. She liked to read our mother's magazines, to practise making herself up til she looked like one of her now despised dolls and to endlessly comb and set her hair. Our mother laughed encouragingly when Laura begged to use her make-up, and she'd been briefly our father's favourite until I came along and turned him off the whole idea of family. Not that I knew any of this then. Not til much later.

Once in a temper, after she and Laura had come back and she and Nana were rowing, mother June had shouted 'If it weren't for that little black bugger I'd still be married.'

'Don't blame me,' Nana said, ''twere none of my doing. Anyway 'er can't have thought much of 'ee to let an accident like that put him off. It weren't as if it was your fault.'

'How did he know that?'

'Then he didn't know much. Ignorant as pigshit.'

I'd been listening with me head under the bedclothes pretending to be asleep. Laura slept in our mother's room since they'd come back. They'd been talking about me. I was an accident. Nana had said 'shit'. I put me hand through the opening in my pyjamas and held onto my widdler for comfort.

'He said even if it were true then the next one might turn out the same.'

'Well 'er took you on. You'm no English rose.'

'I told him we had gypsy blood.'

'And that's all right then, is it?'

That were the year I first seen John Travolta, in *Saturday Night Fever*. June decided we should go into Reading on the bus on her Saturday afternoon off, all of us, even Nana, who never went to the pictures. 'Not since the end of the war.'

She still pined for Pinewood, for names I knew only from her until later when her legs were that bad she couldn't go out and I'd drop in to see her of an afternoon. I'd find her watching the black and white shadow play of *Brief Encounter* or *Green For Danger* and join her in that world of her middle age when there was still the possibility of romance even for ex-nurserymaids. It were because the dancing might be useful to me that made her come with us and pay for us all. Nana could always find mysterious caches of money for special occasions.

Alys Rockwell, ARAD, had kept to her plan of teaching me different styles but of course it were all different when Travolta leapt off the screen at me. If I hadn't a seen him and what were possible I couldn't a dreamt it up out of me own head. Secretly I'd been worrying about not being a Russian.

'Don't you want to do that?' I once asked Laura when they showed the Russian girl gymnasts, those somersaulting human jack-knives, on television, but she just smoothed down the front of the new flares June had bought her and said: 'They're too skinny. They don't look like proper girls,' and I suddenly noticed two small bumps under her yellow T-shirt that I hadn't a been aware of before.

We was sat there in a row in the dark like stares on a wire, passing the cardboard funnel of butterscotch popcorn between us when all the adverts and trailers faded and the real film came on. And straight off I knew I could do it. If I couldn't be a Russian I could fucking well be a Yank or as good as. These was just ordinary high-school kids same as I'd be any day now.

The next Saturday I asked Mrs Rockwell if I could learn the dances from the film. She sighed a bit. 'I'm afraid it's time for you to move on, Gill. Not that I couldn't go on teaching you modern but you need others to practise formation with. The line. And you need the competition. I'll have to think who I could recommend.'

'Will it cost more?'

'I'll see what I can arrange.'

So I'd be changing both my schools. Laura was already at Bedown Comprehensive and had found herself a gang of mates to knock about with, as Nana put it. 'In my day we stayed in the same school until we left unless your parents took 'ee away early to be apprenticed or go into service. Or just to help about the house if there was little'uns and the mother wasn't well, that's if you was a girl.'

'A gang of mates to knock about with' belonged to her days as a young married woman in a downstairs flat in Henniker Road, a tree-lined street of London cottages close to the docks and railways but far enough from the area of rough pubs, doss-houses and red-light girls for sailors to house their wives and families in decency. She had moved there in 1924. Margaret were born the next year. Wilf, her jacktarry husband, went down with his merchant ship into the freezing bowels of the North Sea on a trip to Archangel in the early years of the war when the decks were slippery with ice and frozen mist hung over them like shrouds. When I were very little I did used to dream about him and his frosted pearls of eyes, even though I'd never met him, forever frozen into the skirts of an iceberg drifting endlessly to and fro. Nana mourned this husband she'd only known between ships, and never remarried. 'Though I could have if I'd wanted, once or twice, even trailing a great gawk of a girl as Margaret were by then. The thing about sailors is they ent always under foot and they'm generous to a fault. Never a skinflint among 'em. When they come ashore it's loads of fine presents, some often a bit daft like a parrot or a mongoose, and money to burn til they goes back skint.'

Wilf had met and married her in three days and when he took

her aboard ship in Plymouth to show off his catch the duty officer gave her a fine set of dainty crockery as a wedding present. At one time, when she were still at Gisborne Hall, she were being chased by the Russian horsemaster, who swore to tame her as he tamed the horses and had given her a jet black necklace as a bridle. When his attentions become too hard to evade she decided to move. 'He seemed to think he'd bought us with that old black necklace. I'd never been made up to nanny because the old one were still hanging on there, so I decided it were time anyway to look for a better place.'

She'd had to come down in the world as far as the size of the house were concerned. Gisborne Hall were more of a stately home. The new one were a big town house on the edge of Blackheath, built for an Indian merchant to retire to and passed on to his only daughter. 'It were taking the children to the fair on Blackheath were my undoing. The sailors had just been paid off at Deptford and they only had to walk up Observatory Hill with their pockets jingling to find the girls. Your great-grandfather treated the little 'uns to the merry-go-round and the swings, the coconut shy, toffee apples and candy floss til I was feared they'd be sick.' It was one of my favourites among Nana's tales. The painted horses going up and down on their gilded barley sugar poles, the seesawing crimson swingboats, the gippo-roustabout riding the heaving deck of the merry-go-round among the motor-bikes; the heath itself wide open under a windy sky. The sailors with just one thing in mind.

'I'd been in my new place only four years. There was three children, though only two of 'em was still in the nursery. John, the eldest, were nine and away at school but come home in the holidays and weren't amiss at being made a bit of a fuss of by the new nanny. Sarah were six and the babby, William, just two when I arrived. John were already intended for a soldier. I don't think he cared for it much but he didn't have no say in the matter. So by the time the war came he were a captain. Sarah had married and moved to Scotland and the babby, my little Billy, were called up at once only he went in the navy like my Wilf.

'Even after I left the boys kept in touch. Not Sarah so much once she were married and gone up north, except at birthdays and Christmas. But John came to see me when he were in London and Billy in his school holidays. John brought me a photo of his wedding and said he hoped I'd be nanny to his children. And I laughed and said what would Wilf and little Margaret do if I was to go back? None of us could foresee then what would happen. Though I could a done with the money. Wilf were having to spend more time ashore hanging about between ships. In the end we had to give up our place in Henniker Road and I came home here to stay in this cottage with Great-aunt Martha Bennett til times should look up.'

Nana would pause then and I'd have to wait to see if she'd pick up the thread or if the story too had come to the end for that day and it were the moment to switch on the new telly she'd bought in the hope of luring June and Laura back.

I'd try to take up the tale again the next night. 'Tell us about the war, Nana. What happened then?'

'You don't want your head filled with all that stuff.'

But I did. I sensed a mystery there that concerned me in some way. 'They was out of the run times and ways. You'm not old enough to understand.' I would have to wait. And I did. I waited til our mother June were dead, run down coming home from the Jolly Brewers after work by a drunken driver, and Nana were confined to the house with her bad legs, til I couldn't wait no more. I were desperate, feeling her slipping away.

She were sat in an armchair of brown uncut moquette, watching the snooker with a multi-coloured shawl made of knitted squares over her knees when I called that day, determined that she should tell me everything at last. 'Tell us about the war, Nana, the things you always told me I was too young to hear. I want, I need to know. I got taken to emigration coming back from my holiday. They almost tried to say I was illegal. I must know why.'

28

She peered at me a moment. Then she leaned forward and switched off the pub-elegant players, duelling with wooden lances on the green baize field. 'I loves that Hurricane Davis. Always turned out so smart in his fancy weskits. All right then. Make us a cup of tea and I'll tell 'ee the whole story.'

So she told me at last. How after nearly six months of war the letter had come from Captain John asking her to come back and help out with the new babby in the house in the country they had taken to be away from the bombing, and bring little Margaret with her. And she had let Great-aunt Martha Bennett's cottage that was now hers to some evacuees 'for the duration' and taken up her old job in a house the other side of Reading. 'After all, it were better than being sent into munitions as I should have been with Margaret nearly grown up.'

Mrs John was often away in London in spite of the blitz whenever the captain got leave, which was frequent in the early days of the war. Though sometimes Nana wondered whether she weren't up there drinking and dancing with him not on leave. She reckoned Mrs John would have preferred to stay in London, bombs or no bombs, but he had insisted on the country for the babby, Henry, little Harry. 'That's where I got the news that Wilf had gone down with his ship. It would have been quick in them freezing waters. What else could I tell myself for comfort? Nothing to bury or mourn over. But Margaret took it bad, being her dad's only chick and spoilt rotten every time he come home.'

She'd got in with a wild lot at school and now she clamoured to leave until Nana let her be apprenticed to a hairdresser in Reading. Mrs John encouraged her to try out what she learned at Elsie's salon and even began taking her to London as a sort of lady's maid. Once they only escaped death by a few hours when the London house was gutted by a stray thousand-pound bomb jettisoned by a panicky pilot who'd missed his target zone in Woolwich.

'That put a stop to gadding up there for a bit. But not for long.'

Mrs John found herself a small flat in the centre of London and soon that phase of the war were over anyway. The Germans were fighting the Russians and Major John were driving a sand-spattered jeep around North Africa.

For Nana it were years of minding the babby, eking out their rations and queuing for extras. 'Sheeps' heads for brawn, tongues and trotters, oxtails and, best of all, sometimes a rabbit still in its fur coat.' Tinned pineapple chunks and sliced peaches, chalky powdered milk and gritty eggs. Mending Mrs John's silk stockings with a crochet hook. Turning Wilf's old trousers into skirts for Margaret. Sometimes as a treat, when she could get a babysitter, a trip to the Roxy to lose herself for an hour or two in the dark in the technicolor world of Natalie Calmus. 'That Alice Faye were lovely in *Hello Frisco*.' But little Harry were her chief consolation. 'Poor mite. After Major John were killed at Salerno his mother didn't seem to care. Ran around London as if she was a mad thing and hardly came home at all. And our Margaret were as bad.'

Until one day Margaret did come home. 'I could see what was up at once. She couldn't kid me. I been around too long. "You planning on getting married?" I asked her straight off.'

'How did you know?' she said.

'I weren't born yesterday. Well?'

'He's married already. Got a wife and kiddies in America.'

'A Yank? You daft bitch. Couldn't you wait?'

'We could all be dead next week. A doodlebug killed three people in the house opposite two days ago.'

'Pity it didn't see off something else.'

'You got to help me, our mother. I don't want a baby.'

'You should a thought of that before you took your knickers down. How long is it?'

'Nearly five months, I think.'

'"Then it's gone too far for anything I can do. You'll just have to get on with it and have it adopted if you still don't want to keep it." That's all I could say to her. The mivvy were it hadn't happened before, the way Margaret and Mrs John was carrying on.'

Nana fixed everything: the hostel for unmarried mothers where they could have their babies in secret; knitted bonnets and bootees for the grandchild she might never see; the adoption society. 'Up to the last minute I think she thought something would save her or that she'd made a mistake with the day, so she never told me what she were afeared of. Bring me that drawer out of the sewing machine.' I took out the long thin wooden box and placed it on her knees. At the very back beyond the bobbins of bright thread, pins and spare needles were two or three old snapshots not much bigger than a postage stamp. 'That were your mother when she were born.'

Margaret had refused to see or feed the baby. She wanted it out of the way as soon as possible. But the adoption society said everyone wanted blue-eyed, fair-haired little girls and these days there were plenty to choose from. She would have to go to a children's home. Then Nana put her foot down. She would take June, named for the month she were born in, herself. Margaret could bugger off and start a new life elsewhere. The war was over in Europe. Nana would take the baby back to her own home. She faced Mrs John down. She blamed her for leading Margaret on. 'Fancy doctors take care of them sort when they gets into trouble.' She told her there had been a baby but it had been adopted. The greatest wrench would be leaving little Harry, but in any case he would soon be going away to school at seven.

I stared again at the snapshot of the baby's head. It looked like one of me at the same age: dusky, frizzy-haired, snub-nosed. 'She said the Yank were a darkie. Carl, though, that's a German sort of name.'

'But Nana, didn't anyone ask questions?'

'They dursn't. I fetched her out of the home and brought her back to the cottage.'

'But our mother didn't look like I do when she were older.'

'I straightened her hair with nature's help and kept her out of the sun. But the truth is when she began to lose her babby looks she started to grow like my father in feature. Who knows, you see, but that you might take after that Carl's mother. Sometimes faces skip a generation. At least you don't have nothing in you of that skiver, Ray Idbury, like your sister does.' At that moment I'd have swapped my looks even for lank hair and a thin tight mouth. I got over that later but just then I was going through a rough patch.

Maybe it were just conscience but Mrs John didn't forget Nana. A card came every year and was propped up on the mantelpiece, signed with her full name so Nana would know she hadn't remarried and how to address her thank you. Sometimes she asked after Margaret or told how Harry was taking an exam, going to university. And there were always a note tucked into the card that went up over the years to a fiver, then the tenner I remembered as the value of money went down.

So it were a name I'd grown up knowing, a name written with a flourish you couldn't mistake and strange enough to stick in the mind always: Betony Falk. 'Lady Falk' Nana sometimes called her with her kettlespit of contempt. And I wonder what you'll see when you opens the door, Betony Falk. A bumpkin blackamoor or a dusky prince. I'll know who you are but you won't know who I am til I'm ready to tell you and by then you may have shut the fucking door in my face.


### III


I log on and go at once to the Goethe site to see if there's anything new, a ritual I subscribe to every time to bring me good luck, uncross the wires, avert the electronic evil eye: the bug in the system, the virus, the hacker. What was it the Grand Old Man himself said about superstition? That it was the poetry of life. I wonder what he meant by that. And even while I'm waiting for the image to come up (there's something touching and human about how long it still takes) I'm happy in these thoughts under today's date on my new laptop, liptap, an electronic diary that is really our history, my letter to you, like Kafka to Milena, and perhaps when I finish it, if I ever do, I'll publish worldwide in the hope that someone, maybe even you, will answer at last. I've got Christoff to buy a little tray that fits over the arm of my chair and is just big enough for the machine so that it can go everywhere with me, beating the shakiness of my hands with the help of the keyboard that will give it all back to me instantly in clean characters I can still read.

And today there is something new, unscrolling in front of me, an English version of *Kennst du das Land*, free of the dead weight of the canon, not obsequious, disrespectful even, to be set to music, turned into a rock video perhaps.

> Do you know that country where the lemons flower?
> Among their dark leaves the oranges are on fire.
> A gentle breath blows from the blue washed sky
> The myrtle's motionless and the bay stands high,
> Do you really know it?
> There! There
> That's where I'd go with you my lover.

The translator is twenty-eight and lives in Manchester. I have to admire the iconoclasm that can turn the archaic 'my beloved' into 'my lover'. You would approve of it, Minna. It liberates me to ramble through these invisible spaces, dipping, sampling, dropping a honey jar into a pond on a string, a roving magician in my tower able to conjure up aery spirits.

Christoff is still sceptical. At first he said I would never, at my age he meant, master it. But I said that if the British scientist Stephen Hawking could manage with just his voice, I could surely overcome stiff fingers. That is the true use of these new technologies: to supplement, compensate for our human inadequacies. To remember quicker. To remember forever without manipulation or degeneration; to keep somewhere the clean, the fair copy. To be our hands and our eyes, to take us out of ourselves, elsewhere, to annihilate time and place and put us in an eternal here.

Christoff's real fear was that the machines, now there are two presences siamesed by their printer, would make him redundant, since he no longer has to type or look up things in places I can't get to or in books too heavy for me to hold, but the machines can't bring me my coffee or the warmth of human breath. And its gossip is ponderous. There's also the language, of course. English is the network's language and its grammar the lex Romana, the syntax of cyberspace, that illusory universe which is only a series of conjunctions, seems not is. Those aery spirits chatter with American accents. Christoff's English is serviceable. He finds my greater knowledge of the language a barrier between us that has grown higher since these keyboards for me to play my soundless music on came into the apartment. But that isn't my fault or his. Just an accident of history. When I was a student it was fashionable to study in England. When Christoff was young there was the wall, a divided country I find it hard to believe you never knew since I believe, I must believe, you know everything I do. He learnt from teachers who had never been outside the People's Republic except on holiday to Yalta or to a conference in Sofia, who translated Dickens and Melville, even Philip Larkin and Robert Lowell, without having tasted English ale or American bourbon. Actually, his knowledge of the language is more than adequate. It's confidence he lacks, that's all. If I weren't so infirm I would take him to England to show him how well he could manage.

I would not admit it to Christoff but I find sometimes that I am out of date, that when I have tracked down a new corner of the network the words are opaque. I recognise them but I can't divine their meaning as they have been strung together. The English language, because it has no academy and so little grammar, is essentially democratic, is in constant flux. It's like a net itself flung over the world, stretched and pulled to cover so many cultures and needs. Sometimes it's in danger of breaking, ripped apart by the strains so that those luminous multi-coloured, many-formed sea creatures of meaning and imagination drop back into the dark waters. Sometimes jargonised into ugly formalities that remind me of the lowering architecture of the dictator: oppressive, vapidly flamboyant with a hard-edged uniformity. Or the language of the *Völkischer Beobachter* itself that we used to laugh at together, the snarl of the People's watchdog, the syntax of strut.

Often I take out a word in English or Deutsch, or both, it doesn't matter and hold it up to the light. Herbst: autumn in British English; fall in American. Each word signifying something different about the same season. In my language it's a time of austerity, dry, tart, like its sound. Whereas the British bisyllable is mild, mellow; the American mono is a drop, a death. Playing with words is an old man's game, one I can't share with Christoff. Perhaps out there on the Internet is some equally ancient professor of languages I could discuss it all with, but although I can read other people's texts I have no postbox for them to contact me, no e-mail address for correspondence. Cyberspace is for me to browse in, keeping my own counsel while others fill the ether with their comments and cries. Like a knight on a quest I am vowed to silence. Or perhaps I have seen too much and those I could have talked to once died long ago. If they were to come into the room now as they do into my dreams I should recognise them immediately but they wouldn't know me. They would see only a strange old man in his wheelchair. Christoff knows me as I am now. He has never known me any other way but even he can't see inside me, just the crusty shell. I live inside myself, a soft-bodied hermit crab that has scuttled backwards into a dead animal's carapace inscribed with the salty sprinklings of barnacle tracery.

English was the language of our love, Minna. You perfected yours so that we could talk to each other in public without being easily understood when there were informers everywhere, and so that in bed together we could make love without the compromise of a language, our language, that was being racked into shapes Goethe wouldn't have recognised but Heine had predicted in exile a century before with the bitter clarity of pain. But then he was a Jew.

For some of course, English was the language of traitors, of the resistance, depending on your viewpoint. Trott von Su, von Moltke, Bielenberg were all part of that wave, part educated in England, who'd acquired English manners and ways of thinking, though I never met them myself. They were richer than I was, moved in other circles in Oxford and London. I was still a little reclusive. It was you who brought me out, your enjoyment of all our senses, our bodies. I can see you now licking the spoon you were stirring our supper with, your lips a dark plum in the candlelight, wet with some juice or sauce while you laughed at me, daring me to taste too, a fairy woman offering the cup that would make me invisible or whisk me away for seven years.

And that was all we had, those enchanted seven years, from that first dance in the café beside the lake, the shimmering face of the Wannsee under the summer night sky like a fallen moon. You remember, Minna? That spontaneous end-of-term party we all drove out of the city for; those of us who didn't have cars hitching lifts from better-off students who did. I was one who hitched. Your brother Otto drove. He was in my class but I didn't really know him. I was a student from an impoverished family who had nothing left but their name while your family owned businesses in the Netherlands and Switzerland as well as Germany. As we drove under the summer leaves I was already aware of you sandwiched on the back seat between another girl I didn't know and Anni Reiss, who was also a classmate of mine and your brother's, a girl I had actually kissed when we were both thirteen and experimenting. I knew I would ask you to dance. We'd all been celebrating after the stresses of examinations. Those in my year had been taking the dreaded Abitur that would decide our fates forever. The beer had foamed and flowed until someone, I can't remember who, perhaps I never knew, suggested dancing. We whirled through the city singing and shouting, exploiting the indulgence given to students on their last day before the next phase of their initiation into adult life.

Because my family were poor it was even more important for me to have done well if I was to go on to university and have a career. My father had been killed in the slaughter of the Western Front and my mother let rooms to lodgers in order to provide for us. If I worked hard at my legal studies she hoped I might make a career in the diplomatic. You were a year younger than me. You could simply stay at home when you finished high school and help your father, or you might be sent to a finishing school abroad. You were ambitious. You didn't want to be a hausfrau but to have a career too, to study languages and become an interpreter.

Did we fall in love that night? I think I did, and you always said you liked me at once because I was not as noisy as most of my male contemporaries. We talked about music and plays as we danced. You were so animated, so sure of your own views. So passionate in defence of books I had never read; so dismissive of the popular success of *People Without Space*. My mother paid no attention to politics. She was too busy cooking, cleaning and mending while trying to maintain a façade of gentility suitable to the 'von' we were entitled to, courtesy of Old Fritz, Frederick the Great himself, whose court an ancestor of my father's had once graced. I had followed her example, too busy myself and feeling that politics were either for the rich who had time to play at them or those so poor they had nothing to lose.

Not that we talked politics that night. Suddenly the music changed to an American syncopated beat and you began to dance away from me, scissoring sideways, lifting your knees and moving your arms from the elbow and wrist.

'Come on,' you said.

'I can't. I don't know how.' I longed to join in, to be as free and supple as you were but I was too inhibited. 'Where did you learn to dance like that?' I asked you when we sat down after the music had stopped. And you told me about some American cousins who had taught you on a visit to Europe. Now, you said, the records could be bought in Berlin and you and Otto practised together at home to the new negro music. I thought of my life behind the lace curtains and potted plants and imagined my mother's horrified reaction to such music in the house.

Afterwards we walked beside the dark lake and exchanged plans for the future. You had another year at school. I hoped to be starting at the university. Meanwhile there were the summer holidays. You would be going away to Murnau and then to the mountains while I stayed in the dusty city. But would I come on Saturday to play tennis with a party of your friends before you both went away? Of course. Although I was afraid I didn't play very well. Then it was time to go back. You wanted Otto to give me a lift all the way home but I insisted on being dropped in the Ku'damm and walking the rest of the way. I didn't want you to see exactly where I lived or my mother to be peering from the window, waiting up for me with her questions about the car and its occupants.

Saturday was fine and still and I decided to cycle to your house in the Grünewald and save the train fare. I had recently bought a secondhand bicycle and taught myself to mend the tyres with rubber patches and black glue out of a little oblong tin, to put the chain back when it came off as it frequently did, to fit new brake blocks and keep the whole machine oiled and cleaned. It was to be my passport to more freedom than I could afford on tram and train. And there was something almost daring, daredevilish, in throwing my knickerbockered leg over the crossbar and pushing off with a vigorous thrust down on the pedal. My mother approved of the bicycle too, as cheap and healthy. Her inability to buy me those extras young people needed, in her view, made her often anxious and weary.

I almost shouted with the sheer exuberance of standing on the pedals to force the machine up the tree-lined roads of the Grünewald with the invigorating smell of the pines in my nostrils. The villa Strauss was a modern structure of what seemed at first just glass and metal, set apart in larger grounds than some of its neighbours, behind a wire fence barely restraining a prowling Dobermann. A servant came to my ring at the doorbell and showed me in to a big drawing-room with huge glass doors looking over the lawn towards the tennis courts. I remember there was another boy there, and Anni Reiss, as well as you and your brother. Eventually three more arrived, none of whom I knew, so that we had enough for two sets of doubles. The others began first, having won the toss. 'I always call tails,' Otto said, 'out of perversity. So I always lose. Come and see my lab, while we're waiting.'

'Your stinks cupboard, you mean.' You seemed suddenly annoyed and a little contemptuous.

'Jealousy,' Otto teased. 'Come on. This is for men not little girls.' The little girl stuck out her tongue, a thin pointed pink tip. Otto pulled me away as I tried to make a gesture of resignation. In the hall as we passed through, I noticed there was a full-length photograph of an officer in a long field overcoat and spiked helmet, looking like the Kaiser. 'Who's that?' I asked.

'Oh Papa. You'll meet him later at lunch. We always tease him that he looks the spit of Hindenburg himself.' He took me along a corridor and down some steps to the kitchen quarters, where he opened a cellar door on more steps leading down. When he switched on the light I saw that there was a bench fitted out like the ones in the school laboratory: sink and bunsen burner, tidy shelves with an array of glass beakers, flasks and dishes, a condenser formed from the crystallised alimentary system of a creature from Mars, a glass fumigatory, and jars of different-coloured compounds neatly labelled in modern script. I had expected a rich boy's playroom but Otto's lab seemed to be a place of serious study.

'This is the future,' Otto said, 'not your old law. Mathematics and physics. Why don't you try it?'

'It would be too uncertain for me. I need a safe job in the civil service. That's why I'll do law if I've passed, though you're probably right. That is the future. But how do you know what to do without a teacher?'

'That's the beauty of it. Experiment. You just make it up as you go along. Like poetry.'

We retraced our route to the drawing-room. 'Well?' you asked, no longer the little girl but a grave questioner.

'Very impressive. Otto is undoubtedly the next Einstein.'

'Don't tell him that. His head is swollen enough already. And you? What will you be?'

'Something very boring in the diplomatic, or else the army if the civil service won't have me.'

'Aren't they all "von" this and that in the army?'

'Anton is a "von",' Otto said.

I don't know how he knew for I never used it at school. It seemed too pretentious in juxtaposition with my mother's lodgers.

'Are you a Junker then, Anton?'

'Not really. I mean, we haven't any lands or anything. One of my ancestors seems to have been at Weimar with Goethe and one was at the court of Frederick of Prussia. Both civil servants, flunkeys to princes. So you see it's in the blood. But that was a long time ago. We've come down in the world since then. Not that we were ever very far up.' I longed for you to drop the whole subject.

'You've embarrassed Anton.' Otto came to my rescue. 'It's time that lot finished. They can't hog the courts all morning.' He went to establish our claim and soon the three of us, and that other girl whose name and face I can't remember, were running about in the sunshine. Otto and the other girl were rather good. My greatest achievement was to get my serve in once or twice and occasionally run up to the net and tip one over. You were very patient, misleadingly so. Your friends joined us for drinks on the terrace and then packed themselves into one car with a lot of laughter and drove off.

It was time for lunch and to meet your papa. The best I could hope to draw on was that my father had been a soldier too. I knew about the camaraderie of the Great War. Your father quizzed me on my expected examination results. I felt myself beginning to redden.

'Anton will do well, Papa, he's one of our stars.'

'And what will you read?'

'Law, sir.'

'A good choice. It gives you so many options. But of course it's every young German's ambition. If not that, the Wehrmacht.'

'That's my second choice, sir.'

'It's in many ways an enjoyable life. Especially so in peacetime. I had to give up playing soldiers when my father died, and take over the family business. But the connections I'd made were very useful. Nowadays of course, it's a different story.'

I didn't like to ask what he meant. 'I'd like to get into the diplomatic,' I said.

'You'll need languages for that.'

'Yes. I'll try to find an attachment abroad when I've finished my first legal studies.'

'A very good idea. You should all travel while you're young in case you don't get the opportunity later. It's better to travel in peacetime, too, than as part of an invading army, as we were. You tend to get a warmer reception.'

We had spooned our way through a cold blood-coloured borscht and were now on to Wiener schnitzel. 'Was your father in the war?' Herr Strauss asked me.

'He was a captain in the cavalry, sir. He was killed on the Western Front.'

'I'm sorry. So many good men . . . It must have been especially hard for your mother. Has she married again?'

'No.'

'And do you have brothers and sisters?'

'No sir.'

'At least, whatever happens, Otto and Minna have each other.'

'Papa is full of gloom about the state of the world,' you said.

'So is any man of sense.'

'He spends a lot of time listening to English radio, the BBC, London.'

'It gives me more information about what is going on in the rest of the world. Here in Germany we tend to be too inward looking, to think we are the only ones to have suffered since the war.'

'But surely, Papa,' Otto said, 'that's all changed. Now we are as prosperous as any other country.'

'Just because you can all sit gossiping in some pavement café before moving on to your favourite nightclub to dance the hours away, you think all our problems are solved. But that isn't how they see it in the bierkellers of Munich.'

'But that was a failure, that ridiculous attempt at a coup. Everything has been quiet since then.'

'You think it was like lancing a boil, Otto, but the infection is still in the blood, quietly working away, corrupting the internal organs until it is ready to burst out and plunge the whole body into a fever.'

'What an extended metaphor, Papa,' you laughed, with a piece of schnitzel halfway to your mouth. I grinned across at you, sharing this put-down of the adult world and its apprehensions. 'Papa will be standing for the Reichstag next. He's already practising his election speech.'

I looked from one animated face to the other. I was unused to this kind of discussion, to the heavy family teasing. At home my mother and I ate our evening meal in a silence broken from time to time by a modest question and answer about work or domestic matters. I felt excited by the exchanges, almost holding my breath.

'Why do we in this district all have to live behind a wire fence with a guard dog if there's nothing to worry about?' Herr Strauss asked the table. 'Who are we really afraid of?'

No one answered. 'There is poverty and unemployment in England and America, in all the Western world, but they aren't afraid that the whole state might collapse into civil war.'

'Surely Papa, that won't happen.'

'Well, perhaps it's better if you can't see further than your noses so you can enjoy being young a little longer. Pass the potatoes, Minna.'

After lunch we walked among the pine trees until I had to cycle home to get ready for my holiday evening job, waiting on tables in a little café in Marburgerstrasse. We didn't meet again for months and by then your father's presentiments had become hideous fact with the Wall Street crash, the failure of the German banks and the collapse of the mark, the unemployment and naked hunger that brought personalities of both right and left onto the streets of Berlin in open conflict. In many ways my mother and I had been luckier than most. She had her war widow's pension and I had a grant for my university studies. Waiting at the café I was able to pick up discarded rolls and pieces of cheese while my mother's genteel appearance had qualified her for a job in a fashionable department store. It was there I bumped into you again, trying on gloves.

You said you had often wondered how and where I was. That your father had sent you away to finish your schooling in Switzerland. I hadn't come across Otto around the university because he had decided to pursue his science and maths to America and Harvard. I thought you must see me trembling, and my face and neck flushing as we talked. Until that moment I hadn't realised I was in love with you. Every detail of what now seemed that magic afternoon at the villa Strauss unrolled in my head as if each image had been caught on film. 'You must come over on your bicycle,' you were saying. 'It's so lonely with Otto away. And Papa's too gloomy and preoccupied with business to be any fun. Can you come on Sunday?'

'Do you remember last time we met?' I managed to keep the trembling out of my voice.

'You should hear what my father's saying now. It would make your hair stand on end,' you said, laughing. 'Will you come? What are you doing in the ladies' department? Are you buying something for your girlfriend?' I had forgotten the accepted idiom of constant teasing in your family.

'My mother works here.'

'You must introduce me.'

I hoped you wouldn't think her too dowdy, or she that you were too rich and spoilt. But you charmed her so that when I said you had invited me to lunch on Sunday she began to worry about what I should wear and whether I had a clean shirt. It was February and too cold of course for tennis.

I looked out through the huge glass windows at the court with its pillow of snow, plumped here and there by little fists of wind under the lacy piercings of birds' feet, and overhung by a grey quilt of cloud. I tried to call back the brilliant light of my first visit. But I couldn't quite manage it. We didn't know then it had gone forever. Only you were the same. Your very skin seemed to exude a warmth and energy that lifted me out of my usual dullness in spite of the weather. Unlike most houses I knew, including our own where my mother and I sat huddled in our bedclothes to keep from freezing to death, there seemed to be plenty of fuel to warm the villa Strauss.

'No tennis today.'

'We'll play ping-pong instead.'

Your father shook my hand as if he was genuinely pleased to see me and remembered who I was. But as soon as the maid had served us and left the room, gloom settled on him just as you had described.

'How have things been with you since your last visit?' he asked, carving the chicken.

'Well, sir, I suppose I've been luckier than many.'

'I forget what you were about to do?'

'Anton's studying law.'

'That's right, for the diplomatic. I remember. I hope you'll be able to finish your studies without another war disrupting them. We certainly need those who understand the rule of law.'

I heard myself echoing Otto. 'Surely sir, now we're part of the

League of Nations and the disarmament talks there won't be a war.' I was proud of my knowledge of current events and eager to show off a bit in front of you.

'Those things can easily be repudiated if the communists or the Nazis come to power. I hope you're nothing to do with either of them.'

'They're both too extreme for me. I prefer something more in the middle.'

'Then you're very untypical of your generation. Leg or breast?'

'Either, thank you sir.' I was thinking about what he had just said. When I had time to notice, between my job, my studies and the problem of how we were to make ends meet at home, I realised that not only many of the undergraduates but a lot of the academic staff too, while affecting to despise the rightist thugs, themselves practised a kind of élite nationalism, a yearning for the old days of certainty of the Kaiser and Prussian discipline.

'Suppose for the sake of argument, the communists or the Nazis should seize power, what would you, as a young diplomat-to-be, see as your position?'

'I don't really see what they could do, sir.'

'Both of them advocate a single-party state.'

'But we have the constitution and free elections.'

'Have you ever read the communist manifesto or *Mein Kampf*?'

'No sir.'

'Neither has anyone else except those whose Bible they are. That's the trouble. But I have. Both of them. The communist manifesto may be a blueprint for economic disaster but at least it isn't the work of a raving madman, stuffed with theories about racial purity and Germany's right to swallow up half of Europe. My own fellow industrialists, businessmen who ought to know better, keep their snouts in the trough and pretend everything is fine. Even the Wehrmacht is affected.'

'Herr Müller seems capable, and concerned for the country.'

'But he isn't strong enough to hold the coalition together. They will tear him apart. That will be the beginning of the end for our

45

pathetic attempt at a democratic republic. The wolves are waiting in the forests.'

'Papa is busy making doomsday plans,' you teased him.

'Yes, and they include your safety, yours and Otto's.'

'What about you, Papa?'

'I'm an old man, nearly.' And suddenly he looked it. 'If Germany goes the way I think it will, I shan't wish to live to see it anyway.'

'You mustn't say that, Papa. Even if it does become as bad as you expect, there's the rest of the world.'

'For you, of course. But I don't know if I can begin again.'

'But what could happen, Papa? I don't understand.'

'If the republic collapses when Hindenburg dies and the communists win, all our property will be confiscated by the state. If the fascists win, as Jews our condition will be infinitely worse.'

'But we're not orthodox. We don't practise.'

'To Hitler it isn't a matter of religion. After all, *Mein Kampf* is hardly the work of a Christian. It's a question of blood, of a myth of German racial purity. Back to the Nibelungs.'

'It sounds like Wagner without the music.'

'And you know how that ends.' We all laughed at this and even Herr Strauss's mood seemed to lighten. He left us alone after lunch and we walked in the frozen garden.

'Look,' you said and stooped to pick up a little bundle of feathers from under a bush whose branches were sewn with buds of ice. 'Feel Anton. It's so light it must have died of hunger. We should bury it.'

But the ground was iron hard, and although I poked at it with a stick I couldn't break through the frozen crust that glittered with congealed seams of water, like fools' gold. In the end we covered it with leaves as the birds covered Hansel and Gretel, each leaf crystalline with sugary rime.

I rode home with my face stinging even behind my woollen scarf, thinking about what I had discovered. It had never occurred to me to think of your family, you, Otto, your father, as Jews, or indeed any of my former classmates or fellow students. For all I knew I had Jewish ancestors myself. I had never even asked the question. This was the twentieth century. Ideas of race belonged to nineteenth-century imperialism and the establishment of national states and empires. Africans might be different, of course, and the descendants of American slaves, but that was because they had lived a life apart from the mainstream of Western culture. The Jews of Germany, at least those like Herr Strauss and his family, and countless others I didn't know, were indistinguishable from their fellow Germans: army officers, industrialists, scientists, musicians, shopkeepers, teachers, an endless, largely invisible, presence except for their priests, who wore strange clothes like all religions, and those, mainly newcomers, immigrants in flight from Poland, and persecution, who kept themselves to themselves in their quarters like some of the more extreme Protestant sects. I truly believe, trying to recapture it now, that was how I thought, in my ignorance compounded with bliss.

For I was hopelessly in love and the spice of danger, your father's gloomy prognostications, only enhanced my deep-dyed romanticism and therefore my passion. You understood me so much better, even at the beginning, than I did myself.

Bumping back over the icy tramlines I sometimes stood up on the pedals to shout, now with a new excitement in which the friction of the saddle had its probable share. I was half ashamed, half proud of my need for physical release that led me to the lavatory as soon as I got home, ostensibly to wash but actually to jerk off in acute spasms into a piece of the precious toilet paper mother got cheaply through her job, leaning against the wall as my legs threatened to buckle and stifling my groans with my scarf when I imagined your body held against mine, as you had reached up your arms around my neck and kissed me on the mouth.

'You will come again soon, won't you?'

## IV

By the time she opened the door on the slim figure under its topknot of wiry curls Betony was weary of the whole process. She had been late back from the studio in Twickenham last night, with the lights of the opposing traffic flashing into her tired eyes for what seemed like miles. The shoot had been long and tough. Mysterious failures of power and equipment had meant several retakes. The objects she and Sadie had collected to enliven the pages of *Ruralities* looked dreary and middle-aged: a wickerwork tray, an apron with pockets for hand tools, greenery-yallery canvas gloves she had tried to make more enticing by arranging as a starfish. 'Bring back the garden gnome,' she had said in a moment of despair. And the photographer had reminded her of Mark, with his satirical approach to taking pictures of 'this load of crap', implying that his last and next engagements had been, would be, intensely and artistically fulfilling.

In the morning she had crawled out of bed after the alarm to scurry from room to room, picking up newspapers, plumping cushions, carefully placing newly washed ashtrays, hiding dirty clothes at the bottom of the painted wardrobe that showed a pair of lugubrious overweight pigs in a snowy yard. She had painted them herself as a kind of visual comfort food when she felt that she was getting porky and needed to slim down. 'Trad tat,' Mark had called them, 'sugar piggy banks for good little girls.' That was just before he left. Tearing the plaster off in one go. Kindest after all.

'Betony Falk?' The boy (that was what he looked, still in his early twenties at most, she thought) asked her, letting the name just drop off lips that were so full and sculpted she wanted to put out a finger and touch them to see if they were warm, not carved from some dark wood or cast in bronze. She had abandoned 'Tony' after art school, realising both that it would please Gran Bet and that in the strange world of fashion and ephemera she had entered her full name was a tradeable asset, a fragile artefact itself, an exotic butterfly of sound lighting on the page beside her compositions.

'I'm Gill, Gill Idbury.' He said it almost as if he expected her to recognise the name. 'Come up.' She knew the process so well now, having done it three times already that day. One prospective sharer hadn't turned up at all or even telephoned to cancel. Betony had wandered nervously from room to room, looking at everything with a sallow eye: the avocado bathroom suite she had always wanted to replace but could never afford to; the finger-printed light switches she hadn't had time to wipe; the missing sashcord; a grubby kitchen towel she snatched from its roller and buried in the clothes basket. Mark had called the colour of the bathroom 'bile green'. Bravely she had countered: 'I thought bile was yellow.'

'All right then: sheep shit!'

The first visitor had been a nervous girl in a shaggy jacket whose fabric glistened like permanently wet fur and fastidiously stretched maroon ski-pants. The walk from the station through the mixed and sometimes over-ebullient population had unnerved her. Was it safe at night? She didn't drive. The road seemed long; the tall houses and trees would cast thick shadows over it. Would they each have their own cupboard in the kitchen? Did the work surfaces wipe clean easily? She touched the draining-board with a nervous finger. Betony didn't think she would hear from her again.

The second had been a hearty accountant. Would the washing machine cope with his rugger gear? He liked to have the team round for a few jars after a game or before they went clubbing. She saw herself stuck with a tide of dirty glasses and strewn socks, matted with mud and sweat. Then there was the couple who tried to pass themselves off as a single girl living there alone, with the boy staying most nights and weekends until, Betony knew, she would feel outnumbered, besieged in her own flat.

She remembered Gran Bet's pleas: 'I don't like you sharing with a stranger.' And her answer: 'Everyone's a stranger.'

49

'But a black man, darling?'

'He's more like milky coffee,' she imagined herself saying.

'And what does he do for a living, darling?'

'I'm a dancer. Oh, it's all right. I temp as well. I'll pay the rent regularly.'

'Temp?'

'Mostly inputting to databases when firms get a sudden rush of stuff their ordinary staff can't cope with. It suits me. I'm not looking for anything more permanent because of the dancing. I have to be free when something comes along.'

They were sitting on either side of the electric fan heater with its illusion of living flame. Betony noticed his hands: the very pale palms creased with a darker network of lines; the long bony fingers with their perfect filbert nails steepled in front of his chest. He was dressed in alternating blocks of black and white down to his gleaming trainers. The effect was assured, stylish without being flamboyant.

'Could I get in another wardrobe?' he had asked when Betony showed him the room. 'I've got rather a lot of clothes.'

She made up her mind. 'When would you like to move in?'

'I'll bring my gear round on Saturday if that's okay for you.'

She got up and took Mark's door keys on their metal hoop out of a table drawer. 'Take these in case I'm working.' There came a moment when you had to trust or life couldn't go on. She was glad she wasn't due to visit Gran Bet's again soon. It was easier fielding questions on the telephone.


V


Of course I didn't let on at that first meeting: You might have felt invaded. You had to learn to trust me first. Giving us the key were the beginning; then letting us move in the wardrobe the next weekend whilst you was out. Us didn't see much of each other the first couple of weeks. I were careful not to be around too much and I had a job that lasted well into March, taking me out of the flat every weekday, while in the evenings and weekends I were over to the Dance Arena to practise and work out or at Stomp where the choreographers and managers go to pick up the talent. Time was running out on me. In a year or two I'd be old, over the hill at thirty, pushed aside by the new boys coming up behind, if you do see what I mean.

I like to work out in front of the big mirror at the Dance Arena, watch meself, be me own audience. The mirror, the fourth see-through wall that throws you back at yourself, is the audience. It tells you what they do see when you'm dancing for them. Maybe one day you'll want to see us like that, Betony Falk. I still calls you that in my head. Aloud I don't call you nothing. No name'll come out. As if naming you was some kind of magic. It'd change us, how we are together, and I'm not ready for that yet.

'Keep theeself to theeself,' Nana always said. 'Don't give no one power over 'ee.' So I kept stumm. But I couldn't last out forever. You'd trusted I and I paid you back with a silence that were a lie.

Then came that day you asked what I were doing at the week-end cause you was going to be away and you'd feel easier knowing the flat weren't empty.

'I'll be here.' I'd got a rehearsal for a backing line to a new singer. There were five of us, what Nana used to call 'putting in the dirt', only now it's done visually with dance routines in close harmony. There was three boys and two girls. We'd worked together before, so it were easy to drop into step once we heard the music and before they brought in Jacey and the Toms to put over the lyrics of *Honeybun*.

I got a sweet tooth, honeybun;
You're all sugar and spice.
I'll just make a beeline for your lips
And sip there once or twice.

Philly and Lash were the girls and the other two boys were Jim Blue and Sycamore. I never knowed if their names were real and their own like mine or just something they'd picked up along the way. In this game everyone has a mask, a glossy surface to throw back the light and dazzle the punters, and your monicker's part of it. It says, look at me I'm cool. We're all in it for highkicks. I were looking forward to working again, for a chance to do just that.

'I have to go and stay with my grandmother,' you said. 'I've been putting it off but I must go this weekend.'

'Is it far?' I asked.

'No. Just down the M4. Near Reading.'

I tried to smile. 'That's where I come from. Down that way. That's where I went to school in Reading.'

'So did I for a bit. Nearby, anyway. Until my father died, I came up to London to take my "A" levels.'

'Well I never did,' I said in Nana's voice. But I still weren't ready to tell.

'And I thought you were a real Londoner.'

'I've been here a long time now.'

'She's my godmother as well as my grandmother. That's why I'm stuck with this name, after her.' So Lady Falk were still alive when Nana and mother June, and maybe Margaret herself for what I knew, were all dead. 'She gets very lonely, alone in the house I grew up in. It's really too big for her now.'

And the house were still there too, the very same where Nana had wiped little Harry's nose and arse and mended their silk stockings, Lady Falk's and Margaret's, with a crochet hook so they could go dancing up to London under the great circling globe of mirrors, flowering and darkening as the lights caught them, before our pulsing strobes were ever thought of. Just as I do now. Maybe that's where my dancing do come from if not from darkie, Yankee Carl. Or him and Margaret both, for where else would they have met except on the dance floor. It were nice to have the place to meself. There were always the psychiatrist on the ground floor but she usually went away at weekends, even in the bitter windy cold of that spring that made it hard to limber up after a day in front of the computer screen, earning me bread with columns of names to be made from boxes of faded cards that must have been around in Bob Cratchit's day. Sometimes I wondered what I'd do when all the world was online and there were no more simple inputting jobs that left me free to think dance while me fingers patted the keys automatically.

I didn't envy you, Betony Falk, driving out of London of a Friday. Huddled inside the bus shelter I watched the traffic slowly uncurling like sludge-heavy lava while the wind dragged at me clothes, crept up me sleeves and down me collar. Nana had told of great frosts when she were young, of frozen rivers you could cross on foot and snowdrifts that laid siege to Gisborne Hall for days. I'd see her nurserymaid's peaky face peering out of an attic window etched with frost flowers and framed in a downy border of snow. 'It were that bitter you expected your breath to freeze and fall down in little hailstones at your feet.'

The guy who runs the Dance Arena's wife were once a dancer herself, so he knows the score and lets us members use any empty practice room that hasn't got a class going on in it. The building itself, just on the edge of the street market, did used to be a public bath and laundry for the local people, to encourage the great unwashed to clean themselves and their clothes before there were washing machines and hot water that didn't have to be heated in a copper. It do say so in stone letters outside, and inside there's old smudged photos of how it were so you can smell the suddy steam and hear the echo of the women laughing together as they stirred the huge vats, or folded the sheets, one to each end, sides to middle until they were flat and small enough to be mangled between the big wooden rollers, as I remember Nana doing. 'Take an end boy and don 'ee dare drop 'un. They sheets won't need no ironing if 'ee do do it right and not stand there woolgathering.'

The Arena has classes for everything you can think of, and

some: ballet for kids as young as two and a half, 'Hardbody work-outs', jazz and reggae, trad tap, 'tums and bums', belly dancing, fatburner, historical dance, contemporary, flamenco. I dances me own mixture, free style that come out of eighties break dancing and have got a bit of modern and some jazz in it. Dancing's natural as breathing. Get the feet going right and the rest of the body language flows. Saturday night at a club you suddenly feels the buzz. You'm flying and everyone's focused on you. After, the punter comes up and says: 'Give me your number and I'll give you a call.' You've scored.

'What do you want, then?'

'I'm looking for a dancer,' he'll say and that's all right. But sometimes it's: 'I like your style. Have a drink. Where do you live?' And then you knows 'tain't your feet they'm after. I play it cool then, even if I does fancy 'em.

We hasn't discussed that, Betony Falk, but I reckon you do know. Not that I've hidden it, mind. It just haven't come up. When it do, if it do, I'll tell you. No problem. But maybe it never will and you've just took it for granted, and one of the reasons you asked me in, in preference to all the others that must have come ringing your doorbell, was because you knowed I were safe, or rather you was. I wouldn't be trying all the while to get into your knickers or sheets. I reckon you've had a rough time somewhere recent and you finds me kind of restful.

The bus that takes me to the Dance Arena is one of they little 'uns that flings you all over the shop, even us, who'm young and smart, but if you'm old and brittle could be your death. Nana would have give the drivers a proper tongue lashing if they'd tossed her about like that, but these days you daresn't. So the grey heads get the worst of it, jerked around like broken puppets. That's what I thinks of: *Pinocchio*, under the axe in the puppeteer's jolting caravan, that were one of the Christmas movies Nana found money to take us to, along with our local tatty panto in seventies' steep decline as more and more people grew used to the high standards on telly, *Top of the Pops*, and films like *Grease*, and stopped going out to see the second-rate wallopers trying to reach for the high notes. 'If us don't go and support them,' Nana said, 'why should anyone turn out for you?'

I'd feel for her arm in the Roxy dark and tuck mine under her worn cardigan encasing the slack flesh. It could happen to me. Thrown on a mound somewhere, discarded down the council tip, wasted. She were the only surety and she were old, and because she and the century were the same age I could never forget how old, already well on in her seventies when she took us to *Saturday Night Fever*. And then I broke her heart by going away after our mother were killed.


VI


When I asked my mother if we had any Jewish blood one cold evening after my ride home over the frosted tramlines, parallel silver ribbons leading away into the dark labyrinth of the city, she put down her cup of chocolate and said, 'Is this because of your new friends, the Strausses?'

'I mean, since I didn't know they were Jewish until they told me, or rather Herr Strauss told me, I thought there might be something I didn't know about us.'

'Do you mean your father's family or mine?'

'Both, I suppose.'

'So, on my side, as far as I know, my parents and grandparents were born in Bamberg where I grew up. I suppose I would never have left if I hadn't met your father when he was stationed there after training at the Hanover cavalry school. As for his family I can't say, apart from the stories he told which you know.'

'You never looked into his family after he was killed or made contact with them?'

'I felt they thought he shouldn't have married me, a petit

bourgeois schoolteacher. And they made no effort to get in touch with me or help with your education.'

'Perhaps they're all dead.'

'Your father spoke of a younger brother, Johannes. I believe they lived in Bremen.'

'And the story about Frederick, Old Fritz, was that true?'

'Your father always said so. Although he didn't make anything of it. He never used the "von" until he was commissioned. He said it helped in the army. I thought it might help you too, when I registered you at the gymnasium.'

So that was where Otto had picked it up. My mother took me to her parents' home in Bamberg for the summer holidays sometimes. It was a little old walled town with a cathedral and university and a way of life that flowed smoothly as the river under its stone bridges. The huge and hugely famous equestrian statue of a Teutonic knight in the gloom of the cathedral seemed almost out of place, as if the rider had lost his way and only came to seek shelter from some storm. He looks about as if puzzled, a forefinger pulling the drawstring of his cloak so that it covers his shoulders. The other arm is raised. The ceremonial helmet over the ringlets seemed to me more like a diadem for a king or poet than a serious protection against a weapon of war. Every time I visited my grandparents I would slip away to see him, to try to fathom his seven-hundred-year-old mystery. It was only much later that I discovered that others had been considering his enigmatic presence too. The Stauffenberg brothers for instance, and Stefan George.

I still visited him after the war as long as my legs could carry me but he has never yielded up his secret. Perhaps I shall get Christoff to take me one more time. And there maybe I shall have a road to Damascus revelation in front of his full lips and questioning look, and die at his horse's feet. Romantic nonsense you would have called it, my Minna.

Your father took you away with him in the spring on a world trip that included visiting Otto in the United States and then home via Switzerland. During those months it was as if my life was in abeyance, waiting in the Sleepers' Den for you to return and take it up again for me. I tried to see myself as a knight slumped, slumbering over his sword, guarding the catafalque of a dead emperor under the hill. When you came back like Saint Venus you might carry me off to the Venusberg for Tannhäuser's year of bliss. I used to look at my fellow students and wonder whether their heads were full of such thoughts. I doubted it. They seemed like the proverbial swine jostling to get their snouts in the trough, as Herr Strauss would have said. Most of them were fighting for the few places that might become available for officers in our post-Versailles limited army. And they already behaved with the swagger of that élite, drinking, brawling and roaring out their manly songs as they staggered home together after an evening out.

It was becoming increasingly difficult not to be sucked into the political whirlwind and forced to take sides. I longed not just for your return but for your father's too, so that there was someone, as I saw it, to discuss the situation with. Just after you left, the whole business of whether our ageing president should stand again for election at eighty-five became foremost in everyone's mind. Brüning, on whom Herr Strauss had pinned his hopes, was now called derisively 'the Hunger Chancellor' because of his desperate economies demanded in every sphere of life. I found myself suddenly a committed Republican yet sick of the strikes, street brawls, private armies acting as if they were the official Reichswehr that seemed to be edging us towards a ruinous civil war. At times I felt 'a plague on both your houses' and then I remembered that your father had seen the communists as the lesser of two evils, at least for your family.

I realise I am using clichés. But that was what we were fed. What we are still fed of course. That is the nature of politics. But then there was nothing else. The newspapers ranted against each other on behalf of their parties of 'the coming maelstrom', 'the just demands of the people', 'the evil in our midst that must be rooted out', 'the oppressions of Versailles', until 'the people', people themselves, couldn't think for the clamour and they too began to shout and scream louder and louder.

Suddenly I had a chance to get away from it all. I had entered for an essay prize: the essay to be written in English on some aspect of British jurisprudence; the prize a six-months' secondment to an English university law faculty. My tutor congratulated me. 'You will be able to kill two birds with one stone: improve your English by constant practice, since nobody in England speaks any language but their own, and compare the two legal systems: statute and common law. I hope however, that you will not be contaminated by the English disease: that compound of weakness, greed and hypocrisy which so often characterises a mongrel nation. We shall be waiting for you on your return, to see if you are still a good German.'

Such language was creeping into every mouth, especially among academics, diplomats and the military. I thought how Goethe and Heine would have despised it, but it no longer seemed possible to say so if you were to make your way in the world, especially if you came from a poor family. You will say I was weak, Minna, but then I never had your spirit.

When I told my mother about my good luck she became sad and thoughtful.

'It isn't that. My real worry is whether you should come back at all.'

'You mean because of all our problems in Berlin?'

'I lost your father in one war, Anton. I don't think I could bear to lose you.'

I had never known her speak like this. Usually she kept her emotions carefully guarded. 'If there's to be a war no one will escape. I couldn't run away.'

'You were only a baby so you don't remember the last war. Your father didn't live to tell you and I couldn't bear to speak of it, but you've read *All Quiet on the Western Front*. That wasn't an exaggeration. Far from it. Your father was essentially a gentle and fastidious man although he was a soldier. He couldn't say much in his letters, of course, but when he got leave and came home after he was wounded the first time he was able to tell me. He didn't expect to survive, but even if he had come back I believe he would have been marked for life. Now people talk about another war, to restore German pride, as if it was a glorious game and at the end everyone goes home. I can only say they have forgotten too easily. I wish you could keep out of it all.'

'If I do well in my exams I might get into the diplomatic and be attached to an embassy in a neutral country. Then I can send for you.'

She smiled then. 'Will there be any neutral countries this time?'

'Switzerland will always be neutral.'

'But you will want to send for Fräulein Strauss, not your old mother.' I found myself beginning to blush. 'Perhaps she will visit you in England as part of her grand tour. Anyway, it's right that you should learn English and continue your studies there. Your father said the von Falks originally came from England.'

That was a story I had never heard before. 'From England? But when?'

'Oh hundreds of years ago, I think.' She paused. 'And about Fräulein Strauss. I hope you won't become too involved. She is charming and rich of course. But things are changing. There's much more . . . prejudice, than when I was a girl. You must think of your career.'

I couldn't answer. Instead I asked: 'What will you do while I'm away?'

'Oh I shall go on as usual, only without you to feed and your clothes to wash and mend. You will write to me, won't you?'

And so I went to England for the first time, to the big college in the Strand looking out across the plane trees of the Embankment, down to the River Thames, with its strings of barges bobbing behind the stubby lighterman and its great white passenger ships and blackened, smoky cargo boats making for the acres of dockland from every corner of that empire that was the envy of people at home.

I had never crossed a frontier before or seen the sea. The train took me across Germany and into Belgium. I would have liked to go south and stop at Paris of course but I had neither the time nor the money. And then I reached Ostend and the coast. So this was the sea: this greasy swell of water that cut the British Isles off from the mainland and made them one big floating port. Somewhere there must be other seas that were blue or green with ice, clear and menacing.

The first thing that struck me when I stepped out of Victoria Station was the foul air and grime of the city from the millions of little houses, each with its coal fires pouring their quota of smuts into the common pall that passed for air, the clouds of filthy steam from the trains and the acrid dung and piss of the horses, mingled with the fumes of hundreds of cars and buses. Everything you touched smeared you with its charcoal imprint. The first time I blew my nose I wanted to throw away my handkerchief. My eyes watered and stung with the grits that constantly blew into them and had to be painfully removed with a corner of the same handkerchief or the careful folding of one eyelid over the other. For the sexually laconic British it had become a way of making that first vital encounter with a girl, peering intimately into her face with poised clean handkerchief. Collars and cuffs were lined with greasy smears by the end of the day as if my very skin sweated soot instead of absorbing it from the atmosphere. The miasma that covered the city seemed very ancient. Everyone hawked and spat from the rotted, blackened lungs I imagined inside their sunken ribs with the too white skin stretched painfully over them. And yet they sang and whistled about the streets. I think their poor suffered more than ours physically yet they seemed more cheerful, less angst-ridden. Was it just because they had won the war? I wished I could convey to some of the people at home how they lived.

I soon found that my knowledge of the language was adequate, after a fortnight's acclimatisation, to understanding my fellow students and our lecturers but most of the people in the street, cab drivers, news-sellers, people in shops and public houses, spoke an initially impenetrable argot that I took a whole month to understand.

I was determined to make as much of my time as I could so I threw myself into every activity available to my limited funds. I joined the students' union partly because it was possible to eat more cheaply, partly to be taken quickly into my fellows' way of life. From the notice-board in the union I found a cheap, clean room in a widow's house, the mirror image of my own home, which must have been a great relief to my mother. Mrs Lamb was as gentle as her name implied. Her own son had been killed in the Great War but she carried no grudge against me, especially when I told her about my father. 'Your mother must be a brave woman. She must have had a difficult life alone.' Once a week she lit her copper and stood in the damp or freezing scullery to do her washing, which included mine. Then I took my weekly bath. Never did I have any indication that she did the same. She smelled faintly of musty lavender and her cheeks were a soft pale chamois brushed with the face powder that was probably the source of her scent.

I soon found that the students were very different from those at home. These were clever young men and women from the bourgeoisie. The aristocratic classes sent their children to Oxford or Cambridge where they lived what seemed to be rather rowdy lives. But my fellows at Queen's were necessarily rather sober since they would have to earn a living in the professions once they were qualified, and their parents had little money to give them. They were anti-fascist and inclined, perhaps because of the strong theological faculty, towards Christian socialism. At the weekends they worked in parish halls in the London slums, handing out dinners to the unemployed from steaming pails of thin soup, and coarse loaves of bread. They were also pacifist. Where defeat had made us hunger for the return of Prussian pride and militarism, these British undergraduates spoke of war with universal horror, even to the extent of saying that they would refuse to fight for their country. I thought of my tutor's accusations of weakness, hypocrisy and greed and of how easily he would misunderstand these new companions. I knew there was another side to all this, a world of the so-called 'flapper', but it was even more remote from me than Berlin was becoming. Until you came.

When I wrote to tell you my good news about the award I had no real hope, in spite of my mother's teasing, that we might meet in England. Even so, as soon as I was settled at Mrs Lamb's, I sent my address out into the void. You didn't answer for a month, until I was on the point of writing again. And then one day, when I returned after lectures to the supper Mrs Lamb always had ready for me, normally an English sausage stuffed with bread in a baked batter with boiled potatoes, or minced meat topped with more potatoes called Shepherd's Pie, or smoked fish swimming in milk, none of which I had ever eaten before and had difficulty with now, except that they came with the laundry (and often seemed to taste of it), which came with the room, and I was always hungry, there was a little yellow envelope of dull coarse paper propped against what Mrs Lamb called 'the cruet'. 'A telegram for you, Mr Falk. I hope it isn't bad news. I never like them myself since the war.'

But it was only good news. You were sailing from New York. Had sailed already. Would be docking at Southampton in a couple of days and on your way to London to stay at the Savoy where I should leave a message. Of course, I wanted to rush to you at once but first my suit had to be cleaned and pressed, precious shillings expended on a new tie, Mrs Lamb asked for a clean shirt on a non-washday so that I could present myself at your hotel and not be turned away as a tramp or even a tradesman. 'This must be for a young lady, Mr Falk.' I knew I would blush as I answered. 'The sister of an old school friend. I offered to look after her.' And in a sense I had, with my: 'If you ever come to London while I'm there . . .'

What would we do? Where would I take you? Some things were free. The great London cathedrals, for instance. The picture palaces were within the reach of my student's purse, the new talking films had just hit London, but then you might have seen all the films already in New York. By the time I reached the reception desk and its liveried porter I was ready to faint with apprehension.

You came in the spring of course. If it hadn't been, I would have wanted to turn the seasons forward or back for you, but with all the panache of a Botticelli Flora you arrived in April. Spring had astonished me in London especially in the southern suburbs where I lodged with Mrs Lamb. Now at last I saw the point of all those little villas with their flowery, grassy aprons of garden front and back. They all seemed to break into leaf and bloom at once. Mrs Lamb called up to me one Saturday morning at the beginning of the month before your arrival, when the fierce winds that had rattled the barky branches and had me shivering on my walk to and from the station, where I journeyed backwards and forwards to Charing Cross, had given way to washed sunshine and showers that carried along the grime of winter in the rushing gutters and cleared the dingy clouds from the sky.

'Look, Mr Falk. Spring at last.' She took me to every bursting bush and flower that appeared to have sprung up overnight. The names she told me all sounded like those of minor Greek deities: hyacinth, scilla and narcissus itself, gods that slept through the winter waiting for a warm touch to wake them.

'Does your mother grow these?' And I could only shake my head because I simply couldn't remember, only the hot geranium in the summer in boxes outside our windows.

Then there were the city street flower stalls, kept by women mostly, where narcissus in white and gold lay in neat ranks beside pails full of a flower with a stiff stalk supporting a myriad of flower heads that looked as if they had been stitched together from remnants of multi-coloured velvet. 'Remnant' was a word I had learnt from Mrs Lamb to describe the trophies of cloth she came back with from the big department store of Arding and Hobbs, even bigger than the Strauss shop where my mother now worked.

Every month the weather was a little different; every day even. And I suddenly understood why the English talked so much about it in their little houses heated only with coal fires, and with privies in the back gardens where they waited for signs of the changing seasons. I wondered what summer would be like. It was hard to imagine. I had strayed into the everlasting gloom of a novel by Dickens, which was the city's natural mode.

I passed the Savoy Hotel twice a day at least on my way between Queen's and the station but because it lay back from the Strand in its own cul-de-sac I hadn't really paid it any attention. Often cabs and glossy autos blocked my crossing and dimly behind them I could see uniformed flunkeys guarding the glass doors of the modern façade. Now I had to turn left and walk up to them. No one else seemed to be arriving on foot. I should have got a cab from the station but the distance was so short and the driver might have been unwilling to take me. 'Blimey, it's only a few yards, guv. Not worf you gettin' in. Wot you got legs for?'

I had written my message in preparation, asking you to meet me on the steps of the British Museum on Saturday morning. Mrs Lamb, of course, had no telephone in her house. I should just have to turn up and wait, hoping that my message had reached you and that you weren't already engaged. I left my envelope with its flowing superscription at the porter's desk and turned away. I had had to practise writing your name several times before I was satisfied with its appearance and could transfer it to the clean square of white paper. The note itself had been laboured over like a poem. Should it be: Dear Fräulein or Dear Minna or even Dear Miss Strauss? Already I'd decided to write to you in English although then it was just a way of drawing attention to myself, to impress you.

On Saturday morning I was standing conspicuously on the museum steps above the great forecourt, with its handsome black railings and the elegant houses of Bloomsbury beyond, a quarter of an hour before I hoped you could arrive. Pigeons pecked and courted among the flagstones or rose in a flurry of white water plumage to wheel once or twice before settling again. I felt light-headed. Perhaps we wouldn't recognise each other. And then there you were, crossing the courtyard, very à l'américaine in your check suiting with a white collar under a navy raincoat, and a little hat jaunty on the side of your head. It was as if a rare parakeet had flown down among the dowdy pigeons.

I waved. You waved back and ran up the steps to kiss me on both cheeks.

'Don't let's go in,' you said, looking up at the heavy pediment. 'I've been cooped up in the ship for a week. I want to walk and walk and hear all your news. Otto sends his greetings.' You had your arm through mine and were urging me out of the gate. I steered us away from the rumble of Tottenham Court Road towards the grass and trees of Russell Square. And so it began again, as though there had been no break. But away from home and our families we were freer. Almost breathless. Because we were unrestrained, everything moved very fast, as if we were spooling out our own movie: a lifetime in just two hours.

At the end of the next week, when we had met every day for a film or the theatre with supper in the Savoy Grill, or simply to stroll after my lectures were over, you first mentioned the Walkers. 'Old business acquaintances of Vati. They've asked me to stay for the weekend, so of course I asked if I could bring you.'

'What did they say?'

'Apparently they're always short of young men since the war so they are thrilled. He's a milord. There's just one problem. You'll need some clothes.'

'That's settled then. I don't have much with me. Or at home either.'

'We'll have to hire something for you. There's a dance, you see, and the English are very formal. You'll need die Gala.'

'It will be very expensive to hire.'

'Anton, don't be stuffy please. I've lots of money. Enough for that anyway.'

'I can't take your money.'

'Then I can't go because I won't go without you. Think how good it will be for your English, not allowed to speak German at all except alone with me, in whispers.'

And so I let myself be persuaded and we went to that outfitters in the Strand between your hotel and my college and kitted me out like an American jazz dancer.

I was very nervous as we waited on the station at Charing Cross for the Brighton train. 'Tell me about the Walkers.'

'He's some sort of industrialist: rubber, I think. Originally Walcovitch.'

We had been speaking in German and I noticed our English fellow travellers trying not to stare, with a series of sliding glances quickly averted. I switched languages.

'You said he's a lord.'

'Some charity works, Papa says. That's how it's done here.'

We left the train at Lewes and climbed into the waiting car that took us into the spring countryside. It was the first time I had been outside London, beyond the fog of smuts and smoke. The air washed over us like clear water. It had rained the night before and the rounded hills, fields and trees were a singing green. The car drove through high iron gates, clanged over a cattle grid and on past a landscaped park until it came to rest in front of a big stone house with twin flights of steps supporting a columned porch. A black-uniformed servant appeared and wished sir and madam good morning before calling for others to show us to our rooms.

'His Lordship will expect you for drinks in the library at twelve-thirty,' we had been told. I felt as if I had stepped into a London stage production of a play by some fashionable writer, Lonsdale or Coward.

And that feeling of unreality, of theatricality, stayed with me all weekend as we ate and drank and played tennis and danced to the gramophone.

Dancing took place in the afternoon to the accompaniment of tea with sandwiches and cakes. Then came dinner, and I was glad you had insisted on hiring evening clothes for me. All the expected guests had arrived and the library where we assembled was full of men looking like penguins and women like birds of paradise. You were quite in place in green chiffon with a diamante headdress that sparkled under a wreath of green feathers. The effect of all the male black and white was of uniformity, conformity, where at home such a gathering I imagined would be broken up into the colours of the individual regiments and ranks. This was somehow deliberately civilian: the counterpart of my fellow students' pacifism.

'Let me look at you,' you said and flicked an invisible blemish from my collar.

'There, you look like a Graf.'

'I'm not a Graf.'

'Don't say that. I told them you were. Vati says the English love a lord.'

Lord and Lady Walker were easy and hospitable. He fell in love with you at once of course but I couldn't be jealous of his rosy cheeks of an elderly baby, fluffy white hair and moustache. It was only when I came down to breakfast rather earlier than most on Sunday morning and found him alone with a plate of the same yellow smoky fish that Mrs Lamb sometimes served me, that reality returned briefly. He put aside his newspaper when I said good morning and turned towards the sideboard, where I now knew the silver dishes would be steaming under their shiny covers.

'Good morning, Anton. I hope you slept well?'

'Yes sir, thank you.'

'I'm glad to have the chance of a little talk with you.'

'Yes, sir.'

'I have to say we have found events in your country rather

confusing. I wondered whether you could throw a little light on them for me. I would be most grateful.'

'I'm not sure sir, how I should begin,' I think I said.

'Well for a start then, what will happen when old Hindenburg pops off?'

'I'm afraid I don't quite understand. What is "pops off"?'

'Oh my apologies, dies I mean.'

'There will be great confusion, I think. Perhaps even civil war.'

'That's what Minna's father said but I couldn't believe it: civil war in Europe in the twentieth century, war of any kind after the last one. Russia's different of course. The Orient, the East begins there. And who will win?'

'The communists or the fascists will be the ones fighting each other.'

'So you think one of them will win?'

'Yes, sir.'

'And which would you put your money on?'

'With something so serious, sir, it is unwise to bet.'

'Oh the English will bet on anything. Well Minna said you were going to be a diplomat!' He picked up his paper again while I cut into a salty half moon of kidney.

And it was there, later that day, when we had escaped into the countryside and wandered away towards the sea, that we first made love, lying in a gritty hollow of the dunes with the rough grass stabbing at our skin, our mouths as salty as the kidneys. I remember undoing your coat and then the buttons of your blouse, and you didn't stop me. And then I felt your hands on the buttons of my trousers and warm on my flesh. You lifted your skirt and wriggled down your knickers and I was on top of you, our mouths together in a kind of frenzy as you guided me in. I came almost at once, crying out, and then you did too and we just lay there with all the life sucked out of us.

'Have you got a big handkerchief?'

I fumbled in my pocket, rolling sideways and gave it to you. I watched while you calmly folded it and put it between your legs. 'Next time we'd better bring a towel,' you laughed.

'You've done it before?'

'Of course. There'd be blood everywhere if I hadn't and you wouldn't have had such an easy time. I thought you Burschen had some sort of students' initiation night with one of the Dirnen.'

'I didn't have enough money,' I lied to you.

'Your English wouldn't have done that,' you said as we were walking back across the dunes. 'Too cold.'

'What do you mean my English?'

'Oh you seem to fit in here.'

'My mother says there's a story we originally came from England.'

'So you see.'

'And you?'

'Oh from the East, I expect. After all, in the beginning it must have been Palestine, or Israel as it was once. Hundreds of years ago. But we've been German since the middle of the last century, longer than most of the Americans I met in New York have been American. Otto thinks he might stay. He speaks English better than you do now but with a Yankee accent of course.'

Afterwards we thought of that weekend as our real honeymoon. Back in London the spring bloomed again into heady early summer. Somehow you managed to stay but my term and the award would end with July. Our love-making took on the franticness of anguish rather than the frenzy of passion. One night when we were lying in anxious exhaustion with the sweat still warm between us you said, 'Let's get married.'

'When? How can we?'

'Now. Soon. Before we have to go home.'

'Home.' The news from home was depressing.

Chancellor Brüning, who was at least a democrat and supporter of the republic, had been replaced by the ludicrous von Papen who made everyone laugh. In June a new election was called, the third that year. Bitter street fighting broke out between the private armies of the communists and fascists as soon as Brüning's ban on the right-wing stormtroopers was lifted by von Papen. My mother wrote that she was afraid to go out again at night after returning from work and that Sundays were made impossible by the parties marching and counter-marching, until there were the inevitable riots and pitched battles in the streets, guns and blood.

'We could be engaged.'

You shook your head. 'If we're not married, ways will be found to separate us. It's our only hope.'

I thought of my mother warning me not to get too involved. And Herr Strauss would think I was too poor for his daughter and had too long to wait before I could complete my studies for the diplomatic. He would send you away again.

'Don't you want to marry me, Anton? Perhaps it's all been just a game to you.' I'd never seen you hurting before. And I was the cause. It had always seemed to me that you were the stronger and I followed adoringly behind. Now suddenly our positions were reversed. I was making you beg. I felt an unworthy surge of power and put my arms around you.

'Of course I do. It's only what our parents will think and say. I shan't be qualified for another year and then there's no guarantee of a job.'

'Vati will have to help us. After all, he always said that Otto and I would have each other but if Otto stays in America . . . He ought to be pleased that you will be there to look after me. I know he likes you. I could say I was pregnant.'

'You aren't, are you?'

'No, but I could be,' and you laughed.

'I'll find out how it could be done. I'll ask Bob Weston.'

Bob Weston was one of my fellow students who spent his weekends in the East End. I'd gone with him once or twice before you came. He was studying to be an English priest. He would know. You asked if you could come with us one Saturday.

'It's not very pretty or amusing.'

70

'I'd like to see a different way of life from the Walkers and their friends.'

So you came along with a group of four students who took the trolleybus on Saturday morning to Bow and St Egbert's church hall to help put out the trestle tables and folding chairs, the bowls, plates and soft aluminium cutlery for the shuffling poor who began their slow and orderly advance as soon as the doors opened.

'Do you like my apron? I got one of the maids at the hotel to buy it for me.'

I was worried about how you would endure the stench. The poor of most nations I'm sure stink, but these, crammed together in the gloomy hall, must have been some of the worst: the children often diseased, with crippled limbs, pale faces and inevitably slimy noses which they wiped on their cuffs while their parents coughed and spat. Physically they seemed much weaker than our own poor and perhaps that made them more docile and grateful for the students' handouts of soup and bread. At Christmas, Bob Weston told me, a whole roast dinner was served followed by pudding and custard.

'I shall tell Lord Walker to send some of his charity to the St Egbert centre,' you said when we were washing up afterwards. 'I can't believe anyone needs it more.'

'You'd best try the Quakers, I believe they'll marry anyone,' Bob Weston said. 'Then you take the certificate or whatever to the local Town Hall and Bob's your uncle. I'll be a witness if you like.'

In the end it was in the chapel of a Protestant sect, the Methodists, that we were married, close to the soup kitchen, with Bob Weston and another student as witnesses.

'I'm sorry,' he said. 'I'm afraid my own lot are rather stuffy about this sort of thing.'

Oh Minna, I go through and through it in my mind and in this long letter to you, as if you could hear and read still, although I have few illusions about your individual personal survival. I know I'm doing it for myself, to keep memory intact to the last. That's why I play with my cybertoy, not because I really hope any more that one day I shall find you, that you will answer me, but so that we are both still alive to the last flicker, you in me and me in you and this quest. This recreation keeps my mind and your presence sharp to the final word.


VII


That was the weekend when the daffodils turned their grey-green necks down in a right angle poised for the full sun on their opening trumpets.

'At last,' Gran Bet said, looking out through the long windows. 'When I see that, I know I've made it into another spring. Let's go and look.' But in spite of being swaddled in boots and coats, the cold easterly soon drove them back again. 'When I was young there was no "wind chill factor" that they tell us about now. The wind was "bracing". You were expected to stride out against it. It seemed to be blowing straight across the fens from the North Sea. Even with a heavy tweed skirt it went right through you, especially cycling to college.' Betony had a sudden picture of her in her twenties, short black gown flying, mortar-board pinned firmly to her head, against the wind and the tide of male students who jeered and cat-called. 'It wasn't done to be a blue-stocking. I had no choice, but I was determined to have fun too. I always managed to wear silk stockings, not lisle. "Show a leg," they would call out, but it meant lots of invitations to the college balls. My father didn't like it a bit.' The new beginning had made Gran Bet reminiscent. Betony let her run on, partly because it meant she didn't have to find or skirt dangerous topics of conversation but also in hope of filling gaps in her own and her parents' history. But Gran Bet was going too far back today. Betony's own father, Henry, hadn't even been born. If they were ever to get to the things Betony wanted to hear or ask they must at least reach the Second World War. She realised she would have to lead her grandmother on.

Then suddenly, Gran Bet was off at a tangent that was hard for Betony to dignify as lateral thinking. She had taken an example of her work with her, a weekend magazine she occasionally did things for and that paid well for her coloured display of consumer desirables. As well as Betony's own effort there was an article that caught Gran Bet's eye. 'Of course, I understand that everything has to be made as delectable as possible, and of course there were advertisements when I was young that excited us, I expect, just as much as these do, but now there's so much more, everywhere you turn and especially with television. Nothing stays the same for five minutes. Everything has to change all the time, as if the whole world is in flux. And scientists keep tinkering with things that might be let well alone. Like this.' She rapped the long dismal face of a cloned sheep. 'Dolly, what a silly name. I remember a Dolly Eastwood in the year above me who was sent down for being out after hours. I suppose it means they've created her like a living doll, a plaything. Like that nice young man on the television who was half a gorilla.'

'That was fiction, Gran. Sci-fi.'

'So was this until a few days ago. Why can't they leave nature alone? It's worked quite well up to now. And all this DNA business. How can they possibly tell who's related to whom? This young teacher they say has been traced back to a caveman thousands of years ago.'

'I don't know, Gran. I'm not a biologist.'

'Exactly. We don't know, unless we're experts, what they're up to or the truth of anything they choose to tell us.'

Sometimes the length of her grandmother's life and the changes it had seen seemed too much for the individual unreconstructed organism to absorb, that fragile conjunction of matter, space and time that constituted Gran Bet.

'You think too much about things that either aren't important or are so obvious as to be banal,' Mark had once told her.

Gran Bet had decided on a gin and tonic before they set out for the lunch at the Berkshire Arms that Betony had talked her into so that she didn't have to cook, or Betony pretend to eat, their usual overdone 'Sunday dinner' as Mark called it.

'I got this habit from your grandfather,' Gran Bet said, raising her glass to the light to admire the lift of iridescent bubbles through the ice cubes and perfect round of lemon.

'I thought that was a navy drink,' Betony nudged the memory along carefully.

'That's pink gin, darling. During the war of course, everyone drank gin and lime when they could get it or gin and It.'

'It?'

'Italian vermouth. Martini. Very soothing. How my father would have disapproved. But then again he was so relieved when John came along that perhaps he wouldn't have minded, though if he hadn't been dead before, the war would certainly have killed him. Especially John's death. He thought so well of him sometimes I was jealous of both of them.'

'You never mention your mother.'

'She was a mouse. Elderly and subdued even when I was a child. I can't imagine how they ever conceived me.' Betony knew they had died spectacularly together on a parish charabanc outing.

'How did you and John meet, Gran?'

'Oh I must have told you a hundred times.'

'Tell me again.'

'At a college dance. I'd left and was twiddling my thumbs at home, but I still got asked to this and that. John's younger brother, William, was up at Magdalene and John was visiting him, a soldier, a dashing captain. Except that he was really rather quiet and would have liked a different career, but that's what the eldest Falk boy was expected to do in those days. And I was getting nervous: still on the shelf at twenty-four, with a distinct post-war shortage of eligible men, although things were better for my generation born just before it than for those poor girls born at the turn of the century. And I could see a teaching job in some private school in the deepest countryside looming: live in; most of your meagre pay going on your board; not allowed to escape in the evenings or weekends from one term's beginning to its end, and despised by the girls who would all be coming out as debs and marrying rich husbands while you sank deeper into old maidenhood.'

'I bet they'd all have been in love with you.'

'I liked men. John was a godsend. Good family, comfortably off, handsome in his mess kit. When his mother died he'd inherit the big house where he stayed when he wasn't posted abroad. Then, because he was clever and quiet, not eager for glory in the field like some young officers with fewer brains, he was attached to the War Ministry and the Imperial Defence Committee so he spent most of his time in London. After we were married and his mother finally died I was able to take charge of the house and furnish it as I liked. Not that I threw away any of the things that had come down from his parents, most of their furniture is still here – it's more durable than people. But I let in the light. I always knew how Pip felt in *Great Expectations* when he tore down those dreary curtains. I don't know that John liked it very much but he loved me and in those days the house was a woman's domain. So I held dinner parties for anyone who might be useful to him, and flirted harmlessly with old colonels and ministers as I was expected to do. You can't imagine darling, what an enjoyable life it was. What fun.'

'And then the war came and spoilt it all.'

'The terrible, terrible war. John saw it coming. Even on our honeymoon in Paris he said: "Enjoy it. It isn't going to last." Because in his position he saw so much more than other people. He knew all about German rearmament and Hitler while other people still thought it would never happen. There was nothing he could do, of course. Even more senior people, like Churchill himself, who could see what was happening couldn't do anything. We, most people, didn't want to think about it, you see. Some people even flirted with the idea that a dash of discipline might be a good thing for England too. But mostly we just wanted to go on having a good time. It wasn't until Harry was born that I began to worry.' Gran Bet's thin double slash of lipstick left a last imprint on the rim of the glass. 'Goodness, is that the time? We'll have to hurry if we want lunch. They stop serving at two.'

Betony recognised the point at which her grandmother always broke off. Apart from a generalisation or two about the awfulness of the war: rationing, queuing, the blitz that destroyed the big house, and John who hadn't been able to sit it out with a desk job (not that he'd wanted to of course) and had desert-ratted his way through North Africa only to be killed in Italy in the last days of the fighting, Gran Bet's memoirs stopped with the birth of Betony's father. His whole life, nearly forty years, her young mother's death in childbirth, leaving him a widower with a toddler to bring up, so what else could he do but go back to his mother, his own death, were almost as if they had never happened, as if there had just been the baby Harry Falk, followed by the baby Betony Falk, with the figure of Gran Bet leaning over both their cots.

At this point Betony broke off in her own head, shying away from an image that was almost sinister, an evocation of the bad fairy at the christening. She didn't want to see her grandmother in this posture. It made her realise, too, that in spite of Gran Bet's powers of survival she herself couldn't count on longevity. 'Gather ye rosebuds while ye may', as they had sung at school, seemed to be the prescription but at the moment they were in short supply, long months before even a dog-rose would show itself on the hedges she was driving past, although the banks now shimmered, were quilted here and there with primroses, their pale forerunners. It was the first time for months that she had been driving home in late afternoon light. The fine weather had brought out the Sunday trippers and there ahead was the first tailback from the M4. Betony began to slow down as she approached the slip road, aware in her mirror of the car behind aggressively on her tail. Suddenly the driver in front braked sharply. Betony slammed down both pedals to pull up a few inches short even as she was flung against the steering-wheel by the impact of the car behind. 'Shit!'

'Shit!' She took a deep breath, undid her seatbelt, glanced in the rear mirror to see a door opening and a figure beginning to clamber out. Betony felt in the glove compartment for the envelope she always carried with her – the details of her insurance company scribbled on it. She opened her door and got out. The car in front had pulled away quickly. Drivers behind them were cursing and overtaking the two cars locked together like two copulating dogs.

Betony could see at once that she had come off best. The other car, a rusty Vauxhall, was bleeding green antifreeze onto the road. The Volkswagen had a smashed rear light, and a bent number plate that was hooked over the other car's bumper. The other driver, heavily built, in his forties, she judged, was glowering down at the damage. He turned towards Betony.

'Fucking bitch, why don't you fucking learn to drive?'

'I'm sorry: the driver in front slammed his brakes on. I didn't have any choice.'

'Fucking upper-class cunt. Fucking kraut car. Don't make no difference to you. You can get a new one just like that.'

Betony realised he was probably driving without insurance. 'Look,' she said. 'There isn't much damage. Let's call it knock for knock. If you help me lift them apart we can probably both make it home.'

'Where the fuck do you think I can go in that?'

'There's a service station about half a mile up the road on the other side of the roundabout. You can make it to there. Or we can exchange insurance details and wait for the police.' She was aware of a woman's anxious face swimming behind the windscreen in the interior of the car like an agitated fish in a tank. The woman wound down the window and put her head out.

'We don't want no police, Lew. Can't you get them free and let the lady get on?'

'Fuck!' He turned to Betony. 'Let your fucking brakes off.'

She reached into her car and unnotched the handbrake, knowing that the slightest mistake or hindrance could cause him to turn on her again; shrinking inside from the words or even fists that might be hurled against her. With relief she saw him put his big paws under her bumper and lift the cars apart.

'Brilliant.'

'Yeah. I'm fucking good at that all right. Now get out of my fucking way.' As if the fault hadn't been his but hers, as if he had done her the favour when she had let him off the unarguable responsibility in law of having run into the back of her. Thankfully Betony got into the Volkswagen, switched on the ignition and let in the clutch with a leg that was trembling and wasted as if from a long illness. Suddenly he pulled out and roared past her towards the tail end of cars in front. She would have to drive carefully so as not to attract police attention but fast enough to be home before she had to switch on and her broken rear light became obvious. If she was picked up and had to give details of the accident he could easily find out her address and come after her in revenge for whatever they might do to him.

The traffic edged painfully forward. Betony didn't try to see whether the Vauxhall had turned off into the service station. She was only thankful not to find it stalled somewhere ahead of her where she would have to pass it. She still felt sick, and her head wasn't quite attached to her body, although her heart was slowing its frightening thud. She tried to breathe deeply but it was difficult cramped behind the wheel with the need for a constant lookout in front and to the rear. There was still enough daylight as she crossed Wandsworth Bridge and picked up the South Circular to avoid the telltale lighting up. By the time she drew up and parked in front of the house she was exhausted, drained and near to tears. She couldn't decide what she hoped to find: a silence, an emptiness she could sink into, or the chance to hide her hurt in the warmth of human contact. She turned the key, still not knowing.

At once she was aware of a strange noise, a rhythmical pecking or light drumming. Betony closed the door quietly behind her and began to carry her bag up the stairs. The psychiatrist's flat was dark and shut. The sound wasn't coming from there but from above her head. She saw the strip of light under her door and heard the music backing the other sound. She stood for a moment in the doorway to take in the scene. An area of the carpet had been covered by some kind of board in front of which stood a long mirror. In it the dark shape of the new lodger gyrated and gestured, completely absorbed, to the music coming from a portable player.

'Hi!' Betony put down her bag. Briefly, she appeared beside the figure in the mirror. He turned, reaching for the off button and killing the music.

'Shit. I'm sorry. I didn't think you'd be back yet. I checked out the flat below. I thought I was all on my own. Then I forgot the time. I do that when I'm dancing.'

'That's all right. I don't mind, really.' She was suddenly very tired.

'Hey, you look knackered. Can I make you a coffee? I'll get rid of this shit and put the kettle on.' He picked up the boards, folded them over each other and carried them off into his room. Betony sank into a chair. Then she heard the dull rush of water glugging into the kettle and the chink of a spoon. 'Black, white, sugar?' His concerned face appeared at the kitchen door.

'I think black with sugar.'

'Cool.'

He set the two steaming cups down carefully. 'Do you want company or do you want to be alone?'

'I just had my first taste of road rage. It frightened the hell out of me.' Betony blew on the steaming cup.

He shuddered. 'That's when I'm glad I don't drive.'

'Don't you drive at all?'

'I can. I've got a licence but I don't have a car and I don't really like it. I don't need it. And if they pick on you, think how they'd pick on me. Uppity nigger faggot, shouldn't have wheels.'

Betony found herself laughing. He had said it as if it was a great joke. At the same time she wondered if she sensed a twinge of disappointment in herself. 'I was feeling pretty low anyway and then this guy slammed into the back of me and I thought he might slam into my face as well.'

'I know the feeling. You back down and just hope they'll cool it and you don't have to take a beating. At least the fuzz leave you alone.'

'You get a lot of hassle?'

'They like to find an excuse to feel you up, do you over for drugs. I don't do drugs but I'm always afraid they might plant something on me. It's a bit better at the moment. At one time I couldn't go out without being splatted up against some wall and poked around. They've obviously been told to lay off for a while.'

Betony had a glimpse into a cavern lit by lurid flames which hinted at a world parallel with her own safe, comfortable existence that had only been threatened, not really penetrated, even by the other driver's half-raised fist and brutal language. She wondered for a moment if he beat the woman in the car.

'I'd been to my grandmother's. It always makes me feel edgy. Have you got any family?'

'I've got a sister, Laura, but we don't see much of each other since Nana died.'

'Your grandmother?'

'No my great-grandmother really but she were more like a mother to me. She really brought us up.'

'Like my grandmother. What happened to your mother?'

'Oh, she was around but she was out at work all day and most evenings. What about yours?'

'I don't remember her. She died having me. Then there was my father for a few years and he died too.'

'Mine ran off as soon as he saw me. Didn't want a fuzzywig for a son. It only came out in me. Laura, my sister, looks quite different. You feeling better?'

'Much. But I could do with a glass of something.'

He stood up. 'I'll go up the offo.'

'No need. There's a bottle of white wine in the fridge. Let's have that.' A couple of glasses later Betony heard herself saying, 'Do you know what happened to your father, where he is now?'

'Not really. I've never bothered to try to look him up. Maybe one day I will. It was where I came from interested me and finally I got Nana to tell me.'

'That's what I've tried to do but my grandmother always stops just when it gets interesting, when my father was born. I suppose it's because her husband was killed soon after and nothing was ever the same for her again.'


# VIII


And all the time I were thinking that I could tell you a thing or two even if Lady Falk wouldn't, had chosen to forget her war and that little kid Harry, as Nana had looked after when her and Margaret were off to London, dancing their lives away while that war went on and on til, Nana said, it had changed everything although it hardly touched her in the country. 'I know I can feel Harry is absolutely safe with you, Lilian. I don't have any worries while I'm away.'

It were Captain John as had written to Nana asking her to come back, saying the babby weren't well and his wife were having a hard time with it. And she'd gone because times was hard and she were lonely and poor drowned Wilf weren't coming home no more. And it would be nice to have a babby to look after again. Especially one that his mother didn't seem to want; less than ever after his father were killed. 'He were a quiet good babby. Too young to remember I when I had to take Margaret away. But Lady Falk never quite forgot, with that Christmas card every year.'

I suppose when Nana died I did ought to have written to her, but I reckoned she'd get the message when the card came back returned to sender or she didn't get Nana's usual thank-you letter. I were too grief-struck to cope with any of that, what with the funeral. Just Laura and her husband and me and a couple of old lady neighbours wondering whether it would be their own next. There weren't no music because I didn't know how to arrange it, and that upset me because Nana liked a good sing, would sing along with the morning service although she never went to church, all the hymns she'd learned at school and taking the little Falks of a Sunday to the big grey church on the edge of the heath, making sure they had clean handkerchiefs, sat up straight and didn't fidget.

So much I could have told you but I daresn't. It would have seemed as if I were a great fat cuckoo in your nest, knowing more about you than you did yourself. As it were I almost gives meself away, slipping into Nanaspeak whenever I mentioned her, as if her were talking through me lips and would come out with some message or knowledge you mightn't welcome after all.

It did sound to me as if your dad had a short life and a sad one from what you said and I do remember a saying of Nana's about a child that ent loved not making old bones. After she'd said it, she were sorry and hugged me til all the breath were out of me, and said that I'd live to be ninety she loved I that much and laughed, I think to keep from crying. Old Lady Falk seemed to have tried to make up for it by loving you. Maybe she found girls easier than boys whereas Nana really always liked boys best, as I can see now, and maybe that were because in them days girls could get into 'trouble', as Nana called it, so easy that they was always a worry til they was married. I watched her with our mother June and then with Laura, fretting as the evening wore on and they didn't come home, and that was how she must have been with her own daughter, Margaret, until she came home knocked up, up the spout, in pod, with a bun in the oven, all

82

they phrases we did use to giggle about in the playground as if we didn't see sex all the time on the telly. So what must it have been like before?

Once when me and Nana was shopping in Reading, I pointed out a condom to her in the gutter, a limp pink balloon, and asked her what it was. I went to pick it up and she struck out at me. 'Don't 'ee touch that. You don't know where it's been. Or who with.'

'But what's it for?'

'It's to stop girls having babies.'

'How, Nana?'

'You'll find out in good time when you need to.'

A course I found out later when I shagged a couple of girls just to see if I could and should. That were when I first come to London and took the secretarial course to earn me bread. Before I found out what were what with the clubs and the Dance Arena where I could practise. The course were mainly girls. I were a kind of mascot for the class: a black boy doing wordprocessing. We'd all go down Piccadilly in a gaggle to Santucci's sandwich bar at lunchtime and then, since it was summer and fine, into the park to eat.

It were then Sara Creswell made a play for me. They girls was all very nobby, Sloanes with hairbands who went down to the country and rode about on horses at weekends. If I'd a knowed before I'd never have joined such a class. One day Sara says what am I doing that night because some of them are going clubbing. And I says great by me. They didn't know I could dance. So we all meet up in the Goat in Boots and off we go. As soon as the music starts me feet begin to fly and Sara's very impressed – she'm not bad herself in an amateur way and soon everyone's gathered round, calling out and clapping. Until it stops and she has to sit down and have a drink. But me I'm just beginning. All the girls want a go and then Sara's got her breath back and she's on again. I think she's popped a pill because she's twice the speed, really keeping up with me and learning fast. After that she couldn't get enough and it ended up with her asking me to stay the night in her flat.

I thought I had to do it sometime just to find out, and she were long-legged and fair-skinned, that kind of English rose that's supposed to drive guys wild. She thought I were a bit of all right, too. I could tell me touch of the tarbrush really turned her on. So I gets it up and she puts the rubber jacket on herself so I nearly comes as her fingers is rolling it down me prick and then I get it in. And she's moaning and sticking her nails in me bum and suddenly we're both coming like crazy and shouting the house down. And that's it. I feels drained. She'm caressing me and I'm making a show of touching her boobs but there ent nothing there, nothing inside of me. Willy wilts and won't stand up no more and I say I have to go for the all-night bus. Because although I can do it, it's mechanical and I don't feel nothing. I might as well be tossing meself off. That's the truth. Me heart ent in it.

So where is me heart then? In the dancing I suppose, and as for the other it's in the impossible: they lovely limber shapes that flit through me head and that I tries to catch in the mirror, pretending it ent just meself I can see. Oh I done it once or twice careful like with guys what I fancied. And there were more there than with Sara. I really fancied them and hoped for something more, like they'd call me again and we'd go somewhere – a movie, a walk, a talk and not get ourselves off til later. But that weren't what they wanted. Just a quick fuck and run. You see them round the clubs. The same faces again and again, giving the eye to someone. Going off for a fix in the lavs or a darkened corner behind the lights and then back again. Until one day you sees them gaunt but still leching and then they're gone. Blown away in the dance of death. But there's always new talent to step into their places.

## IX

'Are you pregnant, Frau Falk? Is that the reason for this hasty marriage?' the consul asked as he issued you with your new passport. When I looked sideways at you, you had turned a dull brick colour which I realised wasn't a blush of modesty or shame but a flush of pure anger.

'Not as far as I know, Herr Consul.'

'I hope your parents have given their approval.'

'We are both of age.' I answered this time.

'Oh yes. I have of course seen your certificates of birth. When will you be returning home? In time to vote, I would suggest. I hope your first child will be a German citizen. Healthy children are our future.'

That afternoon we took the train for Penzance and then a bus to the little fishing village of Treffry where we meant to start the walking holiday that was our luxury before setting out for home and the problems that would face us there. The boarding-house was perched on the cliffs, with a long winding road down to a rocky inlet where a few small boats bobbed and a row of cottages threatened to fall into the sea. We booked in for the first time as husband and wife and after flatfish and chips with floury peas, followed by syrup sponge and the custard sauce the English pour over everything, we went hand in hand down that road with the dark rocks that dropped sheer to an opal sheet of sea stretching away until it blurred from sight, to sit on the quayside and write our impossible letters home.

'Dear Muti. There seems no easy way to write this. I have married Minna Strauss in London. Please forgive me for not telling you before but I didn't want you to be worried or to have any expense. I shall of course return and complete my studies for the diplomatic. You need not worry that we shall be a burden to you financially. Minna has some money of her own from her grandmother.'

You had told me this very matter-of-factly. 'So that even if Vati doesn't approve we shan't starve. But I think he will be pleased.'

But I was less sure. It would be another year before I could even begin to support a wife. 'Let's not go any further. Let's stay here in this village. Then we can give them our address and they can write or even telegraph the worst before we leave.' So we arranged our change of plan with the landlady and took our letter to be expressed by the village postmistress. So many women in England seemed to be running things: respectable widows in matching black hats, coats, shoes and gloves, and dark dresses under them with sometimes a little white collar, to show their necks were clean, we imagined. During the day the whole country gave the impression of a matriarchy except for occasional shops like the butcher or the cobbler where a man struck with a shining cleaver or hammer, or a dark blue fisherman tinkering with a boat.

We took the local buses from Treffry in every direction while we waited for answers. One day we went as far as Tintagel, King Arthur's mythical castle with its Wagnerian resonances in the crashing waves and vertiginous steps we had to climb down and up to reach what was more likely the site of a Celtic monastery where there were only the sky and sea to distract from the contemplation of God.

Herr Strauss's telegram came first, of course.

'Congratulations. Good luck. You will need it. When are you coming home?'

'So that's all right,' you said. 'I always thought it would be. Vati likes you.'

My mother's letter kept me fretting until our time in Treffry was nearly up.

'Of course I must congratulate you. And I do understand your reasons for doing as you have done. However, as a mother I must be concerned that you have made things difficult for yourself. It is as well Fräulein Strauss has money of her own. Things are not easy here and you will see many changes even in the short time

86

you have been abroad. Shall you be home for the new election on July 31st?'

When we reached Berlin we took the tram to your father's house at once. From the windows we could see bands of brown-uniformed stormtroopers and heavily armed police blocking the pavements or pushing ordinary pedestrians out of their way like rag dolls. Your father had chilled Bollinger waiting for us. He popped the cork himself and poured us each a glass that foamed over the brim in lavish celebration. 'Congratulations again. May you have long and happy lives and healthy children. Now to the practical. I've had the blue bedroom made into a sitting-room for your personal use when you want to get away from the old man. I hope you'll eat with me when we're all here together but I expect to be away quite a lot. If you and she wished, Anton, we could also make room for your mother.'

'I'll speak to her about it, sir. It's most kind of you but she might prefer to stay among her friends in her own place. She's very independent.'

'Of course. I quite understand. I hope she won't miss you too much or mind you living here. I understood that it would be difficult for you both to live with her.'

I knew but didn't say that it would have meant getting rid of Herr Peers, her English lodger who had given me some extra practice in conversation before I went to London. Probably he wouldn't stay long, they never did, but I couldn't imagine Minna in our chilly, dim rooms or sharing a tiny kitchen with my mother.

'Fortunately you will have enough to live on with your grandmother's money, Minna, though I'm also sure she never foresaw it being spent on a goy. But times change and if I'm right then you will be safer with such a husband. You will both have to make hard choices. Whether to stay in Berlin, in Germany even, or whether to emigrate like Otto.'

'And what about you, Papa?'

'Oh once this election is out of the way I· shall go and take the cure somewhere. Maybe Baden or the Swiss Alps.' I looked at him in surprise and you moved to take his arm.

'Are you unwell, Papa?'

'My digestion hasn't been good lately. But perhaps it's just a severe case of angst.' You remember, Minna, how he looked drawn and thinner. 'Now let me show you your salon. I hope you like the paper I've chosen.'

I think my mother was relieved to have the problem of where we were to begin our married life solved for her. Of course, Herr Strauss insisted that she should come to lunch as soon as we returned. It was mother who chose lunch rather than dinner.

'She's afraid to be out in the evening, especially alone.'

Your father nodded. 'I completely understand. The streets are full of thugs, especially now Schleicher has lifted the ban on the Sturmabteilung. I would naturally send a car for her both ways but even so it might be stopped or unable to get through because of some demonstration, as they call it, though they seem to me more like some barbarous riot. Last Sunday nineteen people were shot dead and hundreds injured, in Hamburg of all places. It's everywhere this violence, not just in Berlin. We are on the brink of civil war.'

'Vati isn't well,' you said when we were alone. 'It's making him even more gloomy.' But when we took a trip into the city we saw that he and my mother hadn't exaggerated. Even the bar beside the Wannsee where he had first danced was half empty and what dancers there were seemed desperate, frantically jigging puppets, apart from a group of stormtroopers getting steadily drunk and raucous, with their insulting remarks about nigger and Jew music. We soon left to walk among the trees beside the water and look at the drowned moon floating face up.

'What should we vote?' We had stopped to light the last of our English cigarettes. The flare of the matches showed me your dark eyes and cloud of hair floating like the moon itself against the night sky.

'Social Democrat, I suppose, though I don't think they have much chance against the extremes. As a Jew, Hitler would say, I'm a natural Marxist.'

'How do you know?'

'I was looking at Vati's copy of *Mein Kampf*. It's impossible to read such vile rubbish all through but I picked up that much. Anton, I may have got you into bad trouble by marrying you if they come to power.'

'You didn't marry me. We married each other. What can they do? We're German citizens.'

And even after the Nazi landslide in that election, when fourteen million people voted for them and they had saturated the electorate with propaganda rallies and marches of massed uniforms, the old president still had the courage to refuse Hitler the chancellorship and instead insisted on a coalition. It seemed like a real reprieve for the republic, as if it might survive after all and us with it, as though sheer weariness would achieve what reason hadn't. Even the politicians took a holiday in the mountains or at the seaside.

Parliament came back at the end of August only to be dissolved by a trick of its new President Goering and yet more elections were called for November. Your father seemed to grow thinner and more haggard every day but he refused to leave for his cure while this uncertainty continued. And now it was bitterly cold. Any kind of fuel was hard to come by and some of those sleeping rough in the Tiergarten froze to death while others merely starved. A succession of greedy, weak intriguers filled the chancellory: von Papen, Schleicher. Betrayed from within by corruption and plotting, even by Oskar, the president's son, by the despair and anger of the unemployed, the republic was finally handed over to Hitler on January 30th. When the Reichstag was burned down in February, Goering said by the communists, Hindenburg, in a pitiful last attempt, as he believed, to avert a civil war, was tricked into suspending those parts of the constitution that had to do with freedom of expression and civil liberties. The whole agonising farce finally ended on March 23rd, ironically in the Baroque theatricality of the Kroll Opera House, when the Reichstag handed over power to the new chancellor, Hitler, and his cabinet for four years, signing its own death warrant. Only our Social Democrats, those who could force their way in past the ranks of stormtroopers, voted honourably against the act.

'In the words of the Christian God,' your father said, '"It is finished." There is nothing any longer in the Nazis' way. This so-called Enabling Act simply enables them to seize all the power they want quite legally. I am most shocked by my fellow businessmen, like Bosch and Snitzler, who are cultured and intelligent but don't seem to understand the monster they have unleashed. They provided the money for Hitler to come to power because they believe he will re-arm and that will be good for their business. But re-armament always leads to a war, that is its natural outcome, and war will destroy us again as it did last time. The army has betrayed us for the same reason. They all want a war and Hitler will give them one because he wants it too. I shall go to Switzerland tomorrow. There's a lot to be done while there's still time and we're allowed to travel. You young people must consider your future.'

Your father left two days later and he was still away at the end of the month when the first decree to boycott Jewish shops and businesses went out. We decided that my mother should leave her job at once rather than try to get into Strauss past the guards and the offensive yellow warning signs. Now we would have to keep her, too, from your grandmother's legacy. Then your father telephoned to say he had transferred the legal ownership to a friend, a Swiss gentile. The guards and notices would be removed but I felt my mother should not attempt to return to work there. Instead, she came to help out in the Grünewald when their old servants felt that they had to leave because it was no longer comfortable to work for Jewish households.

It was clear when your father returned that his efforts to safeguard his business had weakened him further.

'Should we go and look at the shop, Vati?' you asked him.

'Why should we do that? In order that I can see someone else's name all over it? And read the sign: *Under new ownership*? That would only emphasise my loss, my cowardice under fire, not befitting a German officer.'

'You're not a coward, Father. You've beaten them at their own game.' But I could see he was unconvinced. He seemed to shrink a little both physically and into himself every day.

'You realise this is only the beginning. Soon, if I live, I shall have to shut up this place and join Otto in America. I think you should both come too.'

'Emigrate? Leave Germany forever? Surely Papa, that isn't necessary. Anton has his career, and anyway he couldn't leave his mother.'

Your father didn't push it but I thought about it even more when I was called in by my department head and told that my English was about to be useful at last. I was to be entrusted with taking important documents to London and making contact with certain people there who were well disposed towards the new regime.

'Come with me, Minna. We'll have a second honeymoon.'

'I can't, darling. I can't leave Father at the moment, just before he goes away. I might not see him again.'

'Of course you will. We can go to America to see him and Otto.'

'You're such an innocent sometimes, Anton. You don't under-stand. Maybe you won't come back. Maybe they'll find reasons to keep you there.'

'It's only a month, I promise. Then I'll come home and no one will be able to stop me.'

I hadn't known how painful being away from you would be. Not the moment of leaving, when I was too numb to feel any-thing, but the days after. And the nights. During the day I had my commissions to fulfil but at night there was nothing between me and your absence, except for the weekly telephone call I allowed myself. I realise now that your pain was even worse. It's always easier for the one who goes.

London in summer without you seemed merely dry and dusty. Once I had delivered my papers I wasn't clear what I was supposed to do. 'Talk to people. Make friends. Find out what they're thinking,' the minor consular official, my superior, said. 'We are giving a reception next week, for example, where you will be able to use your English. Ask them what they think of our Third Reich. Tell them we want nothing but peace and to take up our just place in the world free from the restraints of Versailles. Incidentally, von Falk, you aren't yourself a member of the party, are you?'

'No sir. I try to keep out of politics.'

'I should remedy that if I were you, for the sake of your career.'

'Yes sir.' What else could I say? Naively, you would have said, I had always assumed that the correct attitude for a diplomat was neutrality in politics, leaving himself free to operate efficiently on behalf of the government. Now I was being told otherwise. If I stayed in my chosen career I should have to identify myself with policies I disapproved of, that might even destroy us both.

The reception turned out to be a sumptuous affair at the embassy. Chandeliers and champagne. Those who had it wore dress uniform, with all their medals glinting on colourful striped ribbons. There was even an Iron Cross. I knew it was my job to circulate and so I moved from group to group, not staying long enough to become involved in what might be an embarrassing discussion. By the time I had made a circuit of the room I caught up with my superior. 'Ah, von Falk, good. Here is a strange coincidence. This is Major Falk. What do you say to that?'

I bowed at the young British officer. 'I don't know what to say, sir. Except that my mother always told me my father's family were of English origin. But perhaps it is the other way around, Major.'

He put out his hand. 'Well both, if I've got the story right. Two brothers went from here to Germany, Bremen, I think, a couple of hundred years ago. And then one of them or his descendant came back. My father had a German aunt or great-aunt, I forget which, but she was called Adelbrit. It stuck in my mind as a child because I'd never heard it before. Are there any Adelbrits in your family?' He laughed. A young man, about my age, with an open handsome face; not as tall as me, and perhaps not very clever.

'After all,' the consular official said, 'it is not so uncommon. Think of your royal family.'

'Oh indeed. Are you here permanently? You must lunch with me so that we can explore this further.'

'Unfortunately my visit this time is only short but I should like it very much if we could meet again before I leave.'

'That's done then. Come to Quaglino's. It's more fun than my club. Let's make it dinner. Tuesday at eight suit you?'

'Very good, von Falk.' My superior patted my shoulder after our English guests had left. 'Excellent in fact. A young officer. You could learn a lot.'

He was already seated studying the menu when the waiter showed me to the table. He stood up and shook hands. 'We'd better get to Christian names. It's ridiculous to Falk each other, I'm John.'

'Anton.' I laughed. There was something about him even more naive than myself though I suspected we were much the same age. If I had intended to exploit him, as my orders were, it would have been easy. As the Americans say: taking candy from the baby.

'I hope you like Italian food. It's awfully good here. Shall we get the ordering over and then we can talk? I think we should start with some champagne to celebrate and toast the Falks. What does that little "von" mean, by the way?'

'It's supposed to show gentility. Apparently it came into the family from Frederick the Great for some service to him by a Falk in Goethe's time.'

'Oh!' He looked blank. I was pretty sure he had never heard of Goethe.

'Frederick the Great was King of Prussia at the end of the eighteenth century. He built up the Prussian army and began the unification of Germany.'

'I say, your English is frightfully good.'

'Thank you. I was here last year on a scholarship. I enjoyed it very much. I even was married here.'

'An English girl?'

'No, my wife is German.'

'I've managed to escape so far, marriage I mean. But I don't suppose I'll hold out much longer. Now, what will you have?'

After we had ordered, the champagne arrived and we raised our glasses to each other to toast 'the Falks'. 'We must be related,' he said. 'I telephoned my mother and she confirmed that one of our lot visited the court of your Frederick and married a cousin Adelbrit. I think this is all great fun. Here's to you, cousin!' He raised his glass again and we chinked the rims together.

'And to you, cousin, or I should say *Vetter*. In German *Kusine* is only for girls.'

'You know if everybody had a cousin in another country or two maybe there wouldn't be any more wars.'

'You a soldier and you say that?'

'I didn't have any choice. There wasn't much money in my family and there were three of us. And anyway the eldest Falk always goes into the army. Only, if I have a son, I hope that won't still be necessary.'

'I could not imagine a German officer admitting all this.'

'My father was killed in the Great War. My youngest brother was born after his death. A lot of us, and more than care to admit it I suspect, would like to go on being peacetime soldiers.'

'My father too was killed. How strange that is.'

'Oh I don't know. There were millions of them. Do you think it will ever happen again? It seems so senseless.'

I took a moment to answer. Could I trust him? Would he go to his superiors and repeat what I had said? Why should they care for my opinion? More seriously, might my superiors come to hear about it? 'Like you, I hope not. Very much. But we have a new government and I am afraid that they and the military and those who make money from arms may push us towards it.' I heard myself repeating my father-in-law's gloomy prognosis almost involuntarily.

'England and Germany might be on the same side this time, maybe against Russia.'

'That is the best we can hope. Then at least we shouldn't have to fight each other.'

'But you're a diplomat, aren't you, not a soldier?'

'In war everyone becomes a soldier. My father was a school-master.'

'That's true. Even women get dragged in. My mother drove an ambulance. I think she rather enjoyed it. It gave her a break from us.'

The moment of danger had passed but I knew I should be questioned about our conversation tomorrow and would need something to repeat. 'Tell me, what do people in England think of our new government?'

'It varies, depending on your viewpoint. Some people think suppressing the trade unions is a marvellous idea, especially since the General Strike. I wish I'd been old enough. I'd have loved to drive a tram. They think it would put the commies in their place. But others are a bit worried by what might happen in Austria. If Germany took over there it could lead to war. I think that's what most people of sense want: no more war.'

'And you?'

'Except for not wanting a war, as I said, I don't mess about with politics. I just get on with my job. You must come and see my mother before you go back. My brother and sister are away at school but I know she'd like to meet you.'

And that was how I first saw the big house on the edge of the heath. I reported the invitation to my superior. 'Very good,' he said. 'This could be an important contact which will give you an introduction to people in high places.' I didn't mention that I already knew Lord Walker. Some instinct told me not to. And yet I acted and reacted not from any preconceived plan or even out of reason but simply because of an apprehension I had that I should be selective in the information I passed on.

Mrs Falk, a widow of course like my mother, seemed still young. Her life had been so much easier, cushioned at least from poverty if not from loneliness. There were pictures of John's father in silver frames, including their wedding. John looked most like his mother. His father seemed stronger, more the professional soldier. Lunch was a rather stiff occasion where the three of us made formal conversation but afterwards Mrs Falk showed me round the house, the family portraits and English Bible with records of births, marriages and deaths written on the endpapers.

'We think these were the ones who went to Germany.' She pointed to two younger brothers. 'The eldest stayed on and took the title.'

'The title?'

'Yes. That one.' She raised her hand towards an elegant figure in shining grey skirted coat embroidered with silver and under a heavy thatch of wig. 'He was rewarded by Charles II for services to the Stuarts during the Civil War. Those are the earliest ones we have portraits of.' They looked like two comfortable Bremen burghers in respectable black, painted by Holbein before he migrated to England. 'And that little boy at the harpsichord was his grandfather's heir. It was his brothers who disappeared from the family tree, though the son of one of them seems to have come back later.'

I stared at them, hoping that something would confirm or deny my descent but no voice came out of a cloud or finger of sunlight reached down to touch me. I should have to do some digging of my own when I got home. Later still, Mrs Falk took me into the brick-walled garden where a man in a sack apron was patiently wheeling a barrow of bright green grass cuttings.

'This is my real pleasure,' she said, leading me between ranks of tall flowers in delicate shades of blue and pink and every tone of cream, ivory, buttermilk and pure snow-white towards an arbour of heavily scented climbing roses. She asked me if I liked it. I said, as indeed I thought, that it seemed a little paradise. Birds chirruped unseen among the leaves and water trickled into a stone basin where white lilies floated on perfect green cushions. 'I had it designed for me by a marvellous woman gardener as a memorial to John's father. A place where there was peace and beauty. You may think it a strange memorial for a man of blood, as some people would call him now, but he loved flowers, and gentle things.' I wondered how much he might have deceived himself and her, this professional soldier.

'Please come and see us whenever you're in England,' she said as she bowed me towards the door.

John shook hands. 'Yes, do.'

'And if ever you are in Berlin you must do the same and meet my wife.'

'Ah yes,' Mrs Falk said, 'encourage John to follow your example and give me a grandchild soon.'

'The English are interested in peace and gardening,' I reported while wondering whether John and his mother were gathering flowers on the edge of a crumbling cliff. Nevertheless I was glad to have met my English cousins. They might be useful if we ever had to leave Germany as my father-in-law seemed to think.


# X


It was unusual for Betony to snake out of London on the South Circular through the abandoned suburbs of Streatham and Thornton Heath, where the pavement and gutters were a perpetual dervish dance of windblown scraps of dirty paper, burger wrappings, chip bags, greasy napkins, and then through Croydon of the glass and steel shopping centre, standstill traffic, darkened theatre, and on again, skimming dowdily respectable Reigate as it seemed through the car windows, with mothers in summer dresses that wouldn't have looked out of place forty years ago pushing low buggies on wheeled insect legs.

'It's just as well we don't still have the family home,' Gran Bet had said once. 'Kent is impossible to get to now and impossible when you do. What it must be like with the Channel Tunnel! Ashford International indeed. Berkshire is barely possible though it's good for girls' schools and I love the racing. It was better when we first came here of course. Now Hampshire's the place. Winchester. But I wouldn't like to move.' She would miss her village cronies and their hot tips. 'This house had been a school when we bought it but they were evacuated to Wales. We were so lucky. It could have been requisitioned by the army and then it would have been hardly worth having back. Nancy Coggan had to sell hers for a hotel, the RAF officers had knocked it about so much. The evacuees saved us.'

'Evacuees, Gran? You've never told me about them.'

'It was a brilliant wheeze of mine. Lily, your grandfather's nanny, came back during the war to help me out and she brought her twelve-year-old daughter with her. So I put them down as evacuees! Then for a while we had two teachers from Reading: very quiet, no trouble, though I expect they were lesbians. Their school had been bombed somewhere and evacuated. So you see, they were real evacuees.'

At Reigate Betony turned east, or left as she thought of it, avoiding the snarled and snarling London circular motorway and opting for the old road through villages and little towns: Oxted, Sevenoaks, Ightham, the Mallings, to Maidstone where there was nothing for it but to submit to the motorway and run down beside the rail link to the tunnel and France, until she could branch off again towards Canterbury and into a web of hedged lanes that led from half-obliterated signposts to hamlets that each had a stone church.

What did she hope to find? 'A serious house on serious earth?' Larkin's poems had been an 'A' level text. She remembered his

experience in the country church as a kind of warning, of emptiness, not worth stopping for.

She skirted Canterbury itself and threaded her way through
Lower Hardres and towards Bishopsgreen where the legend was
that Augustine had preached to the recalcitrant local Jutes. First,
she would stop at the Toad and Hole as the pub had been rechrist-
ened by the chain of eateries that had taken it over in the hope
that tourists emerging from the Channel Tunnel north might
choose to amble through the lanes rather than head straight for
London. Betony got herself a glass of beer and ordered a toasted
cheese sandwich which, when it came, was half buried in a bizarre
salad of apple and orange rings with coleslaw doused in mayonnaise
that was turning the toast to sponge. She studied the fake prints
in their plastic wood frames and the stamped-out brasses that had
never dangled from any horse, and wondered why she could
hardly swallow for the knot of apprehension that contracted her
throat.

Betony picked her way across her plate. The beer that was at
least cool with a strong tang of hops helped her to get the food
down to her oddly cavernous stomach. Then, leaving her Volkswagen in the pub car park, she set out to find the church.

No memory reached down to guide her; no fatherly outstretched hand. She was quite on her own as she walked the village
street, trying to peer over tree and building tops, up alleyways for
the outline of tower or spire, lychgate, or arched door. And there,
suddenly, was a Churchway which must surely lead to it. For a
moment the sun came out from behind dirty freewheeling clouds.
The stiff summer breeze seemed to drop as she walked up an
unpavemented little street between brick cottages whose long
front gardens were given over to cabbages and rows of flowering
bean poles sprinkled with the little red cockles and coarse hairy
leaves of the runners, with here and there a clump of snapdragons
or the blue spears of delphiniums.

Closer to the church whose gates she could now see, were
handsome stone houses that would have held the parson, the

doctor and perhaps those descendants come down in the world from the founding Falk, the conqueror's tercel carrier, unmarried sisters who oversaw the church and schools, the almshouses, the births, sicknesses and deaths in the cottages she had passed. Now they were the country houses of commuters, whose children went away to school as Betony had done, and came home to be driven about by their mothers to each other's parties.

She had reached the gate. A still bright padlock held it fast against her. Unbelieving she pushed at it, shook the rails and jiggled the latch. Then she found herself with both hands on the bars, peering in as a prisoner might stare out. The path was overgrown. There were no notices of services on the board where blurred lettering confirmed that this was St Osmond's. White tufted dead nettles and their stinging cousins fringed the graveyard whose sagging headstones and cracked tomb chests were almost hidden by a rustling curtain of overblown cow parsley. At the far end of the path, where the dark double pergola of yew framed the porch, she could make out what seemed to be a house agent's board.

There must be some way in. Betony set off to circle the grave-yard. Having come so far, and encouraged by the glass of beer, she refused to accept defeat. She rounded the corner of the railings, found a place where one of them was bent and forced her way through into the jungle of weeds, glad of her protective denim jeans and jacket that she had almost not worn in favour of a summer skirt for church visiting, knowing that was what Gran Bet would have approved. Still the dried stalks poked through the cloth into her skin while the nettles let their hairy stems and leaves, dark with summer and topped with beady flower heads, loose their venom over her bare ankles. The churchyard seemed hostile, as if it was trying to keep her away from the building at its heart or punish her for some dereliction, but she couldn't turn back now.

She reached the porch with its Norman dogtooth moulding, recut in the eighteen seventies. The same board sagged beside another padlocked gate. It directed would-be buyers to Strangford and Crisp, property agents of Ashford. Leaving the porch, where swallow and martin droppings had turned the stone floor into a Jackson Pollock in grey and white and yellow, she forced her way round the side to find a window low enough for her to look in but she could see nothing through the dust veiling the intense gloom of the interior. Suddenly, behind her on the yew arch, a bird began to sing. Turning she tried to make out what sort it was from its shape against the grey sky but she could only see a colourless silhouette that might be a blackbird letting its rich sound cascade into the tangle of weeds and stones. Betony went back to the porch and wrote down the name and telephone number on the board. Then she set out to inspect the remaining inscriptions on those graves she could reach, tearing away curtains of leaves and stalks with stinging hands and pecking at moss, and furry grey or scabby yellow lichen with a nail file.

She tried to remember what Gran Bet had told her; how long it was since the Falks had left Bishopsgreen. It might be centuries. Certainly there was no sign of them that she could find. If there were any Falks still here they were in the shuttered church, those half-remembered, half-invented effigies and plaques of her visit with an equally shadowy father. Defeated, she followed the path her own feet had trampled back to the bent railing and then to the gate. Somewhere ahead now a bird sang again. She thought it was the same one. She had read an article in a Sunday magazine that said the yews were older than the churches they seemed to protect. That the buildings had been put there to sanctify, to nullify their old magic and that images of the gods they had been planted for leered from corbel, frieze and gargoyle, tongues stuck out, fingers in ears or nostrils, anarchic, archaic. Sometime she must use them in a design. That would finally tame them.

There was a bench outside the church gate. Betony sat down and took out her mobile phone and dialled the number on the board. Would it work out here? It seemed an intrusion. No wonder the church had been so unwelcoming. What was she doing here? The phone buzzed and a voice offered to help. She was interested in the old church. There had been a lot of interest but it was, of course only a shell, which was why it was so cheap. A mere thirty thousand pounds. Of course planning permission would have to be applied for. Was she thinking of residential or commercial use?

'I thought perhaps a gallery or studio, even a theatre.'

'Ah!'

'I was wondering what had happened to the . . . the fixtures and fittings: pews, the pulpit, monuments.'

'All went to other churches. Although now I come to think of it there was a reclamation firm outside Canterbury that bought some of the more decorative stuff. People like it for their gardens. There's quite a thriving market. And I believe a local museum took a couple of statues. If you give me your address I can send you our brochure on the property.' Betony wondered whether that arch unbeliever Larkin would have been affronted or amused. How had the poem ended? She fished around in her memory. She had an impression of it being something about the very last visitor hoping to learn wisdom from such a place.

'If only that so many dead lie round.'

That was it.

And it was true. There they were. Parked for posterity and whoever bought the place would have to cohabit with them. But they weren't her dead, as far as she could find, except perhaps anonymously underground. And when she was dead in her turn there would be no Falks left. The line would have died out unless she had a child of her own and could give it her name, an AID child, an illegitimate child, a bastard. Turning her back finally on the church she made her way between the rows of cottages to where she had left her car. The clouds were clearing at last. She wound down the window of the Volkswagen which had become very stuffy, and set off towards London through late afternoon sunlight that threw elongated, flickering tracery of shadowy trees

across the windscreen, making her eyes blur. This time she suc-
cumbed to the motorway and let the road carry her past Maidstone
and Swanley until she was deep in the southern suburbs. At some
point, while hardly aware that a decision was being taken, she
had made up her mind to try to find the Blackheath house where
Gran Bet had once been a young bride and a wartime mother.
While she was at it she might as well tie up another loose end
and it would only take her a little out of her way, although to a
part of London she didn't know at all. There was the sign to turn
right, deep in the grimmest part of a run-down area of once
handsome houses, now let out in minimalist flats and bedsits where
the poor were stacked, and flanked by used-car lots and hoardings
that veneered the broken façades of abandoned shops. It was a
shock when the road she was following shook off this detritus
and climbed up into open skies and a stretch of browning common
where several groups, including one in traditional whites, were
playing cricket as if on a village green in Berkshire. Betony pulled
over at the top of the hill to look at her London street map.
Across the other side of the road she could see that a fairground
was already mapped out and the red and gold ferris wheel, swings,
dodgems and big dipper were being hauled up in place for the
next bank holiday.

That was the name of the road, Shooters Hill, once the old
road to Dover, notorious for highwaymen who pounced on the
lumbering coaches and carriages as they strained towards the crest.
She was already part of it. She only had to drive along it or get
out and walk. She drove to where the houses began, hugely
handsome classical cubes with steps and stone porticos, many with
the rash of bells that showed their myriad lives but some with still
just one smart brass knocker and a single discreet push button
alongside it. Betony turned off to park in a metered sidestreet and
got out to walk.

Gran Bet had once shown her an envelope with the address
on it that had been sent on after its arrival from Italy to catch up
with her in London. 'The last one he ever wrote me.' The

unfamiliar hand that had scored out and replaced the original address in boardschool copperplate had imprinted the new one on Betony's memory. Mysore House, one hundred and twenty-one. The steeply rising road was long and very wide. Often a number was difficult to make out unless she pushed open the gate and went up the drive. The one she wanted was sure to be on the other side, where the houses began again after the heath, although they didn't look as grand as the ones she was passing now. One hundred and three. At least she was on the right side for the odd numbers. She passed a huge monkey puzzle tree in a well-kept garden that must have been there since before the war. A slim brown Abyssinian cat drowsed on a windowsill in the sun. A silver Porsche was parked in a finely gravelled drive. And then, where one hundred and twenty-one should have been was a modern infill of two brick semis with the old front garden cut in two between them. 'The house was beautiful,' she heard Gran Bet saying. 'We were lucky to be out when it happened. Otherwise . . .'

So why had letters still been sent there, or had that been before? Would Gran Bet remember if she asked her? Time, its sequence of supposed cause and effect, took on the responsibility for truth. But didn't relativity and so many other scientific theories or discoveries undermine all those old credibilities? If the light from Hale Bop, that radiant time traveller, had started on its way to earth so long before she had stood out on the lawn at Gran Bet's in order to see it clearly away from London's nightlight envelope, let alone that from the brightest star in another galaxy, time and truth were just as distant from each other and it was simply a matter of where you the observer stood. Time was dethroned from its primacy as a measure of the universal to a human invention subordinate to the reality of space, and perhaps space might be an illusion too. Betony had stared at the fluent, flowery, multi-coloured images, sent back by spacecraft blossoming in double spread over the colour supplements and tried to absorb them, vaguely wondering whether there was something among their riches that might be used in her own work, both dazzled and numbed by their opulence. Nothing it seemed was so grand or distant that it couldn't be made to serve human acquisitiveness. She wondered about her own profession that had grown up over night, the frenetic pursuit of the ephemeral, the shimmering, the gossamer. But then couldn't a butterfly's stamp shake the world? Was there any difference in the daily fantasies she created and those we had always imagined for ourselves, a dream time?

## XI

So soon as I seen you come in the door I knowed you'd had a bad day. So I makes with the glasses and bottle of wine, don't I? Little black Sambo to Missy some would say but 'tain't like that really and we'm all little black Sambo to somebody in our turn, fetching and carrying and running your legs off, especially in love, as Nana did for me and in time I did for Nana but not enough, not nearly.

We sits there all polite like and you asks me about me day. 'Did you have a good day?' Making a joke of it to cover your own misery, whatever it were had caused it. And I comes back to keep it going. 'I freaked out, man. I told them to stuff their fucking shit job.'

'You didn't!'

'No, not really. The job I was doing finished. My next one starts on Monday so I've got a couple of days off to work up a new routine we're trying out for some recording company; you know, backing a group in a vid.'

'Maybe if I got more into that side of advertising we could work together.'

'That'd be great. So what's been with you today?' Gently does it, Gill boy.

'How do you know?'

'Oh, us artists we're sensitive like. And gay with it: it's practically obligatory.'

'I've been looking up my past. My ancestors. Trying to, anyway. When I was little my father took me to where the family came from and showed me all these tombs and things in a country church. At least I think he did. But sometimes, often lately, I've wondered whether I made it all up. So I went to try and find out.'

'So?'

'There was nothing there. I drove down to Kent and found the church but it was up for sale, padlocked. I rang the estate agent and they said everything had gone from inside to other churches or to be sold. Now I'll never know. I thought I might recognise, remember something. I suppose I was really looking for my father.'

'I know the feeling.'

'I can't even ask Gran Bet what he died of. There's something so painful there I can't begin to touch it. And anyway she'd put me off in some way.'

'Well, that's one thing you could find out without having to ask anyone.'

'How do you mean?'

'You could look up his death certificate.'

'Surely Gran Bet must have that. But she's never let me see it.'

'She'll have a copy maybe but you can look up the original and get a copy from that.'

'How?'

'Go to St Catherine's House where they keep all those things and just look it up. They've got everything there. Births, marriages and deaths.' I knowed all about it cause after Nana told us who I were and where we comed from I went and checked it all, hoping, I suppose, that she were wrong but she weren't. 'But are you sure you really want to know? Sometimes the answer isn't what you want. Look at me.'

'Wasn't it what you wanted?'

'I don't know what I wanted really but like I said, I think inside I was looking for something else, some other answer. Now the scientists say we're all descended from one old black lady in Africa a hundred or three hundred thousand years ago, whichever it's supposed to be, I don't care so much. I mean, it doesn't seem so important as it did. We must be all the same really or all the races couldn't interbreed.'

'Doesn't everyone want to know, about themselves, where they came from? Especially now we're told it's all in the genes.'

'I think people always knew that. My great-grandmother had a saying about what's bred in the bone will come out in the flesh.'

'Gran Bet says that about racehorses: breeding will out.'

'Nature beats nurture,' I do say in Nana's voice and we both laughs. That were better. She were coming out of it.

'Where is this place, St Catherine's House? Is that what you called it?'

'In the Strand, at the Aldwych. Look, I've got some time off as I said. Why don't I take you? Expert guidance, all that stuff.'

And that were how we found ourselves on the bus in the morning. 'Tweren't no use for to take the car, for the parking were impossible and who knew how long us'd have to be there searching, so there us were, sat side by side on the top of the bus with all the world wondering if us was lovers and making another coffee-coloured baby to grow up on the benefit. Only the chances was, if we had done, 'twould have been like sister Laura and nobody would have thought nothing of it. And then I wondered whether 'twere strange and somehow dismal never to have chick nor child of your own as Nana would have put it.

'You sure you're okay with this?' I asks you as I pushes open the glass door and we were stood inside.

'I'm fine. Where do we go?'

'If you want to start with your father's death it's over there. You see the dates on the ends of the shelves. When did he die?'

'October 30th, 1977.'

'Right. That'll be in that shelf. Come on. We'll have to shove through.' The place were an ants' nest as usual. There's barely room between the shelves full of ledgers and the double bookrest in each aisle, to bend down and lug out the great volumes and heave them up on the rest, with people on either side doing the same thing or trying to. You hung back as if the crowd might be giving you second thoughts.

'I never knew there'd be so many people. What are they all doing?'

'The same as us. Some of the professionals do it for a living; lawyers, researchers and so on. But lots are just ordinary people trying to trace a relative or fill in their family tree.'

'There's Aunt Nelly. 1884. I remember her.'

'I never knew Jack had a second name.'

'It looks as if they weren't ever married.'

And then there's the slap of the bound register on the wooden rest or anywhere you can find a square foot to balance it, repeated all over the building by dozens of pairs of hands at once, while you turns the pages and runs your eye down the columns until 'Eureka'. Or 'Fuck all!'

'You see, they're divided into quarters. So I'll get you up September to December 1977.' I heaves it out, and plonks it down afore you. Then I steps back. It's a very private thing and you never knows what you'm going to find. I watch you turning the pages and suddenly I'm nervous too, me breath coming out hard and shallow and a sort of humming in me head which is more than the noise of the place, though that's all a-hum too with all them working away at once, looking for that honey of truth they do hope'll sweeten their lives.

'Here he is. Look here. Falk. You know, I was really afraid I wouldn't find him. That he never existed and I'd made him up.' You show me the entry with your finger. 'But it doesn't say anything about him, only the date and place: Chelsea. And the first name's wrong. It says "Herman" not "Henry". I didn't see that at first. Do you think it's really my father?'

'Maybe they made a mistake. Couldn't read somebody's writing

I expect.' But I feels that anxiousness rising up in me throat like a bit of stuck, cold potato that won't go down. 'Anyway, if the date's right and the place . . . there can't be too many Falks and the initial's right. You might as well go for it and find out.'

'What do I have to do, Gill?'

I felt as if I were nursing along a babby.

'You have to get a form from over there and fill it in for a complete copy.' And whilst you were gone over to the counter I looked at the entry meself for Henry Falk, who had to be Nana's little Harry, only he were down as Herman which I'd never heard her mention, and wondered what them words was hiding so innocent there. Then you were back and I helped you fill in the details and answer the questions and took you over to the queue for the counter to hand in the form, fill in the envelope, pay the price to one of the clerks behind the grill.

'Now what do you want to do?'

'I might as well look for my mother now I'm here. Do you mind? Have you got the time?'

'I've got all day. I'm getting a bit hungry though. Shall we find a pub and come back after?' I felt as I needed something in me belly afore looking up more entries that might have a timebomb embedded in them, quietly ticking away.

'This is on me. I'm so grateful. I'd never have done it on my own.' The nosh were pub lasagne with a good crusty layer of melted browned-off cheddar. Half an hour later we'm back at the shelves for the dead.

'What date now?'

'She died when I was born, so that's easy.' And she were: Shirley Falk née Lewis aged twenty-two, younger than either of we. Us filled in a form for her too.

'Now what? Or have you had enough?'

'I'd like their marriage certificate and at least my father's birth certificate. Maybe my mother's but I'm not so sure about that. Perhaps I'll come back another day for that.'

This were harder. You didn't have no date for the marriage.

Us could only count back from the day she died, that young girl who weren't much more than a babby herself, back four years quarter by quarter and still nothing.

'Maybe they weren't married, not officially. It was the swinging sixties after all, when people were breaking out. Let's try my father's birth. That was just before the Second World War.'

'We'll start with 1940 and work back again.' And there he were all right, with his proper name this time, Henry Falk, and registered at Lewisham District Office.

'They were still living in the big house at Blackheath. I didn't tell you: I went there, too, the other day on my way back from Kent, Mysore House, but it was bombed in the war and now there are just two modern semis.' I knowed it all a course, so why didn't I tell you then? I likes to think it were for your sake but I can't be certain sure. (Nana would've said 'casn't' there, when I first remembers her and noted the way she did talk, but she gradually left it off as the years went by and the telly and the radio took their toll and the old speech began to die around her till people would've looked at her awry if she'd kept on with some of them things she did used to say, that she held her teacher had told her was royal English when King Alfred burnt the cakes.)

When I come home the first night after I started me new job on the Monday I seed them brown envelopes lying on the hall table where the psychiatrist woman downstairs had picked the post up from the doormat and put out ours, only I never got any except from the Social Security, stuff like that. There was them there waiting for you to come home after a long day away and I were the messenger had to carry them up and lay them out. Then I made meself scarce practising over at the Arena, as if I could dance the questions away or there was only me and me own reflection in the world. I knowed as I had to go back sometime to face what them certificates would tell you but I were for putting it off as long as I could. After, I found a couple of dancers I knowed to go to the pub with and pass another hour before I had to catch the bus back if I were to be on time at me new job in the morning. I climbed the stairs, seeing the light seep out under the door but when I opened it the sitting-room were empty. Either you hadn't come in yet or you didn't want to talk about it and had already gone to bed. I went into the bathroom for a pee and then into me own room and shut the door. Next morning I were up and off early, still chicken, only knowing you'd come home and the letters was gone.


# XII


You were there waiting for me at the Hauptbahnhof, Minna, and we ran at each other like two lovers in the closing frames of a romantic movie and hugged and kissed.

'So at least you haven't become a completely cold Englishman in spite of your new cousins. I wonder how I shall feel at suddenly being married to a foreigner,' you teased.

'This is my home of love. If I have ranged. Like him that travels I return again,' I quoted in English.

You wrinkled your nose: 'Have you become a poet too? That won't advance your career.'

'Oh I don't know. Think how many soldiers and so on are followers of Stefan George.'

This time you brought your head up sharply. I expected you to stamp at any minute as we stood on the concourse with our arms still round each other. 'So you've caught the English disease now. Perhaps we should move to Heidelberg to sit at the master's feet.'

It was all a rough kind of play as you re-established your power over me and I played too, provoking you to show you still wanted me, that separation hadn't really changed us. Lovers always have to remake themselves and each other in their own image after they've been apart just for a few days. It was even strange to me to be speaking German. But once we were home in our own flat above the Grünewald it was as if I hadn't been away, except that we made love with a renewed intensity, a hunger that we tried to satisfy by a second and finally a languorous third love-making. 'Well I can see that at least you haven't been gathering any English roses,' you said as you stroked my skin and gently bit my nipples.

Your father had gone to Switzerland to see if the mountain air would revive him. 'He's dying, darling. I know that. I might not even see him again if they suddenly send for me and I can't get there in time.'

'Is there someone to look after him?'

'You are silly. He goes to his mistress, Francesca, who's Italian Swiss.'

'Shouldn't Otto come home if your father is that ill?'

'Vati doesn't want him to. It's such a long way. He prefers to know he's safe in Boston. He's been offered a lectureship, the youngest ever, with his own laboratory so he can make all the stinks he wants and be paid for it.'

The house seemed empty without your father that night and we were perched in the top of it, two birds who had migrated there out of the storm and stayed as if our lives had come to a standstill. But not for long.

'What are you going to do today?' I asked you at breakfast. 'I have to go and report.'

'I shall go to the school.'

'What school? Are you studying for something? Surely you have good enough results for university already. Have you decided to enrol after all?'

'You don't know what's happened while you've been away. Jews have been forbidden to attend goyim schools or the university so I've become a teacher. We have two rooms in Doctor Jacob's house now he doesn't have so many patients, and I give English and French classes to the older students.'

'Surely the government can't keep that up. Under the consti-tution German citizens must be free to go to school and college.'

'Some people say that, that it will all blow over. Others say it's only the beginning.'

'Perhaps you should go and join your father or Otto.' But I didn't want you to go. I didn't want to lose you, to be alone in Berlin. And yet I had no resources to go with you unless we were to be entirely dependent on your family. I imagined living in New York or Zurich with no job, no prospect of anything. And then there was my mother.

'I want to be where you are.'

My mother, when I went to visit her on my way back from the office that evening, seemed to have retreated into herself. All she said when I told her about the English Falks and their friendliness was: 'Good. You may need all the friends you can get in the new Germany they have promised us.' And I couldn't tell whether she was speaking with irony or out of bitterness, as a reproach to me for not listening to her advice, or simply stating what she saw as a fact.

Yet now there descended that curious and brief lull as if we were holding our breath while the new chancellor and his chief henchman, Ernst Röhm, with his huge rabble of stormtroopers vied in secret for who should be master of the new Germany. When I reported to my superiors I was able to tell them that Hitler's speech in favour of peace had been received very favourably in England.

'Let us see whether they are prepared to translate this into a positive agreement for disarmament until Germany is equal to the other powers and can take her rightful place again as a world leader.'

'Even the taxi drivers in London believe this is fair and just.'

'Ah! The people. But their leaders, the old men who humiliated us at Versailles, that may be a different story. Well they have been warned in that same speech by the Führer. We shall see if they have understood. Incidentally, von Falk, isn't it time you joined the party yourself?'

'I hadn't thought about it, sir. My teachers belonged to the school of thought that said that civil servants should be neutral, prepared to serve the state whatever party was in power.'

'The old school, yes. Well I advise you to think about it. You are doing very well. I have an excellent report on you from the embassy in London. Apparently the English like you and take you into their confidence. But my assessment must include your political reliability. I should like to be able to report favourably on that.'

'Have you thought,' you said when I told you all this, 'that they might not allow someone married to a Jew to join their holy party.'

'Of course I don't want to join their stupid party. I just thought you'd be amused.'

'I can't laugh, Anton. I'm afraid I shall ruin your career, perhaps even destroy your life.'

'You are my life. They may destroy my career but they can't destroy us.'

'Methinks the lady doth protest too much!' You laughed and touched my cheek. We were standing very close. And suddenly we were undoing each other's clothes, dropping them where we stood and going down on the carpet in front of the sofa. You opened your legs and propped up your knees to let me in. 'Hold it, hold it,' you said. I stayed very still for a moment while you put a hand between your thighs. 'Now,' you said, 'yes, now.'

I don't any longer get an erection when I remember these things. My whole ancient body suffuses with pleasure, my breath comes quick and shallow. I can hear your voice urging me on. But, rather like being a woman I suppose, there's no cocky head lifting itself. Just as well, Christoff might come in and find me in such a state and be disgusted. Yet I want to record it all and to do that I have to live it again. The god descends and indwells, like the angel visiting Saint Theresa, and like her I am prostrated, rapt, until the divine withdrawal that leaves me soft, malleable, as if I have died and risen. It's a pity I can't believe in that promise of bliss to come but I know what I feel is simply the pleasure of the flesh, however atrophied.

'Stupid,' you'd say. 'What do you know about how women feel. Of course I felt it here,' and put my hand on your mount of Venus and rub yourself against it like a cat wanting to be stroked.

'Why do you go through it all? Why put it all down? Who will read it, do you think?'

'I need to see if it could have been otherwise, if I could have done things differently. If we could have foreseen.'

'It's history: all over and done with. Let it lie. You've spent fifty years of your life mourning and searching. You should have married again. Got on with life. Nothing could have been changed. The "what ifs" of history are a dangerous game. People exonerate themselves by saying "if only" and wringing their hands. And they learn nothing, no ways of avoiding such horrors even here in Europe. We are tribal animals fighting for survival.'

I put words into your mouth so that I can rehearse arguments we never had. I drag you in my mind through those few years together, looking for answers when I know the only answer is still love, that in Sarajevo there were lovers like us who died in the streets running for a loaf, or a dried tomato, Christian hand in Muslim hand under the bombardment of hatred. Oh the flatulence of history, endlessly repeating itself until it gives up with a final belch and vomits us into oblivion, a puff of gas and particles sucked into an exploding star. Then, as the Christians say, we shall all be as one in that god from whence we came, Helios the light bringer.

Still I go on with my 'what ifs'. If the allies had acted fast enough to give Hitler no excuse for taking us out of the League of Nations a few months later, would that have changed anything? I am, have been, a diplomat. I know how long these things take, especially among democracies. And not just one had to agree but several. The truth is we didn't want their agreement, their recognition. We wanted to be free again. The army and the industrialists wanted guns and the people wanted work and butter. So when they were offered that and a one-party state they took it. I was glad your father wasn't alive to see it.

You went on your own to Switzerland to bury him and mourn.

'I ought to come with you.'

'No darling. It's best if you don't get involved.'

'What is it like, a Jewish funeral? Is it very different?'

'First of all we have to say Kaddish. Otto will come over from America, of course. Then Vati's will must be read.' I felt excluded. They would be together there, the brother and sister with the exotic Italian mistress, taking part in strange rituals in a language I didn't know.

'It doesn't mean I'm going all religious. These are just things that have to be done. I'll be back very soon.'

It was difficult to go to the office every day and sit at my desk, trying to pretend my mind was on my work while it ranged after you among the lakes and mountains, as if you had been spirited away into the forest by some evil presence conjured up by the Grimm brothers or sunk from sight like the girl who trod on a loaf, put down in a puddle to stop her pretty shoes getting wet. At night alone in the flat I heard the wind rub the branches together with groans and creaks. Once I went into town to a bierkeller we had used as students but it was full of uniforms. I drank my Schoppen quickly and left.

You came home in the dark. I heard the front door slam and your feet on the stairs as I went to open the door to our flat. I felt how it must be for you, coming up through the empty house where you and Otto had been children together, of the long gone clink of glasses and laughter, the overgrown tennis courts, the ghosts still lingering in the unlit, dust-shrouded rooms. Your steps were weary on the stairs and even though you let me take you in my arms I was merely holding another ghost. It took a glass of schnapps to bring you back to me a little but we were still strangers, unsure with each other.

'Otto thinks we should shut this house up altogether and that you and I should find somewhere else to live. He thinks it's too easily identified, too well known, and it might be dangerous to stay here. The house is left between us and we could sell but as things are we wouldn't get much for it. And who knows, one day one of us might want to come back here to live.'

I opened a bottle of red wine from Herr Strauss's cellar. You were very pale, your face hollowed and hatched with grief. 'Drink some of this. It will do you good. *Fa sangue*, as the Italians say.'

You took the glass automatically and went on: 'Otto also thinks the house should be transferred to you. That might keep it in the family if things get more difficult.'

'What about the Italian lady?'

'Oh, Papa has left her provided for. She wants to stay near him and keep in touch with Otto and me if possible. She says there is always a place we can go to there.'

'You know Hitler has called for a plebiscite on whether we should leave the League, and for new elections.'

'I haven't been reading the newspapers.'

'No, of course not. It's very difficult. Naturally, I want to vote against but I don't know how secret the voting will be and since there are only National Socialist candidates in the election there's no one else to vote for. Perhaps it's better just to abstain and hope no one finds out.' I was 'chuntering on', in that splendid English phrase, about things that were still very distant from you but it was as if we no longer knew how to talk to each other.

'Let's go to bed, darling. We can leave all that till the morning.'

'Of course. You must be so tired. Please forgive me.'

I got in beside you and turned to kiss you goodnight, thinking you were too exhausted for anything but sleep but you opened your arms and began to stroke my hair and face.

'Have you forgotten so quickly how to make love? Or did you find someone else while I was away? There. I can see it's the prince who falls asleep and has to be awakened with a kiss.' It was our sweetest love-making ever, not wild and fierce but very deep and slow as if we wanted to be fused together by such tenderness, that long slow burn, forever. Afterwards you said: 'Darling, we didn't only lose my father. While I was away we lost our first baby too. I suppose it was the strain. I'm sorry, Anton.'

'Don't be sorry. We've got plenty of time. And perhaps this isn't the best moment anyway, when we have to find a new home and everything is so uncertain. How old was the baby?'

'About three months. I hadn't told you because I wasn't sure. You know how irregular I am.'

'I don't care about anything now you're back.' Which was true. Alone I sink into myself. Only you bring me out. Oh, I can go on. I'm very good at that. Haven't I proved it? But the truth is, it's easy for me to seem to other people to be there, at work for instance, while what they get is an appearance, another ghost. If I haven't married it's because if I can't be with you I prefer to be alone and create you, re-create you daily. As long as I can do that you're still here, and when I'm no longer here to do it we shall both be gone unless someone cares to read this, can conjure it up on a screen from where it lies like all the other lost histories scattered in their secret hiding places in attics and archives, and now in depositories and on disk.

The plebiscite and the election came and went, with their depressing majorities. But not our votes. We shut up the house for the winter and found ourselves an apartment in Berlin-Friedenau, waiting and watching while the wolves took over the forest, snarling at each other's throats. We knew only what we were allowed to know because of the heavy press censorship, except from what I could pick up at the ministry but there it was mostly chatter about our pact with the Poles and the chancellor's meeting with Mussolini in Venice and what they might mean. Until the night you came home with a smuggled copy of *The Germania*, with von Papen's speech about freedom of the press that, it was said, Hindenburg had authorised him to make at the University of Marburg. There was still hope then. The old president himself was disturbed by what was happening to us, to the country. Hindenburg had received Hitler coldly when he flew to Munich for an audience, and for a few minutes only. It was whispered that he had threatened to call in the army. And then the wolves fell on and devoured each other until only one was left and we were all his prey. The only one who had stood in his path, the old grey pack leader himself, died in August after endorsing Hitler's murder of his rivals and enemies.

Still I clung to my reasons for not joining the party although it was now the only one. 'I'm afraid those are typical of the old-fashioned intellectual liberal attitudes that brought about Germany's shame.' My superior shook his head. 'You will never advance, von Falk, with such ideas.'

'We've been invited, commanded rather, to a party at the minister's house. "Bring your wife. I don't believe we've met her," he said.'

'Can't I have a cold or a headache?'

'Why not!'

'But then, why should we be afraid of them?' So we went. Of course you, elegant as some glossy Egyptian cat goddess, turned all eyes and the minister's head. 'Why have you been keeping such a beautiful woman a secret, von Falk? Perhaps you are afraid that someone might steal her.'

I knew how you hated this kind of heavy teasing. 'Why do German women put up with it?' you said as we were undressing afterwards. It was the first time you had distanced yourself from being German. 'All this stuff about Kinder und Küche that you hear now, as if we hadn't got brains. I hope it doesn't start to rub off on you, Anton.'

'I wouldn't dare,' I laughed. 'You were marvellous though.'

'But it won't stop them trying to make you join their stupid party.'

'What can they do to me? I'm not ambitious in that way. I just want to keep my job without getting involved in all that arse-licking and jockeying for position. I wish I could get a posting abroad in England again and you could come with me.'

'Unless you seem to be conforming they'll make quite sure you don't.'

You understood it all so much better than I did, the twists and turns of the political maze. You had your father's quickness and subtlety without his gloom.

'I just hope we don't have to do the social round too often. They give me the creeps with their ponderous flirting and their lack of humour.' But we were bidden to join groups of officials and their wives at concerts, plays and the opera, at suppers and parties. There was no escape if I was to appear co-operative without giving in to more pressure to conform.

The streets were quieter now, except when the state rallies took place. Order and prosperity governed German society while Otto's letters told of the American Depression, and *The Times* reported the same phenomenon in England, with the struggles between communist and fascist groups in the streets of London that we had seen in Berlin. We dreaded that the whole world might fall into line and there would be nowhere to run to. Every day came news of another of your family's friends emigrating as the stranglehold on the country tightened and the propaganda, especially that against the Jews, became more shrill. Still none of my superiors or colleagues at the office, who sat next to you in theatre or concert hall or leaned across a table crammed with elbows and full plates, had even thought to ask.

One rally I couldn't avoid as we had managed so far to be absent for most of them, took place the day after the chancellor had proclaimed universal conscription at the State Opera House. For the first time the growing military presence came out from under wraps for the world to see, with the new air force in its sky-blue uniforms, the old field grey, and the sinister smart black of the expanding Gestapo, Air Chief Marshal Goering's personal creation from the Prussian secret police. As I watched them under the spotlight against the backdrop of a huge Iron Cross, I realised that the country was being made ready for war and that the generals had been given their reward by Hitler for their support. When I got back to our new apartment, exhausted and depressed by the rhetoric, I found you at the window, staring down into the empty street where a strong March wind was blowing rags of cloud across the moon.

'I shall have to join one of the services. Eventually no one will be exempt. Tonight I wondered whether we wouldn't be safer if I made a career of it. My father always said: "The army takes care of its own."' My mother had told me this, and though our lives were hard they would have been worse without his pension and the handouts we got from them from time to time, including help with my education. 'My qualifications and the fact that my father was killed in the last war should make it easier to get a commission.' I didn't mention the little 'von', which would help too. 'If a war comes and we are still here I should have to fight anyway, so I might as well get myself as well placed as possible. And I could protect you better as an officer. No one would dare to look down on an officer's wife.'

'Will you have to wear a spiked helmet like Vati and grow a big bushy moustache? How shall I feel married to a real Prussian Junker?'

'I'm not a Prussian. If I were I should beat you for insubordination. Instead . . .'

'Instead?' You asked teasing, taunting.

'Instead I shall fuck you to death.' And I chased you round the flat until we ended up in the bedroom.

The new law made it surprisingly easy for me. Putting on a grave face I said I felt it was my duty after the Führer's call to arms to enlist in my father's old regiment, first for my national service and then, though I didn't tell them this, as a full-time soldier.

'My dear von Falk I am delighted to see you responding in this way. At last you are identifying fully with our country's future. I shall speak most highly of your abilities if I am asked.'

What I hadn't reckoned with were my long periods away from you in training, except when you came to stay in the town or village near the camp or school as I progressed from infantry to cavalry, even being posted for a time, like my father, to Bamberg where my mother's parents had lived. There I could show you our old home and the cathedral with its stone knight. My mother herself came to stay and for the first time for years seemed relaxed and almost cheerful as we stood on the medieval town bridge, watching the river flow and eddy beneath. She approved my change of career. It brought us closer, made me more like my father, her dead soldier lover, and we were all three able to be together as a family as we had never been before.

It was autumn when I came home on leave to Berlin a lieutenant. The train had passed between fields of fresh stubble and the leaves on the trees were ashen with the dust of harvest. Apart from being separated from you I had slipped easily into army life. My fellow officers, particularly the old military who had had to rise through the ranks under the republic because of the shortage of officer places, were civilised, even satirical among themselves at the new regime, and relieved to find a raw recruit who was also educated and as they saw it cultivated. As I had foreseen, the little 'von' certainly helped. There was no question of being forced to join the party although we all had to swear personal loyalty to Hitler, which I did by mentally substituting the office for the man. All soldiers, I reasoned, had to give unconditional obedience to the supreme commander if there was to be discipline and organisation. I felt liberated by the uniform, as if I was taking up where my father had left off.

We had planned to have supper at our old café by the Wannsee, a romantic evening under the stars by the luminous waters of the lake with the sharp scent of pine needles to keep us alert, but I saw as soon as I pushed open the door of our sitting-room that you were too upset to go out at once as I had intended, walking through the streets from the train stop aware of the effect of my smart new uniform on passers-by and practising my military flourish like a little boy playing at soldiers.

'What is it? What's the matter?'

'Have you seen this?' You thrust a copy of the party newspaper, the *Völkischer Beobachter*, at me.

'What are you reading that rag for?'

'Because I like, I need to know what they're saying.'

'So what are they saying now?'

'There are new laws, National Citizenship Laws. Those defined as Jews are no longer German citizens. Marriage is forbidden between them and Aryans.'

'Thank God we're already married. They can't change that. Laws can't be retrospective.'

'You don't understand, Anton. There's no way round it. Everyone has to be classified. I escape, if you can call it that, because I'm married to you. I'm no longer a Jew but an "Aryan by marriage".'

I didn't know what to say, whether to thank God again or to be angry or weep with you. At least, I thought to myself, your father would have been relieved that his prediction that I would be able to protect you had been right. 'But,' you were saying now, 'our children, if we have any, will be half Jews, mixed race, non-citizens, forbidden to marry Aryans in case they contaminate German blood and honour. Your blood it seems isn't strong and pure enough to wash away the stain of mine.'


# XIII

She laid the two certificates face up, the oldest above the more recent, and tried to make sense of them with a strange silent ringing in her ears as if she might be going to faint. The first, from June 1939, told of a stillborn child called Henry Falk; the second, dated October 1977, of a Herman Falk who had taken his own life at a Chelsea address. Both had the stamp and signature of authority, of the local magistrates of two London boroughs. Henry Falk, born and died of natural causes. Herman, the father Betony now painfully remembered with almost hallucinatory vividness, by barbiturate poisoning. She also remembered the day of the funeral. Gran Bet had said she was too young to attend. She had been left behind in Glebe House, with Maria who came twice a week to clean, while Gran Bet went up to London.

Betony had been fetched out of her English class to hear the news from her headmistress. She sensed that she ought to have burst into tears but she felt only a profound numbness, as if she, not her father, were dead. She was to be sent home to Gran Bet's, where she spent her holidays and where her father came down to see her from his London flat. They were kind to her at her little prep school. She felt safe among the group of girls and a few smaller day boys. Several of the children had irregular families with parents missing: working aboard, divorced, dead. Indeed, it was the holidays she dreaded, alone in the big house with Gran Bet, and her occasional father she hardly knew but felt a sense of failure and guilt towards. Now even that was gone.

She had tried to imagine the ceremony she was excluded from, taking comfort in her own room with its books and assorted animals and dolls until she was called down to pick at tomato soup and baked beans on toast, usually her favourite food, with chocolate ice-cream for pudding. Outside, wind had flung rain hard against the windows all day and threatened to tear the green swags of leaves from the chestnut. Returning, Gran Bet had run from the garage to the house, the wind slamming the door behind her as she stood in the hall in a flurry of streaming mackintosh and droplets shaken from her umbrella. 'Goodness me what a day. Typical funeral weather. Enough to give us all our death of cold,' Betony had heard her say to the departing Maria. 'How has Betony been, Maria?'

'She don't eat much the lunch.'

Later when she was older she had wondered from time to time

why her father hadn't been buried in the village churchyard or whether he'd been taken back to Bishopsgreen to lie with their ancestors. Now she knew. He had been anonymously cremated in some vast London processing plant for the dead. Probably his ashes were scattered in a garden of rest, without even a stone or a bush to mark where she could go and put some flowers. She had never dared to ask Gran Bet, who had fended off the approach of such questions with: 'I always think it's so morbid to dwell on the past. Whatever happens you have to get over it somehow as best you can and go on with life. No good sitting and weeping.' On the day itself she had been kind and reassuring, putting her arms round Betony and holding her against her jutting shelf of bosom until Betony could hear her grandmother's heart beating. 'We shall be all right together, shan't we, darling? Would you like to stay home for a few days more before you go back to school?' And Betony had nodded, lying, the agreement expected of her.

If only Gill had been home he would have helped, but there was no answer when she knocked and no light or sound from his room. She tried again to make sense of the two entries. Perhaps there had been a second baby after the first Henry Falk, following close on because the date fitted with her father's, if it was her father's, age at death. Perhaps if they'd looked later, in 1940 even, they would have found another baby who had lived. What was a year or less? She could go back and search the registers again. And perhaps this Falk who had taken his life wasn't her father. That there was another one who had died of a heart attack and was the real Harry as her father was called by Gran Bet.

She could telephone her grandmother and ask. The telephone was more neutral. They wouldn't have to confront each other face to face. It would allow Gran Bet to evade, to lie. It would give them both time to prepare for what, unless there was a simple and immediate explanation, would be an uncomfortable, perhaps painful, meeting. Betony took up the receiver and dialled. Then she looked at her watch. It was too late: her grandmother would already be in bed. She put back the white handset on its cradle. Then she lay down fully clothed on the double bed she had shared with Mark, put out the bedside lamp and stared into the dark. Sometime later, now half dozing, she heard the outer door open, feet pass her door going to the bathroom, the header tank emptying, and then the feet going on to Gill's room, but she was too drained now to get up and ask for his help. In the morning she overslept and by the time she blundered, still only half awake, into the kitchen to put on the kettle, he had gone. There was nothing for it. She must tackle Gran Bet. But she dreaded it. How could she say: 'Was it your son, my father, who killed himself?' And if the answer was 'Yes', then there was nothing left but the little damning word: 'Why?'

'He missed your mother too much,' Gran Bet might say, or, 'He was ill.' Any explanation like that would make it tolerable even if she was left with a feeling of inadequacy that she, Betony, hadn't been enough to give him a hold on life. Then her grandmother would tell her about the second baby. But why Herman? Maybe there was some family tradition she didn't know about, something to do with that German connection Gran Bet had once mentioned so satirically.

Betony poured boiling water onto a tea bag and dunked it with a spoon until the dark amber swirl had permeated the whole cup and the scented steam rose up like incense. How should she begin? She would phone her grandmother after breakfast. Not too early. Gran Bet found getting up the hardest part of the day. 'I'm fine once I get going.' Betony ate her way through cereal and a banana, alternating the bitterness of grapefruit juice with her tea. There seemed no way round the bald question.

'Gran, how did my father die?' She would listen to the silence while her grandmother tried to assess how much she knew.

'What do you mean, darling?'

'I went to look up his death certificate.'

'I don't understand.'

'You can look up things like that at St Catherine's House.'

126

'Why should you want to?'

'People do it all the time. There seemed to be hundreds of them there. All looking things up. Births, marriages and deaths. Were my parents ever married? I couldn't find an entry for them.'

'I believe so, darling. Your father told me so.'

'And how did he die?'

'I don't think it's something I want to discuss on the telephone. You never know who might be listening. Crossed lines.'

'You don't get those any more, Gran.'

'Is that true? Even so I don't feel safe. These days they can tell exactly who you're talking to. I know because it's on my bill. No privacy. I think we had better have a proper talk. Can you come down this weekend?'

Running this conversation through in her mind as she ate, Betony realised she would lose that round and maybe the next. A call would give Gran Bet time to think, to prepare her answers. She took the certificates out of their envelopes again and willed them to give up their secrets. But perhaps there was no secret. She was just imagining things. Perhaps there was only Gran Bet's unwillingness to be 'always harking back'.

What she should do was check every possibility of mistaken identity before she questioned her grandmother. She longed for it all to be a mistake, for her father to have died of a heart attack or stroke whose classical medical equivalent, cardiac failure or embolism, she had expected to find on the form. Then she could mourn as she had been unable to do properly as a child. Suicide was quite different: an act of rage or despair or a sign of madness, a legacy to be frightened of much more, with its smell of loneliness and violence, than that of physical illness. Barbiturate poisoning. Pills to ease pain or sleeplessness, used to end all pain in a final sleep to death. She couldn't believe it. She must make absolutely sure before she went to Gran Bet with her questions.

A sudden call to set up a clutch of garden tools for a Saturday spread that offered its readers an instant remedy for weekend boredom with the promise of the Chelsea Flower Show abloom in their own backyards, put off her return visit for two days. She gathered her set of trowel, rake, fork, secateurs and two kinds of hoe together and embellished their naked wood and honed metal with a fruit or vegetable to give them more visual appeal, suggest a benign outcome from their sharp edges. Betony did two layouts, with and without, and had the photographer take them both, knowing the innate conservatism of the editor who had commissioned her. As she had half expected, he chose the plain version, finding her polished fruits too suggestive of Eden with its apple and serpent for his readers' suburban plots.

She had seen little of Gill since the envelopes had arrived. It was as if he was avoiding her, mumbling something when they coincided in the kitchen on the day of the shoot about a new job and a new routine he was working on before swinging his ghetto blaster out of the door so that she knew he was off to wherever it was he went for serious practice. Her first impulse to ask for his help had receded. She knew the process to follow at St Catherine's House and she wanted to be on her own this time and able to take as long as she liked.

It was just as crowded as before. Betony elbowed her way to the shelf she and Gill had sampled first and began to work her way back and then forward for three years from their previous find, hauling out and turning the thick pages of twenty heavy ledgers until her back and arms were aching. There was nothing. There had been no mistake and indeed very few Falks. Then she went to the births section and repeated the same actions but no new live Henry Falk appeared to replace the stillborn baby. Suddenly she was weary of searching: her head buzzed with the whispered conversations around her; her stomach yawned with a sick emptiness. She pushed her way out through the glass doors and crossed the road to the little church of St Mary le Strand on its island amid the traffic and went inside. A woman was dusting among the pews and kneelers. Betony sat in the gloom and felt the cleaner's calm movements soothe away her panic, for that, she realised, was what it had been. Gran Bet still went on Sundays to the local church as part of a vanished icon of village life where all things were bright and beautiful, and she would try, and sometimes succeed, to persuade Betony to go with her. But when she did succumb Betony would emerge into the daylight from the dusky interior unmoved except by a faint irritation that her grandmother still depended on such banal and even tawdry props. Still she had wanted the family church at Bishopsgreen to be open, to provide answers, and now she allowed herself to be calmed by gestures of faith she couldn't share.

## XIV

So soon as I heard you come in, me mind were made up to speak. Us couldn't go on like this, not talking and living in the same pad like. I come out of me door and you was standing there looking so down I knowed the moment had come.

'Cup of tea?'

'Great, thanks. You having one?'

'Why not.'

By the time I'd made it the way I knowed you like it and brought it through from the kitchen you'd sunk into a chair and was leaning back with closed eyes, as if to hold down a pain you was afraid might spring out and claw you to bits.

'Have you got an aspirin, Gill, or something? I've such a head-ache. I don't think I can even get up to look for my own.'

'Yeah I got something I can give you. Hold on.' I fetched the pills I takes when I've been overdoing the practice and I needs something to take the pain away. 'There, take two. They'll see you all right.'

'Thanks.' I saw you pause, as if you too was making up your mind to speak while you swallowed down they pills with a gulp of tea. 'I've been back to St Catherine's House today to see if we'd made a mistake. I mean, if there was any chance those two

Falk entries we found weren't the only ones, if we'd been too quick to accept them as right. I went backwards and then forward through the next few years but I couldn't find any more, so they have to be the right ones.'

I wondered whatever they could say that were so what you didn't want to see that you'd go back again to search for something different. But all I said was: 'So you've found what you wanted.'

'Except that all it does is give me a whole set of new questions, things I don't understand. Can I show you what they sent me? You might see something I've missed that would help me to make sense of it all.'

'Yeah, course.'

You went away into your own room and came back with the two brown envelopes I'd seen afore, took out the copies of the certificates and laid them out on the table. I looked at the birth one first and I remembered so clear how I'd opened up mother June's certificate with Margaret's name down as mother and the Yankee GI Carl as the father. This were different though. This baby were dead as soon as born. I switched to the other, the death, and saw that strange name like a sixties pop group, Herman's Hermits, and that he had killed hisself. I picked them up one after the other and stared at them as if I could alter what were written there just by will alone. Then I put them back on the table, knowing now I should have to speak. 'There's something I have to tell you but I don't know if it will help or confuse things even more. And you'll wonder why I didn't tell you before and whether I've got some hidden motive but it's just that I couldn't make the words come out right. You see, I've known your name all my life because it used to be on a Christmas card to my Nana that came every year with some money to buy herself a present. Until she died and then it must have been returned or just lost in a great heap of Christmas post they couldn't deliver. That must happen every year.'

'What do you mean, the card had my name on?'

'Betony Falk. I knew as soon as you said your name on the

phone when I first called you about the room that there had to be some connection. There couldn't be two Betony Falks who had nothing to do with each other. I couldn't believe it at first. It seemed such a coincidence.'

'I don't understand. You'll have to explain more. How could you have a card from me?'

'It wasn't from you of course. And it wasn't sent to me. It was from your grandmother to my Nana. That's what I called her but she was really my great-grandmother. She brought us up, me and my sister, because our mother wasn't around, at least she was out most evenings.' I was gabbling stuff I'd told you already.

'But why should my grandmother send cards to your Nana?'

'Because she was once her nanny, your father's nanny, little Harry and his father before him. You can ask her, ask her if she remembers Lily.' And then I told you everything I could that Nana had told me.


## XV


I see from the calendar that outside these walls where I never go it's summer again. Why can't I die? Other people die but I simply mummify. Like the Flying Dutchman I go on and on as if I am waiting for my release but since I don't know what shape it should come in I may not recognise it. Indeed it may have come already and passed on, leaving me still here waiting. Other people kill themselves. I've thought of that, Minna, as you know but that would be unfair to Christoff unless I were in such physical pain that he would understand that it was just a way out, not a reflection on his care. So I go on searching for some sign, a meaning, an explanation.

An American woman has written a book on modern hysteria. Yesterday when I was browsing, I found a review of it that seems to suggest she believes these religious cults are the latest manifestation of something very deep-rooted, a human tendency to hysteria in the face of what? Fear of death, of the unknown, of the future or the past? Now such a movement can be worldwide through the Internet. People can arrange to die at the same moment, believing they will be swept together into immortality. Is this another manifestation of what we saw induced by flags, a thousand boots marching in goose-step, fifty thousand arms in salute, mesmeric as a chanted mantra. The sleep of reason. And then there's the tribalism we inherit from our ancestors and share with our ape cousins, the bitter legacy of the witch hunt and the Inquisition enforcing conformity, destroying anything other in the name of gods or the race or the people. 'My people,' you began to say, Minna, which shut me out until you explained. 'I never had to think of myself as a Jew before. Now I see us everywhere on the streets. I recognise us by the fear in our eyes. You can protect me, Anton, but I can't protect them. How far can it go? Vati isn't here any more to answer me.'

I felt my own inadequacy in the face of your questions. I clung to the hope that civilised values would prevail, encouraged by what I found in the army of the old concepts of service and honour that were being eroded in the rest of society. That winter was hard and bitter but it brought me a coveted place at the General Staff College because of my knowledge of English, which meant I was near you, could live at home and was very well placed to try to understand and anticipate the future. Even so, the order to move troops into the Rhineland in March took us all by surprise and, I have to admit, filled us with delight. Young officers ran from room to room shouting to each other. 'Come on, von Falk. Aren't you pleased we've got the Rhineland back?'

Of course I was but partly because I hoped, wanted to believe, that this would be enough. Honour would be satisfied. Versailles and its humiliation expunged. Now we would be able to take our place as equals at the world table and there would be no need for war as long as Britain and France accepted that we had simply reclaimed our own borders. Indeed, the other powers seemed to agree. A strange quiet descended, broken only by the excitement over the Olympic Games. When I asked you if you wanted to see some of the events in the great stadium you shrugged your shoulders. 'What does it matter who wins? These are boys' games. Noble young Aryans with their strength through joy cant.'

'Maybe the German athletes are but not all the foreigners.'

'So are you going to cheer them on against your own national athletes because they're black or even Jewish? You'll do what the rest do, especially in uniform. Why should I go and watch that?' And I was ashamed of my own insensitivity, yet when a brother officer suggested a visit I didn't dare refuse, afraid of appearing too different from my fellows.

I saw at once that you had been right. The new stadium was magnificent but it was clear from the hundreds of flapping swastikas that the whole games were simply a huge propaganda event like the rallies and marches. We were unlucky enough to coincide with one of Hitler's own visits, when the specially commissioned music by Orff and Strauss was played and the whole audience rose to its feet in a frenzy of 'Sieg heil'. 'They say in the English newspapers that whenever the Führer attends Germany wins,' my companion shouted in my ear against the din. I had compromised by rising and giving the stiff arm salute in silence, hoping not to appear too conspicuous. The black uniforms of the SS were everywhere and I realised that there were probably dozens of informers among the huge crowd watching for any signs of political deviance. Spying, informing: that was what we had slipped into almost without noticing; a creeping stain of corruption mildewing our society. By the time I could decently leave and persuade my brother officer to come in search of a beer I was exhausted by the weight of numbers, the knee-jerk response to every German triumph and the effort of seeming to conform.

Once the games were over we resumed that deceptively quiet life. You still taught but now your pupils came privately to our flat. The Jewish schools were out of bounds to Aryans by marriage and too risky for the wife of an army officer. From time to time

I had intimations that our high command was unhappy with the regime the government was inexorably putting in place though they were encouraged by the expansion of the army and its weaponry and the opportunities for training, especially the air force, given by the Spanish Civil War. Everyone was agreed that we must help to defeat communism, the enemy without and within. I was kept busy drafting English versions of reports and speeches, more the diplomat still than a practical soldier. If we kept our heads down and our noses clean we could survive. It seemed more comedy than tragedy when I repeated to you a phone call I had taken which had been intended for the general away on leave.

'Give him a message from us,' a woman's voice said with a suggestive laugh. 'Tell him there are plenty more where Frau Blomberg came from if he ever gets rid of his wife.' There were more giggles. Then she put the phone down.

'What did she mean? Who do you think she was?'

'It sounded as if she was ringing from a nightclub or somewhere like that. I don't know what it means. The Blombergs are still on their honeymoon. He's married his secretary. There was a lot of gossip at the college. Apparently he had to ask Hitler's permission. First he asked Goering if he thought a field marshal and com-mander-in-chief could marry a commoner.'

'He was asking the right one there, with an ex-actress for a wife.'

'Of course Goering said yes. But there was a lot of discussion among the officers of the old school. Now nobody knows what's happening but I'm not the only one to have picked up a call like that.'

Later I was able to give you the rest of the story. 'It seems the police have discovered that Frau Blomberg has a criminal record for prostitution and pornographic photographs. The field marshal has been dismissed. He refused either to divorce his wife or shoot himself. The calls were coming from prostitutes but some people are saying they had been put up to it by the SS.'

The tragi-comedy became a farce when it was revealed that General Fritsch, commander-in-chief of the army, was being blackmailed by another ex-convict, male this time. 'He denies it all, of course, and has demanded a military tribunal. At the college everyone believes this is the last straw and the army will take over, arrest Hitler and his gang at the Reichstag when he makes his fifth anniversary speech on the thirtieth.' Instead, he simply took over command of the forces himself, abolished the War Ministry and set up the OKW under Blomberg's son-in-law, Keitel, who had betrayed his wife's father in the first place.

The officers of the general staff seethed with resentment and speculation as to who would be next to go. Anyone who had seemed less than enthusiastic about the regime or had questioned the government's right to interfere with the army was at risk, liable to be informed on by those who coveted their positions. Generals toppled like struck skittles, sixteen of them. There was no more talk of a military coup. We all fell silent, watching our own backs, afraid that even a misplaced or indiscreet joke would catapult us out of the comparative safety of the staff college if not the army itself. The moment when a halt might have been called to Nazi plans had passed. The only effective restraining force, the army, was now completely subjugated, with officers who supported the regime replacing the old guard. And then we reclaimed Austria. Still the other powers made no move. It was rumoured in the office that Hitler had told the generals of his intentions six months before and that their protests had been the real cause of their removal.

'It must mean war in the end. We can't go on like this, or rather we can't expect Britain and France to be silent forever. Austria is one thing. We can argue, make a case for it being part of Germany, but if we go any further . . .'

'Do you really think the British and French will fight for Czechs and Poles? They'll do a deal just as Hitler believes.'

'How do you know what he believes?'

'It's all here in the party rag if you read between the lines. And more. All this inflammatory vileness about international Jewry and Bolshevism. We are supposed to be corrupting the whole state and be in league with all Jews everywhere to take over the world.'

'Who says so?'

'The same rag of course. I read it all the time. Sometimes I can even laugh from my place of safety, hiding behind your name. Sometimes I think you should divorce me and let me go away for your sake as well as mine.'

I put my arms around you, panic stricken. 'Don't leave me, Minna. Say you won't leave me.'

You sighed. 'Only if you tell me to go.'

'Don't you love me?'

'Do you still want me to?'

There was only one possible answer and it wasn't in words. What had drawn me to you in the first place was that very otherness the rest of the world, our world, despised and feared. The braided blonde heads of other women bored and repelled me. They were peasants while you were still the enchantingly enchanting princess. I see now that even in this there was an element of racism but when is sexual attraction, love itself, ever totally free of the so-called impurity of lust that may spring as much from difference as likeness, be rooted in places of the psyche we don't even know exist with our conscious mind.

In the bull sessions that sometimes developed at work I kept all this to myself while my brothers-in-arms, or rather out of them, praised bouncing breasts and buttocks for easy child bearing. Occasionally they would speculate about what it might be like with a woman of another race: a negress, an Italian or even a Jew. Still I kept quiet, finding an excuse to leave as soon as I could, though sometimes the impulse to boast, to speak out of your beauty, the scent and silk of your skin and our passion, almost overwhelmed me and I had to button my lip, as the Americans say.

Then the plans for the invasion of Czechoslovakia began to arrive on my desk, not of course this time for translation but so that I could adjust the reports I wrote for the foreign press. Yet instead of the expected enthusiasm I detected a reluctance for war if that was what it would mean. The army felt itself unready to take on the rest of Europe, which was where we were heading. It had dawned on the senior officers at last that Hitler was determined not just on reclaiming what could be argued was justly ours but on expansion to the East. While the leaders of Britain and France were offering him that part of Czechoslovakia that was German speaking, the Sudetenland, he was preparing to annex the whole country.

It now became my job to translate articles from the British and American press and other documents. One was a letter from an English politician encouraging the generals to believe that Britain and France would march in support of the Czechs. I came to realise that there was the beginning of a conspiracy among the senior officers to strike against Hitler if he should order the invasion to go ahead in spite of the possible threat from Britain and France. It was important for the conspirators to know whether these countries would support them by defending the Czech state against invasion. But my readings from *The Times* of London and elsewhere contradicted the letter and seemed to offer little hope of intervention even before the British prime minister came to Munich and handed Hitler all he had asked for.

'Look,' you said, showing me the newspaper headline. A seventeen-year-old German Jewish refugee had shot a member of the German embassy in Paris. 'The little fool. Doesn't he know how we'll be punished for this?' Three days later I stepped out in the morning to walk to the station through burnt-out embers of shops and homes, over pavements glittering with smashed glass and littered with goods from the shops and with personal belongings: a child's toy, a shoe, a smashed violin. The air stank of smoke, charred wood and cloth and something I was afraid might be burnt flesh. The streets and the ravaged fronts of houses, shops and synagogues were guarded by police and SS, who smiled as they prevented people from searching their own homes to try to find missing family and friends. Other people stood watching in silence as if dazed by the shock, the brutal violence they could see with their own eyes. As soon as I reached the office I telephoned you and warned you not to go out of the flat without me.

'I've been trying to find out exactly what happened,' you said when I got home, 'phoning around old friends of my father. Some of them have been deported to Poland already. That was why that boy shot the secretary at the Paris embassy. His parents were among them. But last night people were burned to death in their own homes or beaten to death as they tried to escape. Thousands were arrested. People have just disappeared. Eric and Liza Goldberg were both shot. It goes on and on. Everyone I contacted knew someone who had died or been arrested. When I couldn't get an answer on the phone, the operator said the line was dead. I knew that house was one of the ones that had been destroyed. Even if they hate us, Anton, they don't have to kill us. I don't want to bring our child into such a world.'

'What do you mean, darling?'

'I'm pregnant. I went to the doctor, to Dr Jacob, yesterday and he confirmed it. Incidentally, he says he won't be allowed to treat me any more but I can still go to see him in secret. He brought me into the world you know. I would have felt safe with him, having the baby. I tried to persuade him to leave but he says he's an old man and may not have long to live anyway. He would rather die here in his own country as he still thinks of it.'

'But that's wonderful.' I tried to take your hand but it lay so limp in mine I had to let it go.

'Is it? Remember our child will be an outcast according to the law.'

'No one would harm the child of a German officer.' I tried to sound confident and reassuring but I began to worry about my own selfishness in keeping you with me. Shouldn't you go as others were doing while there was still time, before that war I began to see as inevitable really got started? It could happen at any moment if someone decided to stand up to us. No, not to us, to Hitler. I didn't believe that ordinary people wanted another war. They were happy to go along with bloodless annexations and the expulsion of Jews from Germany under a daily dose of propaganda that increased with every year but to embark on an all-out conflict with Britain and France, and perhaps America again, filled them with terror and most of us at the staff college understood that our military leaders, especially in the army, the generals themselves, didn't believe we had the men and material to win.

If I sent you away I might never see you again. The days, months, years even, stretched impossibly bleak ahead. Yet I had to consider that it was my responsibility to care for you, especially now, and that child I had secretly longed for ever since you told me how we had lost our first. I had to work out a plan of escape for you both if the situation worsened. How much warning would we have? At least we could be sure that your passport was in order. Already so many had fled that it was becoming difficult to find a country that would take refugees. Other nations required the deposit of securities so that their guests wouldn't become a charge on the state. You knew how hard it was from those friends who had tried and failed or those who had succeeded only after a long struggle with bureaucracy and with the loss of everything they owned, milked both by the German authorities to be allowed to leave and by the unwilling hosts to be allowed to enter.

Otto wrote from America urging you to join him. You showed me the letter without comment. 'Come over and dance at my wedding,' it said.

'He's becoming more Jewish, more Eastern.' You pulled a face. 'Vati would be appalled.'

'Maybe he's right though. Maybe you should go there. The baby would be an American citizen.'

'Are you trying to get rid of us? Are we too much of a burden?'

'Don't be silly. You'll make me angry if you talk like that. But it isn't just you now. We have to think of the baby.'

139

'America's too far and it might be too dangerous to try and get there with that long journey by sea. The ship could be attacked by someone. Anyway, Lore Nausbaum told me it's very hard to get a berth. If you really want me to go somewhere I could go to Switzerland for a bit.'

'But it would be so easy for them to be overrun if this thing gets started.'

'We don't really know that anything is going to happen at all.'

'No, but I want to have a plan in case.' So I renewed acquaintance with my English cousin, John. I wrote him a cheerful letter asking if he was married and saying that we were expecting our first child. 'I hope the political situation won't prevent us making a little trip to England soon.'

His answer told me of his marriage, that they too were expecting their first child, and congratulated me on my change of job. 'You must of course come and stay if you manage to get to England. Do keep in touch. Unfortunately, I'm away from home rather a lot at the moment, visiting some of the far-flung bits of Empire but my wife would be delighted to see you. The two girls could swap baby talk. Not much fun for you, of course.'

So there I had it. An invitation that could be taken up if things looked like getting worse. The most important thing was to judge the right moment. Not too early; not too late. For I was increasingly sure that Hitler's intention was to attack Poland next.

'Why England,' you asked, 'when she will be the enemy?'

'Because Britain is an island and that makes her much harder to invade. You need supremacy at sea and in the air. You can't just drive in as we've done so far.'

'Does Hitler know that?'

'The general staff do. And you have friends there. Lord Walker . . .'

'Hardly a friend. Just an acquaintance of my father.'

'Nowhere on the continent will be safe. It's either England or America.' I sounded cold and matter-of-fact even to my own ears.

'Sometimes I can believe you really are English.' The truth was that I felt as if a deep wound inside me was leaking tears of blood as my heart contracted with the pain of what I knew had to be done. I should be alone perhaps for the rest of my life, which might indeed be quite short once the war began. I should almost certainly die alone. As winter turned to spring propaganda blared constantly from the radio and the newspapers. The Poles were victimising ethnic Germans. Danzig must be returned to Germany. A road–rail link was necessary to reunite East Prussia with the rest of the country. After the fall of Prague the British had reacted with their guarantee to Poland, which would seal our fate. The laws against the Jews were tightened in preparation for war, as if they were the enemy within. Jews were forbidden to live in Aryan houses. They were to be concentrated in their own ghettos. June came with skies of unchanging blue, as Nordic eyes were supposed to be, drained of pity. You sweated in the summer heat that made your pregnancy so burdensome as our child grew heavier. Dr Jacob had arranged his departure for two weeks after your expected confinement but you helped him by being a week early. He telephoned me at the office from our apartment to say you were in labour. 'All is proceeding well, Herr Hauptmann. There's no necessity for alarm.'

As soon as I could I hurried home. These days young husbands hold their wives' hands as they struggle and push but I don't know that you would have liked that, Minna, even if it had been the custom then. When you were in pain or had your period you became withdrawn, distanced.

You wouldn't have wanted me to see you drenched in blood, mucus and birth waters. So while our baby was being slapped into life by Dr Jacob at 10.15 on July the second I paced about in the sitting-room. When he was all cleaned and swaddled I was at last allowed in to see you both.

'What are you going to call him?'

'Herman,' we both answered. My mother had said it was one of my father's family names.

Afterwards, leaving you in the care of the nurse Dr Jacob had brought with him, I poured him and myself a glass of schnapps to toast the baby. 'Thank you, Doctor.' I raised my glass.

'To my last German baby.'

'Where have you decided to go?'

'Palestine.' He paused. 'I wanted to die here. I am a European and I shall find the land of my distant ancestors very alien, very Oriental, I'm sure. But I've been convinced by friends that that is where I should go, where I can be useful. Women will always go on having babies. There must be a need for a doctor in such a place. I have been teaching myself to speak Hebrew, as distinct from merely reading it. Most interesting. Related to Arabic of course, but we mustn't say so. One will have to learn a whole new set of conformities.'

'I am trying to find somewhere for Minna and the baby if things should get worse.'

'That's wise, I think. Perhaps it won't be necessary but I have seen such changes in my lifetime that anything is possible. There was always an undertow of anti-Semitism, if you understand me, but not this open violence of words, and now actions, given government sanction, the loss of all our hard-won civil liberties, even citizenship itself. We are no longer Germans and I'm afraid we shall soon no longer be human. Yet when I think of people I've known like Minna's father, the whole thing seems so preposterous I wonder why I'm going away. We can only hope if there is a god he isn't as the Arabs portray him: one who doesn't care about the fate of individuals.'

Without telling you, I now bought your first-class ticket to London and wrote again to John Falk that, although I was unable to get leave myself, you and the baby were coming for a holiday away from the heat of Berlin and to see one or two friends. I made arrangements for an international money order. You still had funds in Switzerland you could draw on. You would be able to cash the order for your immediate needs in London. I booked a room at a small hotel near Russell Square which didn't object to a baby. I had only to give them a day's notice of your arrival.

Throughout July you and the baby grew stronger while I watched the political situation for guidance. By August little Herman was feeding well and putting on weight. Dr Jacob's nurse had been taken on to help you out. I had heard nothing from London but then there was no reason why I should, unless John Falk should write to advise you not to come.

On the fourteenth of August rumour at the staff college had it that Hitler was in conference with the heads of the armed forces. That could only mean one thing, though nothing filtered out to us of what he had said to them. For once security managed to keep the lid on the discussion. The next day however, anyone who could read between the lines could guess the content. The party rally was cancelled. Thousands of men were sent their call-up papers and the railways instructed to be prepared for huge movements of troops and armaments. There was no time to lose, I decided. You and little Herman must leave at once.

Pleading a stomach upset I left the office early, went to the nearest post office and telegraphed the hotel in London. Then numb but clear-headed, I took a taxi home. It was as if I was in shock or hypnotised. I performed the actions I had programmed myself to carry out as though they had no real meaning, wouldn't inevitably result in separation from everything I loved and needed most. 'Shh,' you said, putting a finger to your lips, 'he's just gone to sleep.' Outside the open window heavy summer leaves swayed in the light breeze. What I had to do seemed, as Dr Jacob had said, preposterous.

'It's come, my darling. War will begin any day. You must both leave in the morning.'

'How do you know? How can you be sure?'

'The orders have gone out for mobilisation. Soon the railways will be taken up moving troops to the East and we shall be forbidden to leave the country. Look if it all blows over you can both come back, but if you don't go now it may be too late.'

All night we lay awake in each other's arms with the baby mercifully asleep beside us. He woke at two and you took him to your breast and fed him until he fell asleep again. At four it began to get light and birds, city sparrows, twittered outside the window. 'I want to give you something to remember me by,' you said, sliding down in the bed above me and taking me in your mouth as I reached up with my lips to your breast. 'Why can't we conceive like this? I'd like to carry your sperm away inside me until it worked its way down to my belly and made us another child.'

Together we took a taxi to the station. You had only what was necessary for the journey, mainly little Herman's essentials. A night's stopover in Paris would give you the chance to attend to him before the last stage of your journey to London. The rest of your luggage I booked in, in advance, for you to collect on arrival in London. I wanted to get on the train with you, of course, to see you at least as far as Paris and spend one more night together, but I had to stay behind to maintain the story that you were simply away on holiday. We didn't cry, only stared at each other through the glass as the train drew away down the length of the platform and then was only a tail, the blunt end receding out of my life.

## XVI

Heavy cream discs of elderflower alternating with pale dog-roses tapestried the dripping June hedgerows as Betony drove down to Berkshire. The endless rain of traditional English summer drenched the heaving bushes and wriggled like translucent tadpoles up the windscreen whenever she switched off the wipers, irritated by their too rhythmic tick-tack across the streaming glass. Gill's story of his great-grandmother Lilian, her father Henry's nanny, had given her the confidence to challenge Gran Bet. At least she knew now what she had almost begun to doubt, that her father had really existed, had once been little Harry who had been fed and washed and lived first at the big London house and then in the country she was driving through now. She had decided not to alert her grandmother by putting questions to her on the telephone but to give her no chance to prepare an evasion.

Now she drove through the gate and pulled up as Gran Bet opened the door.

'Darling, how wonderful to see you. I was just watching through the drawing-room window. Let's have a drink before lunch. Isn't this weather terrible? The roses are being knocked to bits.'

When should she begin? Now, as they sat either side of the fireplace where a jug of summer flowers, peonies, lady's mantle, delphiniums, spread their unflickering cold flames of red, yellow and blue? Later after lunch? Could she keep up this chat of weather and neighbours while the questions burned inside her? She had at least decided how she would begin.

'Gran, you remember Nanny Lilian?'

Her grandmother paused in pouring the coffee. 'Nanny Lilian? Why should you suddenly think of her? She was long before your time. I didn't know I'd ever mentioned her to you. Anyway she was always known as Lily, by me at least.'

'You used to send her a Christmas card every year, didn't you, with a present inside?'

Gran Bet set down a cup of coffee carefully on the table beside Betony and went back to the sideboard for her own. She was playing for time. Considering her answer.

'Yes, I did. But she's been dead for years. That's when I stopped, of course. That's how I knew she'd died. There was no thank-you letter. Lily was very punctilious about that. She would never have forgotten. So she was either dead or had completely lost her marbles.'

'She lived quite close to here, didn't she? Did you ever go and see her?'

'Oh she wouldn't have wanted that. She liked her privacy, her independence. She was quite tough.'

'You told me once, she was my father's nanny.'

'Yes. She'd been John's, you know, and left to get married. Then she came back to help out during the war.'

'The evacuees, you called them.'

'She brought her daughter, Margaret, with her. She became sort of my personal maid. I used to take her to London with me. She got into trouble as it used to be called. A pretty little thing but quite fast. She loved dancing. What made you suddenly think of them?'

'It's an odd coincidence really, but the guy who's taken the room in my flat is Lily's great-grandson. So I suppose he's Margaret's grandson. And he's a dancer. He recognised our name at once as soon as I said it. Lily, he calls her "Nana", brought him up. He went to school in Reading.'

'How strange. What's he like?'

'Rather beautiful. Quite dark. Gay I think.'

'Good lord. Should you be sharing with him?'

'Safe as houses. Much safer than Mark from my point of view.'

'But what about AIDS? That sort of thing?'

'Oh I think he's all right. Anyway since we're not sleeping together I shan't catch it even if he's got it.'

'What about cuts? A broken glass in the kitchen?'

'Honestly, Gran.' Her grandmother was escaping, wriggling off Betony's careful hook. 'He took me to St Catherine's House. You know, where you can go and get birth certificates and so on.'

'Why would you want to go there, darling?'

This was the moment Betony had dreaded but she had come so far now she had to go on. 'I wanted to know what my father died of.'

'I could have told you that if you'd asked me.'

'I didn't like to. It seemed to upset you. As if you didn't want to talk about it. Now I know why, or some of it.'

There was silence except for Gran Bet stirring a half-cold, half-empty cup of coffee. 'He took an overdose, didn't he?

Aspirins or sleeping pills. It only said "barbiturates" on the certificate. Gran, why did he do it? And why is the name on the certificate not Henry but Herman? Look.' She took the two certificates out of her bag and unfolded them, laying her father's on the table beside her grandmother.

'So you know that too. And what's the other?'

Betony laid it face up beside her father's. There was another pause. 'I suppose I shall have to come clean, as Raymond Chandler would say. That one,' Gran Bet pointed to the birth certificate, 'was my own son, mine and John's. This, your father, was a refugee baby I took instead. You could say I stole him. Your father. So you see, you and I aren't related at all, darling.'

'But we must be. I don't understand.'

'John was away in India when my baby was born. I couldn't believe it when they told me my baby was dead. In those days we didn't have counselling, all that sort of thing they go in for now. You just had to get on with it. Pull yourself together and carry on. I was sent home to a house with a nursery all ready to receive my little boy and no one to comfort me. I didn't tell John. He didn't know I'd gone into premature labour. I couldn't say or write the words. I shut myself away. And then one day there was a telephone call. A woman speaking English with a very strong accent. And I remembered a letter John had shown me from someone in Germany with the same name. His cousin he called him. Joking of course. They weren't really related except perhaps a couple of hundred years ago. Asking to come and visit. Then there had been a second letter with the same handwriting and postmark, that I hadn't had time to send on or open before I went into hospital. The woman was asking if she could come and see me, or rather John. I explained that he was away but that I would be very pleased to give her lunch or tea and how to get there. We were still living in Mysore House, in Blackheath you know. After I'd put the telephone down I fetched the letter and opened it. It was a frightful shock to realise that she might be bringing her baby with her. I hadn't wanted to ask her at all in

147

my upset state but the possibility of a baby made it even worse. I hadn't thought to ask where I could reach her, so I couldn't put her off.' Gran Bet paused for a moment while Betony waited for her to go on, almost holding her breath.

'She had dark wavy hair and brown eyes, pretty in a gypsyish sort of way. The baby was very quiet. She sat with him in her arms while I poured tea and passed the sandwiches. I asked her how she was enjoying London. She didn't answer for a moment. Then she said, "We have deceived you." I can see her now, looking so intense, searching for the right English words. She said, "My husband has sent me to ask for refuge for me and our child. I have money. I am not a burden. It is necessary to have someone to speak for us or the authorities will not let us stay." I asked her why she wanted to stay and she told me that there would be a war. "I am a Jew so in Germany our child is a Jew, even though my husband is *Arier*." I said I didn't understand. "Not Jew. Now I am a non-Jew also by my marriage. But if anything happens to Anton in this war that is coming, or if he should be in trouble and cannot protect me, we may be sent to a concentration camp where the baby will die or be taken away."'

'What did you say?'

'I think I only half understood all the stuff about Jews and not Jews. We only knew a couple of Jews. We didn't really mix. I mean, they weren't friends, except for Julia Burnside and she was married to Teddy who was a viscount. John had heard something of what was going on in Germany through some refugee organisation but we didn't really understand what it all meant. There was Mosley and his Blackshirts of course, and that silly Mitford girl but they just seemed ridiculous. Not something you would give up your own country for. But this girl was obviously in trouble. I said she had better stay the night while she explained a little more. Then the baby woke and wanted to be fed so I took her upstairs and opened the nursery door. She looked exhausted. I showed her the bed the nurserymaid was to have used and the baby's bath, the baby clothes in the drawers and then I left her.

When I looked in later she and the baby were both fast asleep. But I couldn't sleep. I sat up for hours until I was forced to lie down. Then in the morning I was sitting in the breakfast-room with some tea and toast when she came down. "Last night I was very tired," she said. "I am so sorry. Please tell me where is the baby?" "My baby died," I said. It was the first time I had said the words and they made me cry. I held my head in my hands and I cried and cried so much the tears made the tablecloth wet. She put her arms round me. "I am so sorry, so, so sorry." Then she sat down with a hand on my arm and waited for me to stop. "I have been thinking," she said. "I don't want to be separated from my husband but I want my baby to be safe. Will you take my baby and look after him until we can come for him? I will know he is safe here. Will you do that, Mrs Falk?" I don't know if it was then that the idea came into my head or whether it had been what had kept me awake all night without my consciously knowing why. This girl was offering me her baby. We both knew that and that she might never be able to return to England.

'Before she left she fed the baby for the last time. Then she kissed him and put him down in the Moses cradle and walked away. "These are some of his things and his papers. If there is no war, and I can, I will come back. Until then I will try to telephone. I shall go back to Germany tomorrow and tell my husband of your kindness." Then she left. I went up to the nursery and looked down at him with a terrible ache in my chest. I didn't make a conscious decision to make him mine, but I contacted the agency at once to engage a nurserymaid, and when she came I let her believe he was mine. Every day I listened to the BBC as we got closer to the war. Eventually John telephoned me from Southampton where his ship had just docked. I told him we had a boy.'

'Gran!'

'He was so thrilled. Once again it wasn't a conscious decision. And in a way it was true. We did have a boy. When I saw how happy he was I couldn't go back on it. He never knew your father wasn't our own child. He died thinking at least he had left a son. I don't believe that was such a sin. But I was punished for it. I never felt your father, that baby, loved me. It was as if he knew I wasn't his real mother or perhaps he sensed something in me. I felt as though my deception had put a barrier between us that we couldn't get over. I know it's a terrible thing to say, but it's you I've loved as if you were my own child. Will you forgive me?'

'There's nothing to forgive, Gran.'

'Even though I'm not really your Gran?'

'Of course not. How did Lily come into it all?'

'John trusted her completely because she had been his nanny. So when the war came and he insisted that we moved to the country because we were afraid Hitler would bomb London, John asked her to come back. It made me freer of course. And Lily loved the baby and spoilt him. Then John was killed and I think I went off my head for a bit, feeling my life was over.'

'What happened to the woman and her husband? And my father? Why did he . . . ?'

'He found out and the shock was too much for him.'

'But how?' Betony knew she was pressing Gran Bet hard but she had to hear everything now.

'He'd never been abroad and suddenly his firm wanted him to go to America. He had to have a passport at once. I decided to give him the German papers his mother had left and I had kept hidden. I posted them to him in London with a letter explaining. I felt I had no choice. The truth had caught up with me.'

'Gran.'

'I didn't think, didn't realise how cruel I was being, what a shock it would be. I meant to telephone first before the letter reached him but we had a storm that brought down the lines and then it was too late. When I did get through there was no answer and then there was a policeman at the door. I've blamed myself ever since. He was too sensitive even as a child. I should have talked to him, explained it all, years ago, not tried to put it in a letter where it all looked so bald. I hadn't realised how much it meant to him to be part of the family.'

'But Gran, he took me to the old church in Bishopsgreen where all the Falks were buried.'

'I never knew. I never really understood. Darling, you wouldn't do anything silly like that? It doesn't matter about blood.'

'No, of course not. But I'll have to find out now what really happened to my other grandparents. Why they never came back.'

'There's something else I have to show you.' She got up and Betony could hear her dragging herself by the banisters from stair to stair. 'There,' she said when she came back. 'I've never opened it and I'd rather you didn't until you are on your own.' She put an envelope on the table, the paper faded and the addresses barely legible. There were two. The first, Mysore House, had been crossed through and Glebe House substituted. The stamp and postmark were German.

'It came after the war had been over a year or two. Lily had left me then. I put it away in a drawer and pretended to myself it had never come. But I wasn't brave enough to burn it or do as I should have, open it and try to contact the sender. You see, in spite of everything I didn't want to give your father up. He had just gone off to prep school and it gave me a purpose and a status with other women to go and collect him at half term and stand around discussing clothes and holidays. I thought perhaps I might remarry and then maybe we could adopt Harry properly.'

'What was his real name, Gran?'

'Herman von Falk. You won't leave me, will you? Even though we're no blood relation you're all I've got. And nothing's changed. This house and everything will still be yours.'

But everything is changed of course, Betony thought as she drove back. She hoped Gill was out. She didn't want to talk until she'd had a chance to think, to read and digest the other letter. She felt weightless, as if drifting in space and barely attached by a fragile cord to anything she had known, including herself. Was she still Betony Falk and what did that mean?

The flat was empty. A note on the kitchen table said that Gill had gone to practise and hoped that her visit had 'gone okay'. She knew by now this was his tactful way of giving her room and time. Betony opened a bottle of Montepulciano and let its smoky richness pour down her throat as if it could flow directly into her veins, before she took out the faded airmail envelope and with a knife carefully slit the top to preserve the address on the back. She took out and unfolded a single sheet of paper. Protected by the envelope, in a drawer away from the light, the writing had stayed firm and clear.

Berlin, January 1, 1947

Dear John

This is a shot in the dark as I don't know whether you came through the war and are still living in the same house. As you see, I survived but my wife did not. I believe she died in a concentration camp while I was a prisoner of the Russians and presumed dead. I am most anxious to know what happened to our son. I realise that he is now your son too in all probability, and I have no wish to upset any relationship you have with him, just to know he is well. In any case Germany is no place for a child at the moment. We have too many problems of reconstruction. But I should like when I can travel to come and see him, if you think that wouldn't be too disturbing, and in any case would appreciate some word from you about his welfare.

I do hope you and your wife have come through these terrible years without too much suffering and that we can eventually resume our friendship. I can never be enough grateful for what you have done for my son. Here he would undoubtedly have died with his mother.

Yours ever,
Anton von Falk

Betony put down the letter and poured herself another glass of wine. The irony of her relationship with Mark suddenly struck her. Suppose she rang him and said, 'I'm a Jew too.'

'You're only accepted if your mother was Jewish,' he had once told her. But what did she know of her mother? If her father could overnight become German and Jewish what might the sad death of that girl who was Shirley Lewis, just twenty-two, be hiding? 'You can't tell from names,' Mark had said. 'Most people have anglicised them if they've been here long enough.' Lewis could easily conceal a Levi. It didn't matter. It wasn't who she was that came first but who she wasn't. She ached for her father's pain, his lonely suffering, brought up as he was in the English tradition, with all its assumptions about the inadequacies of Johnny foreigner, its condescension and readiness to laugh at other customs. Gran Bet herself, had she ever met him, would have been condescending to Mark. Was there anything in blood being thicker than water? Had she herself intuitively sought him out? That seemed mere superstition.

Betony found many of her own views undergoing a violent sea change. She had never understood why adopted children should be so eager to find their natural parents. Now, though she didn't understand with her mind, she felt it deep in her gut. She had to find out more. But how? The address on the envelope was half a century old. She read the letter again and one detail she had missed the first time took over from the rest. Her natural grandmother hadn't survived but had probably died in a concentration camp. Simply disappeared as a rubber wipes chalk words from a blackboard, leaving a smear of dust. Betony had seen the film of *Schindler's List* with Mark. 'How can you be so calm about it?' she had asked him after on the bus. 'Even I want to rage and cry.'

'What's to rage or cry at? It's human nature.' But she knew that he raged inside. 'You can't alter the past. We live with it all the time. You have to learn how to or let it destroy you. Then the fascists would really have won.'

'But why did it happen? How could people, ordinary people, do things like that?'

'They believed a lot of crap about racial purity and filthy Jews. Anti-Semitism goes back a long way, as long as Christianity. Jews crucified Christ.'

'I thought it was the Romans.'

'Jews stole the Host out of churches and used it in satanic cults. Jews kidnapped and killed Christian babies. All that garbage people still believed. There's been a lot of books written about it, trying to understand. Like the experiments in the US where people were willing to inflict pain on others because they were told to. The human race is full of crap.'

Betony remembered an 'A'-level paper on English literature for part of which they had had to study the ballad. Among the tales of abandoned girls, ghostly children, drowned lovers, border warfare was *Little Sir Hugh*, the medieval boy saint murdered in Lincoln for kicking his football through the Jew's window.

> The first come out was a Jew's daughter
> Was dressed all in green
> Come in, come in, my little Sir Hugh
> And have your ball again.
>
> She sat him up in a gilty chair
> She gave him sugar sweet
> She laid him out on a dresser board
> And stabbed him like a sheep.

'They needed an excuse to kick the Jews out of England so the king could get his hands on their money,' Mark had explained.

Betony looked down at her green silk T-shirt. She had become the Jew's daughter. 'How did they get back?'

'Same reason: money. Cromwell invited them in. He needed their cash.'

There was that other Jew's daughter, Jessica, whom Betony had also encountered as an examination paper and then again at art school where part of the course had been to design a production, including the costumes, and to make a maquette of a chosen scene. It had been like being asked, ordered even, to play with a doll's house or to be Alice peering through the little door into the sunlit garden. She didn't know why she had chosen *The Merchant of Venice*. Perhaps it was something to do with the current obsession with serious money, epitomised by the young traders on the stock exchange doubling their ducats with a flick of their fingers, that made the concerns of Antonio and his gang of young Venetian speculators seem so contemporary. The project meant that she had to read the play again and it was still fresh in her mind. She had chosen the moment when the eloping Jessica steps onto the ladder, a more dramatic version than the simple 'enters below' of the text, while the masquers wait, their beaked faces turned up at the moon. Betony had been the goddess midwife of her little world, bringing it into being so that it seemed as if the toytown figures would move and speak.

Now she reconsidered the play in the light of the letter in her hand. She couldn't remember anything about Shylock's wife, Jessica's mother, except that she was dead, but presumably she wasn't a Christian or some point would have been made of it in the play. Jessica was determined to convert to her husband-to-be's faith, to join the majority. There was no question that Lorenzo loved her, found her beautiful and clever, though he was also happy to let her steal her father's money as dowry. Without a portion a girl couldn't marry. His friends accepted her as his wife. The difference then wasn't one of race or blood but religion and the personality of the individual. Shylock was a skinflint and a tyrant. Leave aside for the moment the question of why. Old killjoy parents who tried to stand in the way of the loves of bright young things were always thrust aside to please an audience of youthful courtiers and aspiring cits, the forerunners of the yuppie dealers.

Jessica would be assimilated, her children grow up good or bad little Christians by baptism, but for Betony's father and his mother even that would have been no protection and then she, Betony, would never have been born. The inescapable logic chilled her. 'Here he would undoubtedly have died with his mother.' Sunk in misery as she had been after the loss of Mark, Betony had never wished herself dead or unborn. Now she tried to peer through into her father's mind but the window was too narrow and opaque. She hadn't been old enough to know him, to understand why. Was it simply the loss of his long-accepted roots, of his supposed mother, or was there some terror of a more generalised kind that had tipped him over, the bestial horror she had seen in *Schindler's List* of cattle trucks, camp and crematorium that had made her feel sick and faint when she had stumbled out of the cinema searching for Mark's arm. This was what she couldn't escape. This was now her inheritance as it had been her father's.

The letter had been written a couple of years after the war had ended, so it was possible the miraculous had occurred and her grandmother had been found alive after all. Perhaps she had been too ill to go back at once. Or she hadn't been able to find her husband because their flat had been destroyed, like Mysore House. Betony realised how little she really knew about what it had been like in post-war Britain, let alone Germany. She wasn't even sure how many had died. Four million, six million? She thought she remembered forty million for the whole war from every country. That must be nearly the population of England itself.

Mark was right: the human race was crap. Against this was her own instinct for survival, her own need to believe if not in the perfectibility of humankind at least in some residual human virtue, compassion maybe. If people were nothing but crap then the whole of life was pointless and perhaps that was the cause of the despair that had overwhelmed her father. Yet Anton von Falk, like Lorenzo, had loved his wife. She read an indelible pain behind the dignified statement 'my wife did not' and in the search for that child given to Gran Bet for safe-keeping, even in his understanding that his son now belonged to someone else. Then again perhaps it had been Gran Bet's inability to love that child she had made hers that had killed him in the end.


## XVII

Late as 'twere you was still sitting up when I comes in, with a half-empty bottle of red wine and a half-full glass in front of you, staring at an old blue envelope, so I knowed you wanted to talk.

'Hi. How did it go?'

'I don't know where to start. She remembered your grand-mother, of course. I think that was what decided her to tell me everything, otherwise she might have lied. She wasn't sure, you see, what else I might have found out. To cut it short I'll just tell you she isn't my real grandmother. My father was a German refugee baby she took in just before the war started. I think I need to get some books from somewhere and read up about it all before I can understand what happened.'

'Try the library. They'll have a whole section on the war. You have to take some proof of residence with you to join, then you can borrow the books you want straight away. It's cool.'

It were Saturday next day so I were able to go along of you and show you how 'twere done. As I'd thought, there was a whole stack of shelves on World War II but you seemed to be looking for something special. You made a little pile of them just from one shelf labelled 'The Holocaust'. One I could read the title of were *Refugee Children in Britain 1939–45.*

'Now I need a map of Berlin.'

I knowed about the library cause us did used to go there from school when us were doing projects. I always done something on dance a course: New Rave, the Kirov, the life of Fred Astaire or African and Caribbean, limbo to hip hop. Libraries hadn't changed much in the years since I hadn't been going to them. Now that I didn't have to do exams and projects, I didn't read much neither.

Never a book. Music and dance mags, that were all. But when I looked around at all they shelves it made me a bit sad for what I were missing. Still, we never been great readers in our family. 'There's them as does and them as sits on their backside reading about it.' Now I saw they was lending out all kinds of music on tape and CD, and even old vinyls in their big shining record sleeves with full-colour pictures. Libraries and secondhand shops looked like being their last resting places. When I were a kid there was still they little forty-fives the size of a tea-plate and now they'm all gone too and you can't buy a machine that would play them. Soon it'll be the end of cassettes and we'll be downloading music online from some great databank in the sky or out at sea on a disused oil rig or even nowhere in the world that anyone can see.

Of a sudden there, me legs ached to be dancing under the strobes with everyone watching and clapping til I falls in a heap on the dance-floor, the sweat pouring down me face. Hey man, cool man. And a punter, a producer, clapping me on the back with an offer I couldn't refuse. So I think as how they'm got it all wrong with their bloodless virtual this and that threatening to blot out the living and breathing, the throb of blood, the stamp of feet. 'Enjoy theeself when thee do be young, boy,' as Nana would say. 'Look at me, with legs like black puddings, unable to stir out.'

We checked all the books through and took them home. Then you spreads out the map and runs your finger down the index of streets. 'Look, it's still there. The street the letter came from. I wonder if he could be living there now.'

'Who?'

'Anton von Falk, my grandfather, at least I think he is. He must be very old though, if he's still alive. As old as Gran Bet or more, I expect. I've been wondering . . . if you've got a name and address you can ask the operator in this country for a telephone number. Do you think that works for abroad?'

I got up and fetched the directory and flipped over the pages to the international service on pale blue paper, the colour almost of the faded envelope you was holding in your hand. 'Look.' I pointed to the information section. 'It says here if you've got the name and address you can ask for the number, just like in Britain.'

You took the book from me.

' "Dial 153." Shall I?'

'Go for it. Then you'll know if he's still living there.'

'But if they say there's no one of that name I still won't know if he's alive and just living somewhere else, perhaps not in Berlin at all.'

'Then you won't be any worse off than you are now.'

I seed you take a great gulp of air before you could pick up the phone and dial.

'International directory enquiries. Oh Germany please, Berlin.' You gave the name and address. Then you began to scribble down a number, said thank you and put the receiver back.

'Fuck it, Gill, he's still there. Unless he had another son and gave him the same name, he must be still alive.'

'Why don't you just ring and ask?'

'No. I thought of that, but he might put the phone down on me or not understand English or even drop dead with shock. It's better if I go myself. How do you feel about a trip to Berlin?'

# Part Two

# XVIII

I still remember how heavily I climbed the stairs on that evening, after a day when it had become clear that we intended to invade Poland, and no declaration by Britain and France that they would defend her would make any difference or be believed, that there would be no eleventh-hour rebellion by a conspiracy of generals to stop Hitler. I had one confidant in the building who had a contact at High Command, Lieutenant Wild, who was as appalled as I was at the approach of war. Wild had come into my office in the afternoon to say that he had just had an anonymous call from his source with the news that they had received a personal order from Hitler by telephone to be ready to attack on September 1st, in less than a week.

The house seemed very quiet, as if all the inhabitants were dead, as I let myself in. The family on the first floor, party supporters, had taken their two children to the mountains away from the summer heat. I suspected the Remers of being informers, only too happy to spy on their neighbours, and was glad not to see Frau Remer's eye at a crack in the door checking when I came in and with whom. I turned the key in the lock, swore because I must have left the light on in our gloomy kitchen when I went out early, and then you came through to meet me, to put your arms around me and your mouth on mine. I was so glad and stunned I couldn't breathe or speak.

'What are you doing here? Why have you come back? Where's little Herman?' At last I was asking all the questions.

'Herman is with the wife of your English cousin. He will be safe there. Even if Germany overruns Britain. Mrs Falk will pretend he is her own and nobody will know he is Jewish. It's easier for children to stay in England, especially if nobody knows they are there. But it would be hard for me even with someone to vouch for me, I was told. I might be interned if the war comes.'

'It's coming. Unless Britain and France back off again.'

'They won't. Not this time. There is a feeling even I, with my bad English, could understand. They are determined now because they believe Hitler will never stop until he has conquered the whole of Europe, especially since the pact with Russia.'

'You shouldn't have come back. If anything happens to me . . .'

'Don't you want me, Anton? I want to be here with you as long as we can be together. Now I know our baby is safe I want to spend as much time as I have left with you.' You smiled and stroked my face. 'I know you always think you are the one who loves most.'

Later that night, you remember, Minna, after you had told me all about your visit and we tried to telephone Mrs Falk but got only her servant, we made our plan. The Remers' absence gave us a chance to find a hiding place where we could leave notes to await the other's return in case we were unable to speak directly. With a great deal of noise I managed to remove a couple of bricks behind the stove and make a hollow in the wall before replacing them. It was crude but it gave us both a little comfort.

'I don't think I'll be able to keep my easy job at the staff college once the war starts. Everyone will be mobilised for the front line. Unless I can get a transfer to the High Command; that might make it possible for me to stay in Berlin. At least I can try.' So I applied and was eventually turned down. Meanwhile we had been told to be ready to join our regiments. Only the politically safe would be kept to train the new troops who would be needed if we went to war. English language teaching wouldn't be wanted and translation would now be part of the intelligence or propaganda services.

Those last few days of peace we took every chance to be together, like bees storing up nectar against winter. In the evening was went to the Wannsee, where there was more breeze beside the lake. The weather was sultry with overhanging cloud as the negotiations between Germany and Poland and the allies of both stumbled towards their inevitable end. Even the Berliners, apart from a few young recruits, usually drunk, who saw it as a great adventure, had no stomach for a new war, fearing that the city would be bombed, that we couldn't win. Mostly they stayed indoors or sat glumly in the corner of cafés or bierkellers, talking in hushed voices. We tried to telephone London again to ask about the baby but were told that all communication with London, Paris or Warsaw had been cut. It was the morning of Thursday August 31st. 'This must mean the war has begun or will have by tomorrow.'

In the afternoon I had an anonymous call. 'Canaris says Germany is doomed,' the voice said and then the receiver was replaced. I knew it must be Wild but didn't dare ring back and ask him the source of this information. I couldn't believe the admiral himself would have confided in some junior officer. It must be just one of the no doubt many rumours circulating at the High Command as the last hours of peace ran out. It showed me, with its expression of defeat, that there would be no rescue for their country by the German military without British and French support.

On Friday morning we woke to hear Hitler's proclamation to the army broadcast to the nation. Poles had fired on Germans. From now on we would return bombs with bombs. We had therefore invaded Poland. I decided I should go to the office as usual. I must seem to conform as much as I could, even to the point of becoming a diligent, patriotic officer. There was a pile of stuff for me to translate: reports from the foreign press about the deteriorating situation, speculation about last-minute attempts to avert a war by Mussolini. They didn't know it was already too late. No cheering crowds lined the streets as the chancellor drove to the Reichstag to explain to parliament the necessity for this war which he described as merely a series of engagements, as a counter-attack.

Now we all held our breath to see what Britain and France would do. Were you right, Minna, in your assessment that this time Hitler's gamble wouldn't pay off? News came from the front line of our rapid advance and heavy bombing by the Luftwaffe that had destroyed the Polish air force on the ground. Was it already too late to stop the war? Paris and London were taking their time to react. Perhaps once again there would be no response. On Saturday night we even went to the cinema, partly to take our minds off the fact that it was still impossible to get through to London. The film was only a piece of propaganda rubbish with Christian Soderbann as usual floating away to a watery grave in the last reel while the audience laughed and clapped, but it was a relief to be anonymous, among people who could manage to look satirically on the approved party line being offered to them.

We were wakened on Sunday morning by a beautiful late summer day outside our bedroom windows and made love for the first time since the birth of our baby. Your breasts were full and aching with milk so I became your child and drank a little from each. Then we fell asleep again. When we woke once more I dressed and went down to buy a paper while you made coffee and heated rolls for breakfast. I was stunned to find they were already giving away extra news-sheets proclaiming in huge head-lines that England had declared war on Germany. I grabbed one and hurried back. 'Look at this!' I thrust open the door. You turned towards me. 'Sh!' You had your ear up against the wireless set with the volume turned to a whisper. We had been forbidden to listen to foreign broadcasts two days before. We heard the weak voice of the British prime minister saying, 'This is a sad day for all of us . . .' I put my arm around you and we clung there together, listening until the broadcast ended.

After breakfast I telephoned the office to see if I was needed. 'You should already be here, von Falk. What does Sunday matter when we are at war? There are important texts which need to be translated. Dr Schmidt has asked for your assistance.' To be asked to help out the official translator would fit in well with my plans to stay in Berlin near you if I possibly could. I hurried to present myself and was sent to the High Command, where I was kept busy until two in the morning compiling a dossier of world, especially American, reaction to the outbreak of war which was to be dispatched after Hitler who had already left by train for the Eastern front. A few days later I heard that my bid had failed and I was to follow him. 'It has been noted that your wife is less than satisfactory for an officer of the Third Reich. You can prove your loyalty by your behaviour in battle,' I was told when my application to the High Command was refused.

Our last night together, Minna. You said, 'There are things I may have to do while you're away, Anton. I shall be very careful not to compromise you and so it's better if I tell you nothing about them when you come home on leave.' I begged you to be careful. 'Don't worry, I don't want to die. I want us to survive. One day we may be able to live freely again and bring our son home. You have to believe in that.' What you were saying was that we must work and prepare for the defeat of our own country. Already the laws against Jews were being tightened, a curfew imposed on them, their rations more meagre than those of the rest of the population, the cards stamped with a red J that excluded them from buying any food that wasn't rationed. I knew you wouldn't be able to stand by if things got even worse.

'I shan't come to the station to see you off. It's better if we say goodbye here.' And so I was alone among my uniformed colleagues with their wives, children and girlfriends clinging to them, proud and desolate in my isolation. There was no cheering or flag waving as there had been when the troops left for the Great War, as my mother had told me, just the pain of so many partings.

My life became a series of snapshots, postcards to and from the front, censored, enigmatic, a sequence broken by leave when we had conquered Poland and I was allowed home to you, to try to pretend there was no war and walk hand in hand, scuffing up the fallen leaves like children while we invented code words to use in case the telephone should be tapped. 'Aunt Gertrude' who might pay you a visit was the Gestapo; 'taking a trip' meant you had either been ordered to move or were going into hiding. You were already sure Frau Remer reported on us in return for delicacies not on the ration cards. Then it was back to my regiment for two months where the word was that we would soon attack the French by way of Belgium. The easy victory in Poland had made us seem invincible. The invasion was put off after a faked attempt on Hitler's life. It was bitterly cold when we were suddenly told we could all go home for Christmas, and that postcard, seen through a rubbed gap in the steamed-up windows of the train as I was carried towards you, is lodged in my memory forever, with the looping arms of trees in their thick white sleeves of snow fringing the track under a frozen moon.

We had Christmas with my mother on the extra provisions I had been able to bring home with me, including a bottle of Polish vodka. I didn't tell you of those other snapshots: of Jews being herded into the Warsaw ghetto where they now had to live like rats in a warren; of the pale face of a little boy, no older than eight or nine, I had seen sneak out after curfew and had caught up with, of his terror and then disbelief as I gave him money and the bag of food I happened to be carrying, and sent him back again. It was only a moment of respite for him in the struggle for survival, and for me one small act of humanity, of defiance and hope that one day this bestial madness that had overtaken us all might end, the nightmare swept away by some dawn we couldn't even begin to imagine.

Sitting round the table in my mother's small flat away from the Remers' prying eyes we decided that she should go back to Bamberg, which was less likely to be bombed and where she still had friends. I didn't say but I also thought her Berlin address might be useful in the future, although I couldn't at that time foresee how. Like everything that was now happening to us and the

168

country it was impossible to predict any outcome. Poland had fallen in a few weeks. It had been too easy. Now the hard times must begin, surely. There were rumours of peace that Christmas lightening the city's winter gloom, of special envoys from England and secret negotiations. You shook your head. 'The English would never allow Germany and Russia to keep Poland. They would lose too much face. And Hitler will never give Poland back. Don't forget *Mein Kampf* and that his Reich has to last for a thousand years.'

You were right, I saw, as soon as I rejoined my regiment, which had been moved West again. My next postcard showed Hans Andersen's little mermaid in Copenhagen in spring, closely followed by the tulip fields of Holland and the royal gardens in Brussels. Again we seemed unstoppable. Soon I was sending home the Eiffel Tower and Montmartre by night. This last earned me a sharp reply. The same card also told me that Aunt Gertrude had paid you a visit, and said that you were not a good hausfrau and an impediment to your husband's career. I too was sent for by my commanding officer, who suggested that it would be easy for me to divorce you. I complained that my wife was being harassed in my absence and that such action was illegal. I am still proud that I fought for us then, Minna, as you told me you had fought back when I managed to telephone you at my mother's flat. Surprisingly my commanding officer was sympathetic when I spoke of my honour as an officer that would regard divorce under those circumstances as desertion, the act of a coward. 'Quite right, von Falk. There is too little respect for the old virtues I was brought up with. Honour was not to be bought or vows cast lightly aside. The oath of allegiance to the Führer, for example, is binding on every officer even those who believe they know better what is good for Germany. But now that it is realised in some quarters that your wife is an Aryan by marriage only you will not easily be promoted.' I didn't want promotion for my own sake but for yours. I thought that the higher my rank the more I could protect you.

My next postcard would have shown you the English cliffs I could see through my binoculars as we waited on the French coast for the order to invade while the two countries' ships and planes tried to pound each other out of existence. Was our son still safe or had he already been destroyed by air bombing? My commanding officer sent for me again. 'We need your skills as a translator, Leutnant. We want to know, I want to know, how the English are responding to our attacks.' So I was set to translate newspapers, broadcasts and intercepted messages again. I knew you would be listening to my mother's old radio, with your ears against the speaker to try to catch the BBC, and that talk of invasion would make you sick with worry for little Herman. Fortunately I wasn't required to analyse the material, merely to translate it. It told its own story. The English were not crushed or dispirited while we, waiting for the order to sail, were subjected to daily and severely damaging bombardment from the sea and the air. How delighted I was with the superficial burn from one of these raids that sent me home to Berlin on sick leave. That night, the first English bombs fell on the city but instead of going to the shelter we clung together in mother's little bed and made fierce love. I almost hoped a bomb would obliterate us together in that wild climax and though we never spoke of it I have always believed you hoped so too. When we were still alive in the morning we decided to visit my mother in Bamberg. The medieval streets and ornate baroque houses, the bridges and the half-timbered city hall looking down at its reflection in the river, seemed like another world in the late autumn sunshine. As we walked beside the old canal you told me of so many of your family's friends who had been sent away to labour camps, their property confiscated, their families wrenched apart. How I wished you had never come back while at the same time hugging you to me as the only thing that made any sense of my life. Then again I thought that any day we would invade England and you wouldn't even have been safe there. So we walked, ate, drank and made love in Bamberg as if in a dream of peace, like the blindfolded statue of 'the Synagogue' in the cathedral, smiling above her stone draperies. Then it was back to Berlin, where I was pronounced fit for service and we were saying goodbye in our own bed again. We didn't know it was our last time together.

I found that the invasion of England had been abandoned and we were pulling back from the Channel ports. Instead my post-cards show Belgrade, a heap of smoking rubble, and then the flat plains of Eastern Poland again, looking toward Russia, the falling snow blotting out the onion domes of Moscow, the waters of the Don where I was captured the following year, but not my descent into the hell of captivity, starved and degraded as our captors had been starved and brutalised by us.

## XIX

They had arrived in Berlin the evening before, taking the train from the airport to the modest modern Hotel Tauris in the Messedamm, and after they inspected the clean and serviceable box-rooms with separate shower and lavatory, wandered out in search of supper. Betony found herself drained of emotion, wondering why she had come and what she expected to find. 'See you in the morning. I'm shattered. Breakfast at nine for me, I should think. If you're not around by the time I've finished I'll ring your room.'

She had thought the official inspecting the passports of European visitors at the airport had lingered over Gill's, staring over his glasses to compare the face with the photograph before passing it back. On the train itself Betony had been aware of the whiteness of everyone else's skin, unlike a London underground compartment where a significant number of faces would be some shade of brown.

She supposed it was her sudden exhaustion that made her unable to manage the square plastic key, which she seemed to have inserted in its predestined slot the wrong way round, for the door didn't give when she turned the handle. She took out the key card and reversed it. This time there was a click and she was inside. The room was narrow and spartan, with the obligatory modern accoutrements of mini bar, telephone and television set but only a chair, a spindly chest with an unkind mirror that showed her a sallow face, smudged with the prints of fatigue, and a very single bed. There were no prints or pictures. She could have been anywhere in the world. Betony switched on the television to give her a sense of place and found she was watching the BBC with subtitles, the end of the nine o'clock news an hour behind local time.

There was a telephone directory in the drawer of the plywood dressing-table-cum-chest. She turned to the section beginning with F and saw, quite soon, her own name looking back at her followed by the address she already knew and the number she had been given in London.

Betony studied the instructions for making a call, picked up the receiver and dialled. There was a high-pitched single ping, repeated three times before a male voice said: 'von Falk.' Panicking she put back the receiver. Her heart thudded and her hand shook as if she had just braked in time to avoid a smash. The voice had been younger than she had expected: perhaps it was a son, who would be, presumably, her father's half-brother. How would he feel about an unknown niece on his doorstep? Perhaps there was no point in such a meeting. She should have telephoned from the safety of London and not come all this way to expose herself to disappointment or indifference. Still, at least she could see the house that the letter had come from. That might give her a greater feeling of reality. Ever since Gran Bet's explanation she had been in danger of losing all sense of who she was. Here in this anony-mous room she felt as if she was floating again, adrift from herself, even from her own body. Maybe this was what people meant by jetlag but she'd never felt it on trips to Italy or Greece, holidaying. It was the nature of this visit rather than the physical fact of flying

172

that was the cause of her sense of having been cut loose from everything that defined her. 'I am still Betony Falk,' she told the uncaring walls. The nightly ritual of undressing, cleaning her teeth and having a last pee before stretching out on the strange bed with a glass of water and a tot of whisky from her duty-free bottle of Glenfiddich relaxed her a little. After all what did it matter? She could only be refused a meeting, sent away. But if she had never come, had never tried to find answers, then she might be adrift for years until someone came along like Mark, a lover to redefine her, and even then she would always be insecure in herself, her selfhood, waiting for doubt to rise up and engulf her. Betony turned onto her right side, facing the small curtained window that she had discovered looked down only into a well or across at other heavily curtained windows, drew her knees up into the foetal position and fell asleep.

In the morning her anxieties seemed silly. Nobody could hurt her if she didn't let them. She showered and dressed and went down to breakfast, working her way through the lavish buffet of cereal, fruit, yoghurt, eggs, bacon, sausages, cheese and rolls. By the time she had reached the strawberry jam and honey Gill had joined her, still yawning.

'Man, if you ate all this lot you could save on lunch.'

'Enjoy it, you're on holiday. What will you do today?'

'Well, if you don't need my company I'll look at some of the sights. I picked up this map from the desk. It tells you what to see and how to get there. Like Checkpoint Charlie if there's still anything left and Kreuzberg where the artists and the Turks hang out. And there's a whole palace just down the road from the hotel.'

'I suppose it's better if I go by myself. I tried to phone last night but when somebody answered I lost my nerve. I wish I spoke German. That would make it easier.' She had picked up a little dictionary at the airport. 'I shall ring the bell and when somebody answers I shall say: "My name is Betony Falk. Mein Name ist Betony Falk."'

'Cool.' Gill forked up a piece of sausage.

'But then if they answer in German I'm done for. I don't know what to say or do next. Now if you spoke German you could come as my interpreter but they, he, might be even more confused by two new faces.'

'Especially if one of them's black or at least brown. Anyway, different. I expect I'll get back for supper and you can fill me in then. Good luck. I'm going to have some more coffee and toast.'

Betony left him still munching. She knew that if she wasn't going to lose her nerve again she must make a start. It looked on the map as if she should take the train to Nollendorfplatz and walk from there. As she set out from the station she rehearsed her sentence in her head. 'Mein Name ist Betony Falk.' There was the name beside the second bell. Before she could back off again Betony forced herself to press the button. She realised she was holding her breath and took in a gulp of air as a voice said: 'Ja?'

'Mein Name ist Betony Falk.'

There was a pause, a long pause as if the person on the other end had gone away. Betony waited. The voice said 'Herein!' and the entryphone buzzed. She leant against the big door and pushed it open. Inside was a marble-paved hallway, with one door and a staircase railed by ornate iron banisters. She climbed up slowly, holding on until she came to another door which was open. A middle-aged man in a dark suit was standing there.

'Bitte.' He waved her forward to the open door. She heard it close behind her. She was in a short corridor with polished doors leading off. Light came through the one at the end. Conscious of the man behind her she went forward. As she entered the room she saw a figure in a wheelchair parked in front of a computer screen. Betony hesitated. Then the chair's occupant wheeled round to face her. His hands clenched on the arm-rests as if he was going to lever himself up. Betony could see he was very old, at least as old as Gran Bet.

'Minna!' he said. 'Minna!'

# XX

I've lost your voice, Nana. It's gone from inside me head. As soon as I sat down in the plane and fastened me seatbelt I knew it had gone, perhaps because you never flew during your lifetime. Oh, I can still hear you, but coming from a distance. 'Ketch I going up in one o' they tin cans.' Not my voice any more. I'm on me own. Maybe that was why I never took a plane until now, because I was afraid of leaving that part of me that was you behind. Always the ferry, because it was cheaper I told myself. Or perhaps it's because this city is raw, new, with building sites everywhere. You don't get that in London except with some of the old tower blocks they've brought to their knees with a dose of Semtex. Nobody's sorry to see them go but in their place it's streets of little houses again, fitting in English style. Here's more exciting. You could call it the grand style, more like the stuff the commies and the nasties put up. More like one or two things in the city of London that make it seem so alien. Temples to money. You could say, too, they're plastering over old wounds, the gaping lots in the middle of the city where that old wall came down, pasting it together again with new laws and signs, papering over the cracks.

The first thing that strikes you though, is the people, all casually dressed but looking rosy and well fed. No beggars in their door-ways. All white too. Well nearly. I've seen a couple of Africans who look like students and some Japanese. People's eyes slide over me and away, partly because of me hair I think, and partly because of me clothes. I'm all in brown and white today. Snappy, cool. If they only knew it's because that's what I am, the two parts that make me up. Not black or white but coffee and cream. Like Tiger Woods and Eartha Kitt. Not to be codified, ghettoised. Just ourselves. I wonder whether when the scientists finally make contact with whoever's out there it really will be like *Star Trek*, with everyone able to shag each other anywhere in the universe

175

but maybe sterile, like mules. Still, the way they're going with cloning and all that, anything'll be possible.

I want to say to some of these people in the street, sitting at little tables on the pavements as I pass by: 'Hey guys, we all came out of Africa, you know. That Carl who was my grandfather could have come here as a GI soldier in the American zone and got himself a Fräulein after his English miss. There might be cousins of mine around and I wouldn't know. There's a lot of cabaret and nightclubs in this town, I've read, and some one of them might be dancing here; even pretending to be the real thing from Harlem. That's a jazz, a stunt I could pull and no one, I bet, would suss – I could be a Yank for a couple of days. Except with Bets of course.

I wonder how she's doing, if she's found her family. The war stirred everything up, brought the descendant of an American slave to England along with Bets' father, sucked everyone down like a great whirlpool and then spat them out. There must be a better way of mixing up the ingredients than first having to kill each other. Here's a bit of wall with writing on it all chipped and hacked about. The guide says souvenir hunters knock bits off it but what would you do with them when you got them home? Use them as paperweights or doorstops? I can understand wanting to take away something beautiful, a piece of painted tile or a bit of a Roman pot, something to hold in your hand and look at that'd remind you of the place and the civilisation that could make it, but a memorial of horror and death, who'd want that in their right mind? Worse than playing among the gravestones, as we used to do when we passed the churchyard on the way back from school. There at least you can think of the lives, not just the deaths.

West of here the guide says is the Jewish museum and I know I ought to go in for Bets' sake but I can't. It's right it should be here, of course, but just thinking about it makes me feel sick in the guts. If they'd ever got to England how many of us would have been for the chop? Mother June for sure, and it wouldn't have done any good for her to claim gypsy blood. 'And that's all right then, is it?' Nana asked her. But it would have been just as liable to get you arrested and sent up the chimney in smoke. And I wouldn't have escaped, with my looks. Besides, a lot of faggots went to the flames as well. This town was full of gay bars just like in Liza Minnelli's *Cabaret*. Still is, says the guide. Well where are they then? How many of those old queens and queers ended up behind the wire? Some people, and not just here, would still like it to be that way. I could do with a cold beer. Maybe if I head towards Kreuzberg.

This looks more promising. A lot of darker faces here but not with my fuzzy wig, and women with black scarves over their heads. It's got that romantic grottiness of parts of London, Brixton or Shepherd's Bush. Now I could live here and not stick out like a sore prick at a wedding. Families all together, sitting at their windows or ambling along, smaller, dark-skinned but not like me, more Paki in colour. Oranienstrasse, that looks as if it would have a bar I might dare go into.

This one will do: I can sit outside on the pavement at a table on a plastic chair under the striped awning. I don't even have to go inside, and if I sit here long enough someone will come and ask me what I want. That's it, man. Just relax, chill out. Let them see you're really cool.

'A beer please.'

'Welche Art? What beer?'

'Just a beer, man.'

'Fassbier?'

'If you say so. Ja.'

'Stein?'

'Ja.'

I thought all Germans spoke English. I wonder what will turn up. I don't think this can be a part of the gay scene. Too mixed but young. I should have looked Berlin up in Spartacus before I came here but I didn't think of it. He's coming back with a little round tray and a huge mug of frothy beer. He puts it down saying something I don't catch. 'Bitte.' Then the bill and he's away to another table. Everyone's talking and laughing and I can't understand a word but the beer's very cold and good and goes straight into the bloodstream by the feel of it.

Am I overreacting or is that guy by himself over there giving me the come-on? Must be my imagination or my funny looks. Maybe it isn't rude to stare here, like it is at home. Shall I stare back, make eye contact? Hey, he's getting up and picking up his glass. Looks like white wine. Nice looking. Long thick blond hair and a bony face, big nose. Like a Viking. Taller than me. He's coming over.

'May I join you?'

I wave at the empty chair. 'How did you know to speak English?'

'I guessed. You are American?'

For a moment I think I'll say yes and see if I can get away with it. But it's hard to lie. The word sticks in my throat.

'No. British.'

'You look like an American.'

'I'm from London.'

'Ah, swinging London. Britpop. The mecca of young persons.'

'Some people seem to think it's swinging again.'

'You are a student?'

'No.'

'You like the beer?'

'It's cool.'

'Cool? Not cold?'

'It means it's good.'

'You will have another?'

And I think, why not? This guy is after me for something and I'm in a strange town where nobody knows me, on a crazy kind of holiday, and I should go for it. Chill out. Let whatever it is happen. The sun is very bright and all around people are talking, laughing, drinking. Why not let it all hang out for once without fretting over the consequences?

'Why not? Thanks.'

He whistles up the waiter and orders another round.

'You are here on holiday?'

'I'm here with a friend just for a couple of days.'

'Where is your friend?'

'She's busy.'

'A girl.'

'Just a friend. I'm gay myself.' I say this quite deliberately. Handsome as the guy is I'm getting a bit pissed off with the interrogation tactics. 'What do you do?' Time to turn the tables in case he thinks I'm some kind of trade or just a dumb nigger who might have a big plonker, be good in the sack, as they often do when they see me dance.

'Do you mean, am I gay? Yes of course.'

'I really meant, what is your job, work? How do you earn your bread?'

'I am an artist and a teacher of art. And you?'

'I dance. When I can, that is. Otherwise I work in an office, doing different things, short term. We call it "temping".'

'Temping?'

'Because you're only temporary, as long as the work lasts. When you finish one job, like putting all the customers of a big company onto a new data file, you go somewhere else and do something else.'

'You can use a computer?'

This guy is going to ask me when I came down from the trees at any minute and hand me a banana. 'Yeah. Computers are nothing. They're cool.'

'I cannot work one. I do not know how to begin with it.'

'Well first of all you have to plug it in. Then you have to switch on.'

'You are making a joke of me. Then what happens?'

'The magic box, the screen, lights up and then it shows you its menu.'

'Like a restaurant.'

'More like a cookery book.'

'Have you ever thought that what really makes the difference between man and other animals is that we're the only ones who make fire and cook? Scientists try to say it's speech but it's really cooking. If you are a dancer you must have a beautiful body. You must permit that I draw you.'

He's hoping for a piece of chocolate. He'll be very let down when he sees how light I am. Just me face and hands dark from being in the sun. 'Oh I'm no Mohammed Ali, man. You might be disappointed.'

'I think not and I would like to try, if you permit.'

Not so fast, man. I'm not for rent or a pushover. I've got to like you first if I'm going to ditch two years of celibacy. You could be some sort of sadist or serial killer of gays for all I know.

'This is your first time in Berlin? If you like I can show you something of the city. I have my car. A car is necessary to see everything in a little time. Then we could have some lunch and go to my flat, which is close by, for me to draw you. It is not easy to find good models who have working bodies. I mean, there are those who do it for money, like the old who are interesting of course, and then there are those who go to the gymnastics two times every week but their bodies are false.'

'I've never posed for anyone, especially in the nude.'

'It is nothing for you. Only to keep still and as a dancer you will have the control. Come, we drink up and I show you Berlin. We begin in the South West with the Gleinicke Bridge where they used to exchange spies and prisoners between the Russians and Americans, only now it is open, of course. But the woods are beautiful and there is a good restaurant in an old house of wood built for a German princess, Charlotte, who married a Russian Tsar.'

I'm wondering if he always takes his pick-ups on a guided tour first and if they end up buried under the leaves in these woods. But the guy's growing on me as we cruise the city in his Honda.

'Why do you have a Japanese car?'

'Because it was the first with a catalytic converter. I am of the Green Party. What have you seen? I don't want to bore you.'

'The wall, you know. Checkpoint Charlie.'

'We don't have time for the museums. We will go to the Tiergarten and then to my favourite place, the Zoo. This is the Brandenburg Gate, where the wall at last came down, and our most fashionable street at this end only, Unter den Linden. At the other end of town, not fashionable, lived the English writer Isherwood before the war.'

I nod but I've never heard of the guy. We pull up in a big square. 'Over there is where Hitler killed himself in the bunker but there is nothing to see because the neo-fascists would make a souvenir of it. Now we go to the Tiergarten. There is the Berliner Ensemble theatre of Brecht. You have seen *The Threepenny Opera*? I have seen it in London better than here.'

The gardens go on for miles and then we come out on to a main street he says is the 'Ku-damm' and to a square surrounded by bars and cafés. 'This is Savignyplatz. We will have lunch here at the Zwiebelfisch. I will treat you, please, because I hope you will permit me to draw you. But you don't have to.' He smiles and it's a good smile.

The café's very full but he gets us a table and I even spot a couple of black faces. 'You will drink more beer?'

'I'd like some wine now, if we're eating.' That's it, Gill. Don't let him think you're just a beer-guzzling slob.

'So tell me about your dance and your life. Who is your girl-friend?'

'She's a girl I share a flat with.' I don't say she's in Berlin to look for relatives who might have escaped the gas chambers. I'm beginning to fancy the guy and I don't want to put him off. After all he can't be more than forty. He wasn't even born until it was all long over. And he's a peaceful Green but quite tough, I think. Do I let him pay or would that give him the wrong idea? I'll worry about that later. Right now the wine's going down cold and crisp and I'm beginning not to care.

'You would like a roll–up?'

I realise he's offering me a joint, but I don't do drugs, not even soft ones. 'No thanks, man.'

'You object if I do?'

'That's your affair. They just make me sick, that's all. I don't have a moral stance about joints. Can you drive on that stuff?'

'I only have a little, what you say, puff? I am used to it for many years. It doesn't affect me. I won't kill us. But if you are worried I take it away.' He stubs it out carefully and puts it back in his tin of tobacco. The grub when it comes is good but too much for me. The plates piled up with salad and chips and fried fillet of pork. It stops the conversation for quite a while.

'We will have coffee in my flat. First, we go to the Zoo.'

Whether it's the wine or the strangeness of it all I don't know, but I'm feeling like you're supposed to on a good trip only I wouldn't know because the only time I tried I got a bad one, which is why I won't try again, even when they're offering the pills in the clubs that can keep you dancing all night. The streets swim past. The people all look relaxed and well-fed, even the animals when we finally get to them don't have that mangy anxious look I associate with zoos.

'I am coming here often to study and draw them. I am paid to make postcards. You like them?'

'I'm not too keen on zoos myself but this lot look cool.'

'They make many baby animals here so they must be happy, I think. I like to watch how they are together. Maybe we learn from the animals to be better to each other.'

'Isn't it all survival of the fittest, dog eat dog?'

'Ja. But sometimes the best way to survive is to be nice to each other. Like the elephant. They help each other and protect the baby elephants.'

'You don't get much of that among humans. Look at Rwanda and Bosnia. We're more like those animals that go in for genocide. I saw this programme about chimpanzees and man they were murderous, beating up the next tribe in the forests, hunting their monkey cousins and eating them raw. And they're our closest species.' We're at the chimps' enclosure by this time and they're making the most of their space to swing and play and socialise.

'That is true. But now there is this new little Schimpanse they have studied for the first time, small, like little men in Africa.'

'Pygmies?'

'Ja, is the same in German: pygmy. These little Schimpansen are just as close to us genetically as the big ones but they are quite different in their Benehmen.'

I'm looking blank. He's lost me. 'My English is so bad. What they do. They don't fight. When there is trouble between two of them, males or females they have sex instead. They,' he makes a tossing-off gestures, 'each other. You know?'

Yes, I know. And I'm enjoying this come-on that's all talk not the quick fuck and run. 'Make love not war.'

'That's it.'

'Well, that's lucky for them because they'll never be able to put them in zoos where kids and little old ladies might be upset by it.'

He laughs. 'That's so. Because they are having sex all the time, these little fellows. Men, women and children. So now the scientists say who have studied them that nothing is unnatural because somewhere the animals are doing it in nature. It is us who make it unnatural. So now, you would like some coffee? We go back to Kreuzberg where I live.'

The zoo has sobered me up. I don't know what I feel about what he wants. I'm beginning to recognise a few landmarks now, like Checkpoint Charlie where I was this morning, a light-year ago. Soon we're in the run-down Turkish quarter of tenement blocks and dusty roads again because he drives his Honda like it was a Porsche. He pulls up in front of a tall house, switches off the engine and I follow him through a doorway into a hall, dark until he puts on the light, and we climb up to the top of the building just before the light goes off. Sunshine streams into the flat which is a penthouse with white walls covered in paintings that give it its only colour.

'Sit down. I will make coffee. Unless you want to go outside on the terrace.'

'I'm fine here.' I sink onto a cream sofa. I can hear him banging about in the kitchen. After a minute I get up to look at the pictures. Many of them are of the animals we've just seen. His name is Rayner Nauheim. The pictures are stylised, abstract patterns that still somehow contain the nature of the animal.

He's come back into the room behind me with a tray. 'You like my work?'

'I think it's cool.'

'I am much influenced by Douanier Rousseau.'

'And your name is Rayner? I'm Gill, Gill Idbury.' We shake hands.

'I have brought some schnapps to have with our coffee.'

'I need to use your bathroom.'

'Of course. It is there.'

I want to pee, badly, but I want to wash my prick too, just in case. When I get back he's poured out the coffee and little glasses of pale liquid.

'You drink it like this.' He throws it back in one. 'You mind if I smoke now?'

'Go ahead.'

'Gill, I want so much to see you, to draw you. Will you do this for me? Look I show you some drawings in my portfolio.' He fetches it from another room. 'In there is my studio. The light is especially good.'

I look at the drawings. I can't tell how good they are but there are stacks of them of all ages and sexes. It's a genuine collection. He pours us another schnapps and I think, what the fuck, I'm used to an audience. It's just getting the clothes off that's a problem.

'All right,' I say. 'Here's how we'll do it. I'll go in there and undress and you don't come in till I call you. Agreed?'

'Agreed.'

184

I go into the next room which is bare except for an easel, a bench with brushes, paints and stuff on it, a chair and a couch. There's a sort of raised bit like a mini stage. I strip off my clothes and drop them over a chair. Then I take up a classic position learnt years ago from Mrs Alys Rockwell, ARAD, and call out. 'Okay.'

For a moment nothing happens and I wonder if I've been set up. Then he's standing in the doorway. 'You are beautiful, just as I knew.' He comes forward. 'Forgive my hands. The paint gets on them and I can't get it all off.' His nails, as I've noticed on the steering-wheel, are outlined in a very dark green. He puts both hands on my hips to swing me round a little. 'Das ist kein Mann. Das ist ein Traum.' And suddenly I'm halfway to the ceiling with the feel of his hands on my body. He bends and kisses my prick. I look down and see the top of his head with the fair hair falling over my groin like a visiting angel or a sea anemone. Then he takes me in his mouth and I explode almost at once, spending as if I been saving it up forever, pressing my hands on his shoulders in order not to fall down and hearing myself groaning out loud.


# XXI

And when I saw her I thought for a moment it was you come back to me, Minna. If I believed in reincarnation I might have gone on thinking so, but of course after the first shock I knew it wasn't and I didn't know whether to be glad or to weep because I knew too, inside myself, at last, that you were never coming back. This girl who is so like you when you were her age half a century ago is the messenger I have been waiting for.

Christoff had said that there is someone called Beate Falk below, presumably wanting to come in. I thought it must be some distant unknown cousin, some descendant of my father's family, who had ignored my mother when she was widowed and left to bring me up on her own. So I was not impressed. They could only be wanting accommodation for a stay in Berlin, or even money now that the little half-orphan, destitute as we had been, my mother and I, was an old man with property to be bequeathed. I didn't even turn away from my computer screen when I told Christoff to let her come up. I thought I might have a little game while I found out the motive for this sudden visit. I expected some middle-aged hausfrau in matching jacket and skirt with thick legs. Instead, when I turned there was your likeness and I called out your name. I almost stood up and then my legs wouldn't hold me and I sank back again in my wheelchair.

She stood there quite calmly, giving me time to recover, and then she said: 'My name is Betony Falk. Do you speak English? I am from England.'

'Yes,' I said and I could hear my own voice like a whisper from the dead. 'I do speak English. Please sit down. Christoff, bring that chair forward, please.'

She sat down in front of me, put her bag on her knees and took out a letter in a blue envelope which she opened. 'I am looking for Mr Anton von Falk who used to live at this address.' She unfolded the letter and held it towards me.

'I am Anton von Falk. Where did you get that letter? May I see it, please?' But I knew what it was at once.

She got up and brought it to me. There was my own handwriting, Minna, looking both familiar and strange, as if I had written from another planet or in another life. 'I wrote this letter many, many years ago to someone I called my English cousin John Falk although we were not related, not immediately that is.'

'John Falk was killed in the war. His widow eventually received the letter but she never answered it.'

'When I didn't get an answer I went to England as soon as I could, but the house I had visited in London before the war was gone.' You remember I told you, Minna, how I had gone to look for our son and found only the shell of the house, shored up with wooden bulwarks, light coming through the empty eyes of window sockets, the garden a fire storm of tall red weeds. Then I knew why my letter hadn't been answered and that little Herman had probably been killed, that I had lost the last part of you that was half of him.

'It was bombed,' the girl said, 'but the family wasn't there. They had moved to the country when the war came, to be away from the bombing.' We were fencing with each other, approaching cautiously as if over a crevasse that might suddenly crumble and drop us to our injury or even death. 'What were you looking for in London?'

'It's a strange story, perhaps hard for you to understand. You see, when we knew there was going to be a war my wife took our baby to England. My idea was that they would both stay there in safety. My wife was Jewish. But she came back. She left the baby behind but she came back herself to be with me, in spite of the danger. She said the English Falks would look after the baby. In Germany, you understand, he would have been classed as a Jew under the racial laws. She said that even if we conquered England, and the same laws were applied there as everywhere else in Europe, then he would still be safe because no one would know he was Jewish. Whereas if she had stayed with him he might have been recognised. I didn't completely understand, but she was so firm there seemed no point in arguing since our world was falling apart anyway and we had so little time together. My wife was very strong. Do you know what happened to the baby? Was he in the building when the bomb fell?'

'No, he was quite safe in the country. He was called Harry Falk. He grew up as the son of the family.'

'But he is no longer alive? Somehow I think that is what you wish me to understand.'

'He died in 1977.'

'And you, if I may ask?'

'I am his daughter, Betony, named after my English grand-mother, or rather the woman he always believed was his mother.'

There was a silence. Then I said: 'So you are my granddaughter.'

'I think I must be, if that is what you think too.'

'And why have you come to see me now?'

'Because I have only just found out that my father was your son not my English grandmother's, and that I am someone different from what I'd always thought. I needed to find out the truth.' In that moment she looked so like you, Minna, I couldn't doubt what she was saying and that her motive was what she said it was. Oh, Minna, why have I become so suspicious? Is it because I'm so old? If I'd had you with me it would have been different. You would have said: 'Don't be silly, Anton, you can see she's telling the truth.' And I would have seen it through your eyes. And yet I did believe her. You would be, must be, proud of me. That sometimes I can see not through a glass darkly but with your clear vision.

'Do you believe me?' she asked. 'Do you believe my father was your son?'

'My dear child, you are so like his mother, my wife, that I can't help believing you, and besides you have that letter. How else could you have got it?'

'In the letter you wrote that you thought your wife had died in a concentration camp. Did you ever find out?'

'Not for sure. But if she had been alive she would have found her way back to me somehow, I know. That's why I've waited and searched all these years. Now you're here and I have to accept that she really isn't coming back, that she died long ago. There's something I have to show you that I've never shown anyone else before.' I wheeled myself over to my desk and unlocked the lid to find the spring for the secret drawer. Then I took out my treasures, a handful of old photographs, a lock of your hair and mine woven together and your last note to me.

'These are my souvenirs. I shall leave them to you. This is the last thing she wrote to me. Do you read German?'

She shook her head. 'I will translate it for you. She didn't put my name on it so that it couldn't be identified. That was part of the arrangement. We had also arranged a hiding place behind the stove in our apartment where we could leave messages for each other. I was a prisoner of the Russians for four years. When I finally got back to Berlin I went straight to the building where we had lived, hoping of course to find her. I found instead that it had been badly damaged, especially the upper part, though our neighbours were still living on the ground floor. You have to understand that much of the city was in ruins. I knocked and asked about my wife. We had always thought they were informers and now they seemed guilty and frightened. They said my wife had gone away. They knew nothing about it, of course. They said they had assumed she had gone to join my mother in Bamberg. They suggested I look for her there. I knew they were lying. My mother had died just after the war, before I was released. She caught influenza, which in her weakened, undernourished state turned to pneumonia. The neighbour who had nursed her had sent me the news through the Red Cross. If Minna had been with her she would have written herself. I climbed the broken stairs to our apartment, keeping close to the wall because the banister had been blown away or taken for firewood. The door was hanging off and the place was stripped bare either by the police, the people downstairs or ordinary looters. Even the stove had been wrenched from the wall but the bricks were still in place behind where it had stood. I felt sick with apprehension as I went forward. Perhaps I wouldn't be able to find the right brick or someone had been there already and sealed it up. The Remers downstairs had told me the flat had been requisitioned by a member of the Gestapo before it was destroyed. Then, even if I could find it, the space might be empty. But when I dug around in the mortar with my penknife I found a soft place where the blade slipped in and I prised out the brick. This letter was inside.

"Darling,
They came today to tell me that you had been killed on the Russian front and that therefore I am no longer in a privileged

marriage and must report tomorrow to the collection point at Schulstrasse. I shan't go of course. I have been ready for this for months and tonight I shall go underground. I have false papers in a different name so that if I'm caught there will be nothing to link me to you. I don't believe you're dead. So many people are missing for one reason or another. I think this is just a way of rounding up those of us who are left, even though Germany will lose the war. She is like a drowning man who tries to pull others down with him. I think I was spotted when I joined a protest of German wives whose Jewish husbands were being taken away at Rosenstrasse. There are, sadly, Jewish informers who hope to save themselves in this way. You can't even thrust people you grew up with or were at school with. I shall do my best to survive, as I hope you are doing, so that one day we can be together again and go and find little Herman. Next week he will be five years old. When we find him he won't know us but it will be enough if he is well and happy. Perhaps we will have another child together. Whatever happens I will always love you. If I am alive when all this is over I shall come and find you, even if you have a wooden leg, and make you dance again. If not, then you must look for our son alone and find someone else to love and take care of you. Be happy my darling.

Your Minna"' '

'But you didn't marry again?' she asked.

'It would have been the final betrayal. Anyway I never gave up hope. And I wanted so much to find our son. It was as if she had laid that duty on me. Do you know the singer Joan Baez? After the war she was very important to us. She seemed to symbolise a new life that wasn't based on the old nationalism but was more universal. She had a song on one of her albums that in some strange way I felt was for me. It's about a father coming to fetch his son and take him away. But the father is a seehund, a seal. He has to teach his young son to swim. If I had found mine I would have had to teach him to be a German or at least not English. You say he died in 1977. That was very young.'

'I don't remember him all that well. Sometimes I'm not sure if I remember him at all. Meeting you makes him seem more real.'

'Look, I can show you a photograph I took the night before they left for England when I was afraid I would never see either of them again. I have had to live with the knowledge that if she hadn't come back to be with me, Minna would have probably been still alive after the war and we could have started again. Or at least tried. Too much might have come between us perhaps. See.' I wheeled myself closer and gave her the photographs. 'You can understand why I was a little shocked, shall we say, when I saw you. That's Minna when we were in England before our wedding. That's the one I took when . . .' And suddenly I was weeping as I have never been able to weep, the tears running down between my fingers until she put a hand on my knee and eventually I was able to stop. 'Would you like some coffee?' I asked her then. 'I have so much to tell you.' I rang my little bell for Christoff and he brought us coffee, little biscuits and schnapps. He had been anticipating my call. 'This is Christoff who looks after me.'

I knew he would be both curious and nervous. 'Das ist meine Englische Enkelin.' He bowed to her in his very formal way and she responded with a simple 'Hallo', as young people do now all over Europe, I believe.

'Was this the flat you and Minna were living in?'

'No. She never lived here. Our flat was in the old East Berlin. After the war, when I came back, I was lucky because my knowledge of English was needed. I had learnt Russian as a prisoner and now I was required first of all to translate for the Russian occupying forces and then to translate from Russian and German for the Americans when I moved to West Berlin, to this place, as soon as I could. I wanted to be in Berlin, in case Minna should return. I posted missing notices everywhere I could, contacted every organisation for refugees, had Minna's name and details broadcast on the radio. But I could tell how things were going in the Russian zone and as an ex-prisoner and officer I knew I would eventually fall under suspicion. When no answers came to my initial enquiries I crossed into the American zone, offering my services as a translator, passed my de-Nazification test with Minna's help, I mean the fact of my marriage, and found this apartment. That was when I felt safe to write to England to try to contact your father. Tell me something about him.'

'He was brought up largely by a nanny, not by my grandmother. I still call her that.'

'Of course. You should. She's lucky to have you. You shouldn't, mustn't, take that away from her.'

'Then he was sent away to school and eventually he went to university in London where he studied economics and married a fellow student, who was my mother. But she died when I was born. That was why I was brought up by my grandmother too. My father worked in London. He had a flat there and came home at weekends.'

'And he believed he was English?' I thought she hesitated for a moment before she said. 'Yes. He once took me to the Falk family home, the village that they came from, where they lived for hundreds of years. I remember family tombs in the church. But when I went back recently it was all closed up and for sale.'

'We have that in common of course. Those would have been my ancestors too. They still are. And yours.'

'I'm trying to understand it all. To get used to the idea of being someone different.'

'But you aren't. You are you.'

'Am I? Don't we all make ourselves out of what we know as well as what we inherit? You know, all the genes stuff you read so much about? Don't I have to remake myself now, especially since I've met you? Or at least rethink things I've taken for granted, like my grandmother's house that she's always said would be mine when I grew up.'

Then I thought I had to tell her. 'She will still want you to have that one day, I'm sure. After all, she has known about your father all the time. But there are other things that should be yours from your German grandmother. Minna made a will, you know, leaving everything to our son. You are his heir and so it should come to you.'

'But I don't really need anything. It isn't that I even want Gran Bet's house. It's she who wants me to have it.'

'Minna would want you to have what was hers.'

'Wouldn't she have wanted you to have it?'

'She left it to our son, your father, not me. She knew I wouldn't need it. It was important to her that her son, who would have been killed if he had stayed here, should have something of hers. It was taken from her twice. First by the Nazis who sent her to her death then by the communists who destroyed our hopes again. She would want you to take it back. It is the apartment where we lived together. She bought it with her family's money even though later, when Jewish property was being confiscated, we let it seem as if it was mine. And now there is something else, something that even I didn't know about. Let me show you. Come over to the computer screen.' I wheeled myself across the room and switched on. Then I searched for the site I wanted, the list of dormant accounts held by Swiss banks, nearly two thousand names, some with a country attached to them, others starkly alone, most of them recognisably German and Jewish. I began to scroll through the alphabet. 'There,' I said stopping at your name: Falk, Miriam. And above it Falk, Herman.

'I don't understand,' she said. I must learn to think of her by her name not yours, Minna. But it is a strange name, 'Betony'. In my Oxford Dictionary where I looked it up after she had gone I found that it is the name of a plant used in healing many years ago.

I said: 'It means that before the war someone, perhaps Minna herself although it was more likely to be her father, who had business connections in Switzerland, opened a bank account in her name. Then she followed his example when our baby was born and did the same for him. There are thousands of these accounts that are only just coming into the open because, of course, no one has drawn on them or known about them since their owners died or emigrated. Then there are other moneys deposited by the Nazis who had confiscated, stolen them from the people they conquered or destroyed.'

'What do you mean?'

'Mostly unidentifiable. Gold bars that were once piles of wedding rings or teeth for example.' For a moment I thought I had been too harsh and that she might faint so I added something less evocative: 'Jewellery, even perhaps paintings.' I am so used to it all, have lived with it so long that it has perhaps lost the power to shock me. Now I saw it through her fresh eyes and was ashamed of my thick skin of familiarity.

'That's what's so hard to get used to, what I inherit from both of you, your lives and histories, things I don't know about. Gran Bet says you should always study the bloodline to pick out a winner. People aren't that different from horses.' She laughed and then said: 'Honestly, I don't think I want any more from anyone. It's somehow dirty, that money.'

'But not Minna's inheritance, she wanted your father to have. If you feel that then you are rejecting her, and that part of yourself.' Even I felt my arguments were somehow spurious.

'No, no of course not, I didn't mean that. It's just the thought of taking money from someone who may have died a terrible death.'

I felt myself wince as if she were wounding me, as I had wounded her. 'I try not to believe that she did. I've made my own story of what I've learnt from so many years of searching, of study. Do you know, there are hundreds of pages and thousands of names I can call up, accounts of arrests and deaths, of labour camps, trains to nowhere, death camps, death marches when the war was nearly over and the prisoners could have been left to survive. And yet five thousand people lived on as U-boats in

Berlin itself. Someone helped them and they helped themselves, as Minna did. That's why I tried not to give up hope. She would want you to have what is hers. It would be a kind of justice. Will you let me show you tomorrow? For many years I couldn't go there, even to look at the outside of the building, but now of course we can go anywhere. Will you come with me? Do you have time?'

So today, my darling, for I was too exhausted to write to you last night, I am going out for the first time since the wall came down. It always seemed too much to bear that you weren't here to go back with me when it became possible again, that it would be wrong to go alone, a kind of second death for you. Now I've asked Christoff to get out the old outdoor wheelchair and check it for safety, the folding one I used to put in the car when I still drove. He grumbles that I am too weak, that the light will hurt my eyes, and the traffic fumes poison me. But I am going out, Minna. I am going out with our granddaughter to visit the past.

## XXII

'What would you do?' Betony asked. Gill hadn't been in his room when she had got back to the Hotel Tauris. It was in some ways a relief. She felt drained by all she'd had to absorb. When she'd set out that morning she hadn't known what to expect. She might have drawn a complete blank, been refused any meeting or admittance to the flat. Instead she had been buried under a mudslide of information riddled with emotional demands that cried out for her attention like the lost souls in a painting by Bosch.

Perhaps the most shocking part was that Gran Bet had met Minna, however briefly, and had still kept her silence except for the fatal letter to Betony's father, all these years. Wasn't her silence and Anton von Falk's (she still couldn't think of him as her grandfather) retreat into denial of the present like being buried alive?

He had lived entombed as if he had been guilty of murder, or a war crime, himself. There was something almost unhealthy, life-denying about such faithfulness? But then wasn't she still mourning Mark?

Betony called room service for a sandwich and orange juice, sensing that she should keep off alcohol for the moment if she didn't want to crack up completely, and then she closed the curtains and lay down in the room that was even more box-like by daylight and let sleep overwhelm her. The telephone beside her bed, on the table that was also a radio, and where the pith from her orange juice was now clinging in yellow shreds to the glass like dried sick, woke her hours later.

'Hey man. I'm sorry I been so long.'

'That's all right. I was asleep, a great sleep. What's the time, Gill?'

'It's seven-thirty. I'm going to shower. Then how about some food and we can swap stories. See you, downstairs eh, in half an hour. I'm pretty starving, man.' Betony showered too and then took the lift to the ground floor. Gill was leaning back in one of the beige, fake leather sofas with his eyes closed and a half smile on his face. A flock of Japanese tourists was being rounded up to be bused in search of pleasure while a pair of backpackers in shorts, woolly socks and climbing boots haggled over a map.

'You look more like you need sleep than food.'

He opened his eyes and got up, stretching. 'I noticed an Italian place on the way back. Let's go there.' They sauntered out into the warm evening. 'It's some place, this Berlin. Let's go towards the Ku-damm.'

'The what?'

'That's what they call the main street, at least I think it's the main one. You get it. Like us calling Piccadilly, the Dilly.'

'I didn't think anyone did any more. Wasn't that in the Dark Ages, music hall, that stuff?'

'Now you say so, I think I got it from Nana.' He laughed and danced a couple of steps.

'I hope you're going to be able to tell me about your day. You look high to me.'

'I was offered a coupla smokes, yeah. But I turned them down. I'd take you to the Kreuzberg, they've got really cool spots there, but it's too far for now.'

'Suddenly you're the expert on Berlin in one day.'

'There's short cuts you can take to learning. Let's try this.'

Once inside the trattoria, Pizzeria Francesca, the ubiquity of the surroundings, the dishes, the smells of garlic, herbs and cooked mozzarella, was reassuring. They might have been in London. 'Let's have a bottle of red straight away,' Gill said.

Betony was glad now that he was there. He would be able to tell her whether her day as she remembered it could have been just a bizarre dream. 'Okay,' he said when their first glass of wine had been poured and they had settled on starters and main courses with the Italian waiter, gondolier in black waistcoat and trousers with a flouncing white shirt, 'so you found the place and rang the bell. What happened then?'

She told Gill about the very old man in the wheelchair with his manservant and computer who claimed to be her grandfather. Of her grandmother's death and will. She had persuaded her grandfather to make a copy of Minna's precious last letter which she showed Gill, précis-ing what she remembered of its contents.

'It's like holding history in your hand, man. She must have been a helluva woman for him to go on loving her. What did she mean "going underground"?'

'Apparently some Berlin Jews, quite a lot really, managed to disappear, with false papers, hiding out in people's houses or empty flats or sleeping rough or even escaping from the country altogether.'

'Always on the run, always afraid of being caught but determined to survive. Anything to avoid the camps. Did you know there were tens of thousands of gays in the camps? The guy I met today told me. I knew there were some but not that many.'

'My grandfather, he wants me to call him Anton, showed me a photograph of his wife just before they were married. Do you believe in reincarnation, Gill? When he first saw me he thought I was her come back, you know.'

'No, I don't believe in all that crap. It's like the Rasta jive about Ethiopia. I'm sorry Bob Marley went for that stuff because I think his music's second to none but I can't follow him down that route. Sometimes I wish I could. It might make life easier to be able to identify with a religion, not be always on your own. But there you go. Did you see any likeness to you when you looked at her picture?'

'Yes, yes I did, I have to admit. I was a bit shaken by it.'

'I guess if I'd seen a picture of that GI, my grandfather, there'd be a resemblance there. Nana once showed me a snap of my mother when she was a baby and looked more like me but she grew out of it. I think that's all there is, just simple genes, nothing spooky like people back from the dead.'

'I wouldn't like to feel I was being taken over. Anton, my grandfather, wants me to go and look at some places where they lived and that sort of thing tomorrow. He says they really belong to me.'

'How can that be, Bets, when you didn't even know about them?'

'Apparently my grandmother, Minna, left them to her baby, my father. He wants me to claim them back. What do you think? Should I go?'

'There's no harm in looking, as Nana used to say.'

'Would you come with me? It's a bit frightening, with him in his wheelchair and that creepy manservant like someone out of a Hitchcock movie. Are you busy tomorrow?'

'I said I'd see this guy again.'

'Oh yes. Tell me more. Did he offer you the joints?'

'Yeah, but he's cool really. He's an artist, Rayner. He's got this fab penthouse studio in Kreuzberg. He's started making drawings of me, so he wants me to go back.'

'That's how you became the Berlin expert in a day. I take it he's gay.'

'How is this old guy going to show you places if he's in a wheelchair?'

'I don't know. Maybe the creepy valet, nurse, whatever he is, has a car. Please come, Gill. Tell your artist you'll see him later.'

'I'll ring him in the morning. But won't your grandpappy object to me tagging along? He might get the wrong idea and not be completely crazy about you having a darkie for a boyfriend.'

'I don't mind what he thinks. Well, that's not true really. I don't want him to be hurt but it's all so strange, like some surreal film, that I need something familiar to help me cope. And just now, that's you. But I don't want to cock up your love life, if you see what I mean. Is it a holiday romance or anything more do you think?'

'Man, I can't tell. It's too soon. But I don't think it's just a one-night, I should say one-day, stand. I think he'll want to see me when I ring him. At least he gave me his number, even though I'd already copied it off the phone when he was out of the room, and sort of almost begged me to call. He's a real dishy guy too. Mature, you know. About forty. Not some rent kid.'

'I hope you're being careful.'

'He isn't that kind of guy but yes, I am. I'm not in the dying game if I can help it. Not yet anyway or through acting stupid. He wanted me to go clubbing with him tonight but I'm too shattered.' He yawned hugely. Betony laughed.

'Lucky sod. I wish I felt tired for the same reason. Anyway, at least now you're not sorry I made you come with me.'

'You didn't make me. I fancied a spot of travel to broaden me mind.' They paid and left. Outside, the evening had become a warm enveloping darkness that they strolled through. Stopping to look in shop windows as they passed they compared the goods on offer and the prices with their London counterparts, indistinguishable by streetlight from the other loiterers filling the pavements with a sluggish stream of mingled tourists and residents.

Betony felt the pressures of the day oozing out of her pores, leaving her light and easy, as if she too were nothing but an unconcerned visitor.

Back in her room she sat on the downturned lid of the lavatory and stared into the cruel bathroom mirror that showed every smudge of fatigue, every open pore in relentless close-up. She'd told Gill she had seen a likeness to herself in that photograph of over half a century before of a girl with her dark hair falling in waves to her collar. Did she look foreign then, Jewish? What did that mean anyway? There'd been a girl at school someone had whispered one day was 'a Jew', Rosemary Sherman, whose parents owned a private bank. She had thick corn-coloured wavy hair, blue eyes and very pink cheeks, like a Dutch doll Betony had among her toys who wore clogs and an embroidered jacket over a puffed cream skirt and blouse. Ros, as she was called, always had tuck from her parents that she shared among her room-mates. Betony could see her now, very upright at the piano, as she played for dancing on wet afternoons when there was no chance of tennis or a walk. If only Betony had kept in touch with more of the girls from her school she could have written to Ros or rung her up, arranged to meet, had lunch. Asked her what she thought, what it meant. She thought she remembered that Ros had gone to Birmingham University to study medicine. Perhaps next time there was a school reunion, an occasion she'd always despised and avoided, she would try to go in the hope of meeting Ros, whose name probably wasn't Sherman any more, making it hard to trace her in any other way than through this long-neglected connection of school song and the smell of damp wellies in a chill stone passage.

She wondered how much her father had known or understood. He hadn't seen the letter Gran Bet had kept, only a German registration document his real mother had left behind with him, and a letter from his supposed mother giving him the bald facts. He wouldn't even have been a British subject, Betony suddenly realised. He would have had to begin at the beginning to try to establish who he was with the German embassy perhaps, searching for records in a language he didn't understand. He had needed, wanted, a British passport to travel for his firm. What could he have told them to cover the fact that he hadn't got one, couldn't have one, wasn't British at all? Could he even have been deported if the police or immigration had found out? Betony wasn't sure when it had become legal for Europeans to live and work in Britain. But then, she realised, he wouldn't even have had a German passport. He would have had to begin to unravel and then explain. It could have taken months. His company might have begun to question the suitability for a responsible job of someone who suddenly didn't know who he was and might have been lying about himself all this time. It would have seemed such an unlikely story to conventional, cynical British ears. Gran Bet's thoughtlessness, for that was what Betony had to believe it was, had left him not only without a past he had always taken for granted but with a present in limbo. Perhaps if Betony's mother had lived she would have been able to help him through it. As it was he had been completely alone in his empty flat. She couldn't blame him now. He had looked into that black hole and let himself be sucked down. That was all.

You read about it in the paper from time to time. Someone had been brought over to England or adopted and believed they had the right to stay until the knock on the door, the removal to a police station, the start of proceedings, the desperate appeals. Or the hand on the shoulder at Heathrow. 'Would you just step aside.' The detention centre. The flight that would take you back to punishment or poverty. Her father had been too young to know he was an asylum seeker, a refugee.

There was so much she didn't know. Suppose Gran Bet had adopted him officially? But then she didn't want anyone to know she had lost her own baby and taken someone else's. Women whose babies died sometimes tried in their desperation to steal other people's out of their prams. Gran Bet had been given a baby by its own mother, handed it to bring up. The real sadness was that her guilt had made her unable to love it, unable to think of it either as hers or as in trust. If only her father had left her a letter, Betony thought. But then if he could have explained how he felt perhaps he wouldn't have needed to kill himself. Why hadn't she been able to tell Anton von Falk what had really happened to his son? She had evaded the truth, just like Gran Bet. Because she hadn't wanted to hurt him, to spoil what for the old man was a homecoming, a reunion. Would she ever be able to tell him now or would it always lie, a lie, between them? She imagined Gill's Nana would have had something to say to cover the situation. 'What the eye don't see the heart can't grieve over,' ran through her mind but she wasn't sure where it had come from. Perhaps she had heard Gran Bet say it, uncharacteristically, as if she was quoting Nanny Lilian. There was a line of descent in speech as in everything, words, sayings from another age handed down unthinkingly. She must be very tired for her thoughts to be rambling like this.

How could she ever come out with the words and see the shock and pain that would be there in his face, in his tears even, like those he had wept today. It had been hard to put out a hand and touch the bony shank under the cloth that gave the impression of being nearly as old as its wearer. She felt no kinship with the old man, no surge of 'blood thicker than water'. But then, often, she felt little for Gran Bet except an irritable compassion. When she had understood that her father was dead she had thought that she ought to cry but couldn't. All her upbringing had been against it. Only now that she was so old and often lonely and frightened did Gran Bet overturn the practice of a lifetime and let herself cry out: 'You're all I've got,' before she resumed her jaunty mask of controlled defiance. If she was ever to get to sleep she must stop this roller-coaster. Betony undid her bottle of duty-free whisky as she had done the night before.

Gill, when he joined her at breakfast, had all the appearance of having slept like a baby. 'I rang Rayner first even though I thought he might not be up. But he was. He's a really cool cat. Said all the right things. Couldn't wait to see me, that jazz, that makes you feel great. Says he'll drive us if you don't mind him coming too. What do you think?'

'I'll have to ring my grandfather and see what he says. His man might be a bit put out if he thinks we're taking over.'

But Anton von Falk said he would be delighted to meet her friends, especially if they had a car. He had thought they might have to hire one for the day since he no longer drove or had a car of his own for Christoff to ferry him about.

'Is there room in it for all of us and my wheelchair?'

'I'll ask.' Betony covered the receiver with her hand and poked her head out from under the telephone hood. 'He wants to know if he can bring his wheelchair?'

'It's a big Jap car with a big boot. I guess that'll be all right if it folds up.'

## XXIII

Thinking about Bob Marley when I get up to my room I realise that when the guy wrote and sang about Babylon, it was just as much Babel he and the other cats meant. Wasn't Babylon a land of palaces and hanging gardens where they'd asked for a song from the people, Israel in exile? Whereas London is like that great tower of different voices trying to understand each other, where I feel at home as I never did before in the place I was born and grew up.

I wonder how early I can ring Rayner in the morning. Is the cat an early riser or a slugabed? Maybe he'll pretend not to know who I am. Fuck and run. Well, it's best to know, Gill, so you've no chance to stuff yourself with illusions, like a kid on candyfloss, that you're anything more than a piece of arse. So I pick up the phone and dial.

'Nauheim.'

'Hi, it's Black Beauty. Are you awake? Is this too early to call?'

'No, it is perfect. Where are you?'

'In my hotel room.'

'What are you wearing?'

'Nothing.'

'Beautiful. When can we meet? Where would you like to go today?'

'There's a problem.'

'Oh?' The guy's voice has been eager and happy. Now it drops an octave like a ballerina whose partner's just failed to catch her.

'I have to go with Betony, that's the girl I came to Berlin with, to see her grandfather this morning. He wants to take her to see some place he used to live but she wants me to go too because he's very old and she's a bit scared of him. He's in a wheelchair.'

'Wheelchair?'

'Yes. He can't walk. He has to be pushed everywhere in a chair. He's like a cripple. How else can I put it?'

'Ein Krüppel. Ja. But how will you go?'

'I don't know. Maybe in a taxi.'

'Tell your girlfriend I will take you and the grandfather. At what time shall I come?'

'I'll find out and ring you. Thanks, Ray. Bitte, is that right?'

'Danke. Don't mention it.'

So here we are, me and Bets, waiting in the hotel foyer behind the revolving glass doors for what looks like being a real Dad's army of an outing complete with wheelchair. I'm nervous of this meeting of Rayner and Bets. I hope they won't hate each other on sight. But there's nothing I can do and here's the silver car drawing up at the kerb. Rayner jumps out, slamming the door behind him, and strides towards us as if he's on camera, determined to make a forceful impression, not come on as some limp queen.

'This is Betony.'

For a moment I think he's actually going to click his heels and bow. Then he puts out a hand, smiles and says, 'Rayner, Rayner

Nauheim. Happy to meet with you. Would you like to go in back? You must tell me, please, the address we go to.'

I climb in beside him as he's arranged, so our hands can contact as he changes gear. He's driving the saloon like a sports car today, revving up through the gears, starting away like a greyhound out of its trap at the lights.

'You know, it's not Green to drive like Fassbinder.'

'I know, but sometimes it's necessary to be a little brave. I will be more careful with the Grossvater. Here is the place. I will wait in the car in case the police try to move me. Then I can explain about the chair.'

Bets and I get out because the old guy is going to have to sit in the front. Bets rings the bell and in a couple of minutes disappears inside while I hang around on the pavement talking to Ray through the car window.

'You have slept well?'

'So well.'

'I also. We must do it again. It is good for the health.' He grins at me. 'Tonight I take you to a club so that I can see you dance.'

'Cool, man.' I feel like a cat myself, stroked by his eyes and his tongue. The big door opens behind me and coming down the steps are Bets, the old guy in the chair and the creepy manservant hanging on behind for dear life to stop it running away down the steps, bump, bump and dumping the grandfather on the pavement like some Bonfire Night guy letting his stuffing burst out of his clothes and his stick bones poke through. Rayner gets out of the car to open the doors.

'This is Gill,' Betony says and I shake hands.

'Rayner Nauheim,' Ray says with a bow and a flood of German. The nurse, for that's what he really is, pushes the old man up to the open door and together they lever him out of the chair so that he can hang onto the roof and let himself down backwards onto the seat.

'Splendid,' he calls out. 'Now the legs,' and the nurse lifts them like the slack trousers were empty and puts them inside. I can see by his face he disapproves of the whole expedition and I think: Maybe he loves the old guy, truly loves him and is afraid for him or afraid to lose him. And I think, Gill, you're so lucky to have dancing legs. But one day soon, quite soon, they'll have run over the hill and not be able to dance any more.

Ray helps the nurse fold up the wheelchair and stow it in the boot. I realise he's already taken out the shelf above it so the back poles can stick up in the air behind our heads. I get into the back with Bets. Now the nurse is standing there on the pavement, looking so forlorn I wave at him and open the door. He squeezes in, murmuring what I take to be thanks. I'm in the middle with me feet straddling the gear box as Rayner pulls the old man's seatbelt across his chest and plugs it in. Then he starts the engine, lets off the handbrake and draws away smooth as a new Central Line train out of Notting Hill Gate. We drive along as well behaved as a hearse, Rayner and the old man swapping sentences Bets and I can't understand. Maybe they're talking politics or the weather, which is fine and bright this morning as we go through the streets in our royal progress, streets I know I haven't been through before of big buildings all like town halls and then streets of grey blocks of flats, grim as inner London estates everyone says they would like to pull down if they had the money. 'This is the old Eastern part of the city,' the grandfather says over his shoulder. 'You see the television tower.' It's like an elegant spaceship pointed at the sky. 'And this is the famous Unter den Linden, the heart of the old Eastern part and also before the war, very fashion-able and popular with many big shops and buildings.' His English is nearly perfect, with hardly a word out of place and the accent very precise old-style BBC like you hear on black and white news clips.

Rayner pulls up. 'Now we can't go where Herr von Falk wishes exactly because of the one-way system. So I will stay here with the car while you take a little walk only.' We all scramble out, Rayner unlocks the boot and sets the wheelchair on the ground. Basically it's like a director's folding chair of canvas and struts with wheels on the legs and a footrest that comes across the front. The nurse wheels it up to the door. It's harder to dig the old guy out than it was to lower him in. I'm hoping to stay behind with Ray but Bets, reading me like an open book, says, 'Please come with us, Gill. We might need some extra hands.'

So away we go down the street that must have missed the bombardment because it's still got the original houses and even trees, a sort of oasis in the wasteland of these estates. We're bowling along, with me and the nurse both on the chair pushing because old Guy Fawkes is heavier than he looks and the nurse is soon in a sweat. I expect people to stop and clap as if we're part of the alternative Olympics and I suddenly remember a scene from a fifties or sixties movie way back where kids were pushing a bed along on its castors through the streets. I want to laugh out loud at the spectacle we have to be.

'That's it. Stop, stop.' The nurse and I dig in our heels because this old chair doesn't seem to have any brakes. We're in front of an elegant house with balconies, like something you might see in Chelsea but more modern. The old man points up the black and silver cane he's brought with him. 'That was our flat, up there on the first and second floors. That should be yours.' The hand holding the stick is trembling. Betony takes the other and holds it for a moment till he calms down.

'Who lives there now?'

'I don't know. It will be rented out. The state took it over. Now perhaps it belongs to the City Council or to no one. We shall find out.'

'I couldn't turn people out of their homes.'

'Perhaps not. Although they may be ex-party officials who were once ex-Nazis.'

'It has to stop somewhere.'

'It's perhaps harder for you to understand because you haven't lived with it. We shall see. We'll talk about it later. Now back to the car. There is something else to show you.' So we turn him round and we're bowling back again to where Rayner is waiting.

He and the old man go at it hammer and tongs in German.

'Unfortunately I can't take Herr von Falk where he wishes to go next because the area is for pedestrians only. I will take you a little way and then wait.'

I'm beginning to worry that he'll get pissed off with all this hanging about but he seems calm and still smiling. Away we go again and then Rayner drops us off and it's back to the wheelchair, this time over the stones of a pedestrian precinct where the old guy's bones must be getting a terrible jolting. Rayner has decided to leave the car and come with us so we're quite a procession. All we need is a few placards or balloons. I expect people will soon start asking what it's for and if they can join us. He calls a halt in front of a posh eaterie all plate glass with fish swimming in the windows, crabs and lobsters on the bottom and little see-through shrimp darting about. The main window is a huge aquarium where the fish look out at us and blow bubbles. 'This was once the department store of Minna's father, Strauss. The windows were all broken in the Kristallnacht riot when the SA smashed up Jewish shops. The next morning I stood here on the pavement in a depth of shattered glass that might have been the smashed pond ice of a children's game. Then, after the war, it was requisitioned by the state. Now it has been privatised, sold off. Under the Nazis it was leased to an Aryan partner of Herr Strauss but I believe it is still by right yours. Now it is owned by an international chain.'

'Ja,' Rayner says. 'This was the place that was prosecuted and nearly closed down for serving live animals.'

'How disgusting.' Bets looks as if she might throw up.

'If you tried to do anything here you would have all the power of an international company against you. Clever lawyers, the best money could buy.'

The old guy is beginning to sag. You can see this trip down memory lane is getting to him now.

'I think you've had enough,' Betony says. The nurse looks relieved. 'If Ray doesn't mind we'll take you home.' This time

Ray and I push him between us back to the car and then when we reach his home we drag the chair up the steps and into the building.

'It's the first floor.' Bets points. 'There's a lift through the door. The other day, yesterday I mean, when I came here I didn't realise it was there.' We wheel him in with the nurse while we walk up the stairs. 'I'll just see he's all right then we'll go and find some lunch.'

'As long as it isn't MacFish,' Rayner laughs. 'I'll take you to a Turkish place for couscous.' That meant we'd be near his home. I'm wondering how the rest of the day is going to work out. The manservant is waiting with the door open. The grandfather has gone for a leak and comes back in his regular chair, wheeling himself along.

'I think you should have something to eat now and a rest,' Betony says.

'You will come back tomorrow? When must you return to London?'

'In the afternoon. I'll come in the morning to say goodbye.' The old guy looks like an abandoned kid. Betony takes his hand. We all say goodbye and shake hands. Then we're out in the street again where the light is blinding after the gloom inside.

Soon we're sitting in the Omar Grill. 'The past is a burden always,' Rayner says while we're waiting for our food. 'Always with someone that age you wonder. What was he doing in the war?' I hadn't had time to tell him the story. For one we'd been too busy with other things but also I wasn't sure how he would take it or how much Bets would want him to know. I should have trusted my instinct that the guy was okay. After all he fancied me.

'He was in the army, an officer. But he must have been all right, I mean not mixed up in camps and that sort of thing, because his wife, my grandmother, was Jewish.'

'So what happened to her?'

'She disappeared. The police, Gestapo, told her he was dead

and therefore she wasn't protected any more. He was a prisoner-of-war. She went underground, hid out somewhere, but they must have got her in the end because she never came back. Unless she was killed in the bombing.'

'My father also was a prisoner of the Americans. He was very young and only called up when Hitler was pulling in old men and boys to defend the city. He said the American GIs made a kind of mascot of him.'

'My grandfather was captured by the Russians. He hasn't told me but I think he had a pretty rough time.'

'The Russians had not the food of the Americans, therefore their prisoners didn't have much. But also they were angry because of what we did to their country. It was easier for the Americans to be kind because they had everything and their country wasn't invaded. Then it was politics. They wanted Germany to be strong as quickly as possible against the Russians. Now we are all Americans.' Rayner suddenly seems his real age, as if Bets and me were only kids still.

'What do you mean, Rayner?'

'That restaurant we visited, for example. It is for the rich to consume. It doesn't matter if one day there are no more fish or animals in the sea as long as we all consume all the time. They said in the newspapers that the customers, the consumers, were cutting pieces from the animals while they walked on the tables.'

'Like frogs, where they don't kill them before chopping off their legs but just throw the part they don't want onto a pile to die.'

'Do you mind! I might not even be able to eat my conscous and beans.' Betony takes a long swig of foamy beer.

'Do you know the first Western genocide?' Rayner asks.

'Was it the Romans? They killed off a lot of people, destroyed whole cities if they rebelled,' I remembered from 'O'-level history.

'Ja, of course. They first killed the Jews and dispersed them. You know what Goethe, our great poet like your Shakespeare, said? I tell you. He said once: "The Germans should be scattered and resettled all over the world like the Jews in order to develop the great mass of good that is in them." He also said: "Germany is nothing but every individual German has great value. Yet they believe the opposite." That was nearly a hundred and fifty years before Hitler. But that, too, has its problems. It leads to democracy, yes, but it also leads to nackt individualism. I, I, I, only. Everyone must have his car even if the ozone layer is destroyed. I know I am bad also in this way. I admit. I love my car and to drive fast. It is very difficult for humans to be always good.'

'What are you going to do now?' I asked Bets when we'd eaten.

'I think I'll go back to the hotel and flake out.'

'I will drop you there,' Rayner offers.

'That's kind. But I think I'll walk a little way and then take a taxi if I get fed up.'

I can't decide whether she really wants to do a Garbo or is just being tactful but she's quite firm about it. Outside the restaurant we arrange to catch up later and she goes off down the street to be quickly swallowed up in the crowd. 'Will she be okay?' Rayner asks and I like him even better for it.

'I think it's all been quite a shock, a lot to take in. One minute you're one person and then suddenly you're someone else.'

'Isn't this happening all the time? Some people have the theory that we are not one person but a bundle of sensations.'

'But they all belong, my sensations, to me. I mean, I'm the one who feels them in my body. When I'm dancing I know it's me.'

'Have you never felt you might be becoming someone else?'

I think he's teasing me but I'm not sure.

'I've never got that close to anyone.'

'Come back to my flat and I will try to prove it to you.' Now I know he's teasing. 'I want to tell you more about those pygmy Schimpansen. You know, when the males get angry with each other instead of fighting they rub their penises together like sexy sword fighting.'

# XXIV

When she came to see me to say goodbye, our granddaughter said her friend has decided to stay on a little longer so she is going back alone. She has promised to telephone me and to let me know what she decides. I showed her the website where everything is catalogued. There's so much she doesn't know and perhaps she shouldn't. Let the dead bury the dead. She asked me if there were any other relatives she should contact. I told her how after the war I heard that Otto had been killed as a test pilot, that he had died unmarried so that was the end of the line. There is nobody else. She also asked me why I hadn't made any attempt to claim what was yours. I tried to explain that I didn't need it. I had my own work as a translator and then at the university. But most of all I couldn't bring myself to profit from the loss of you. It would have been somehow obscene.

Why then, she asked, was it different for her? I tried to explain how I see it, how in her case it would be a kind of reparation, of justice for you, how some people, like Simon Wiesenthal for example, have devoted their lives to the pursuit of this justice so that what happened to six million people could never happen again, at least not in that way. I gave her the address of the man in London she should contact. Now it is up to her to do as she wishes. Somehow, I suppose because she reminds me of you, I trust her to make the right decision.

I gave her copies of the photographs too that I got Christoff to have made. Anything can be copied now in a fraction of time. I told her how I had carried them in my wallet to Poland and Russia and in the prisoner-of-war labour camp, how I had believed that if I could still keep them next to my heart I would find you again. You would have laughed at such superstition. The irony is that if you came back now, rang my telephone number or answered the message that is still hanging out there in cyberspace, we wouldn't recognise each other, two old people with no shared existence for half a century and nothing to say. Should I give up my dream then? I can't. I have to go on with it. If you aren't in England, you must be in Israel or the States. I can centre my fantasy there. But if you had been in America you would have found me again. No, only Israel is a real possibility. But you were such a European. How could you go to a place of conflict and more fear except out of bitterness and anger. I would have to accept that you never wanted to see me again. That would be almost worse than accepting death. You see, I've learnt nothing. I still can't let you go, even for your own good.

I remember my last gleam of hope when that ex-prisoner wrote that you had been in a camp with his daughter who was now in America, but all she could tell me was that you, or the person she thought might be you, had been moved on. She and her mother had escaped by climbing through the window, though her mother had died later in the forest like in some terrible story by the Brothers Grimm, except that there was no happy ending for the daughter. 'I try to forget but I can't,' she wrote me. 'I find it hard to love my husband and children because of it.' She saw the woman she thought might be you beaten, fall and get up again. She had told her that her real name was Miriam and she had been married to a soldier who had died on the Russian front.


# XXV


They were held in a waiting pattern above the city like a bomber in a searchlight cone. The pilot, 'your captain', had told them jokily on the address system that because of congestion over Heathrow they would be going round again, passing above the web of lights waiting below to catch them and anchor them to the ground. The plane wheeled north and east, the dark sky becoming earth, the pinpricks of lamps, stars, as they banked slowly. Below, late commuters were driving home, heading west.

Betony found herself almost grateful for the suspended moments before she had to act, decide, make her way back to the empty flat. She didn't blame Gill. She would have done the same if she had found a new fling instead of an old grandfather. She hoped he was being careful. She hoped he wouldn't get hurt. Not too soon or too badly.

When at last the plane was allowed to land she gathered up her bag and the remains of her duty-free, relieved that she didn't need to wait beside the carousel of circulating baggage but could head straight for the customs exit and down into the long bowel of tunnel leading to London's underground intestinal network, be shuttled towards the city, changing at Victoria for the last leg of the journey south under the Thames. If it's all true I could afford to do this by taxi, Betony thought. It was the first time she had allowed herself to toy even unconsciously with what her new circumstances might mean.

'You are yourself,' her grandfather Anton had said, but she felt completely different as if she were the kind of animal – she didn't like to think too closely about which sort, not a cuddly mammal anyway – that had to change its skin if not its whole body in order to grow. Didn't caterpillars dissolve completely inside the shiny hard case of the pupa to be reconstituted for flight and mating? Yet surely they kept some innate sense of being. The tailpiece jerked automatically when she came across them at Gran Bet's, overwintering in some dark corner hoping to be un-noticed.

The tube retched her out at Clapham Common and she began to walk up Lavender Hill. Gangs of boys and girls in every shade of pale and brown clustered around the lighted windows and entrances of the video exchange, the fish and chip shop, Lily Roots, the Chinese takeaway, the doner kebab turning slowly on its spit like a haunch of elephant. Pizza couriers revved beside the plate glass of the launderette where a woman in a green overall rhythmically mopped the floor from a clanking pail in the last rite of the day. The street life seemed as strange to her as if she had never lived among it, as if what she saw was a backdrop video for the figures to gyrate in front of, a piece of installation art, ephemeral as the fluid it swam in, a dance without music except when a door opened to let out a customer on a wave of sound or a car went past with the window wound down, and an inarticulate bass thump thumped out into the warm evening.

There was a light on in the downstairs flat and a murmur of voices in the hall which suggested that the psychotherapist had a late client. She had once told Betony that she supplemented her National Health Service work with stressed businessmen who wanted to be taught to relax, 'a kind of mental prostitute you could call me'. She looked forward to the day when she could leave her full-time job, concentrate on her private patients and spend long weekends at her country cottage. Betony was comforted by the knowledge of a presence in the house but not one she was required to respond to. She knew she would soon have to telephone Gran Bet and answer questions. But for tonight she would shut the door and pretend to be still away. She picked up a thin summer mail from the hall table and climbed the stairs.

The flat seemed both known and strange to her. Did she really live here, whoever she might be? Sadie's voice chattered into the silence from the answering machine with details of a shoot they had been asked to do. Would Betony be free or should she go ahead on her own? 'Give us a buzz a.s.a.p.' For once Betony hadn't confided the details of her trip and its purpose. Since Gill had moved in she realised she had had less time to linger with Sadie at the end of an exhausting day, catching up on each other's lives and lovers. Partly she shied away from trying to explain herself, this new inheritance that she barely understood.

The telephone shrilled at her. 'Hi Bets, how you doing?'

'I'm fine. How're you?'

'Just great. Cool, man. I'll send you a cheque for the rent. If the agency calls could you tell them I'm on holiday. Oh, and I forgot to give you my number, I mean Ray's number, where you can reach me. I'll let you know when I'm coming back. Maybe a week or so.'

When Gill had finished speaking she sat for a moment or two before she went to see if there was the remains of a bottle of white wine in the fridge. She found an open Pinot Grigio and smiled at the remembered difference between an optimist and a pessimist: half full or half empty. The call, Gill's voice, was a link to what she had left behind. Slowly she drank her way through the pale wine, wishing that like most of her acquaintance she could enhance her pleasure with a fag. She turned on the news to be soothed by the sleek voice of the announcer. She remembered, though she couldn't recover from where, perhaps Grandfather Anton had told her, that it had been an offence in wartime for Germans to listen to the BBC. She must ask Gran Bet what had happened here. How little she knew. How little most people knew. And yet it didn't go away, all that history. It went on being passed down in the mind and in the blood of millions of people. She was part of it too. She couldn't turn her back on it.

In the morning Betony felt stronger. The wine had made her sleep and she didn't remember any disturbing dreams. The books she had got from the library with Gill were still there in a pile. It seemed so long ago. They must be due back or even have already overrun their loan time. She began to look through them and was confronted at once by a series of photographs of horror and imminent death that made her feel physically sick. Most disturbing was the close-up of a young woman's face, not yet eaten away by starvation but still fresh, as if she might have been about to go shopping, who had just stepped out of a transport and was being herded by a uniformed official; a young woman like herself, not poor or wearing strange rabbinical clothes, shawls, long beards and hair as the men were in some of the photographs, but a woman you might see going through the swing doors into Peter Jones and forget in a second after you had held the door open for her. On her face there was a look of complete incomprehension. Other pictures were more superficially frightening, with their neat marching uniformed columns or equally neat rows of emaciated cadavers. It was the very ordinariness of the young woman's photograph that was so chilling. That could have been Minna, or me. She would contact the London lawyer whose address her Grandfather Anton had given her and see whether he could help her.

'How can I be of assistance?'

'I believe I may be entitled to some family property in the old East Germany. I wondered if you could advise me.'

'How did you get my name, may I ask?'

'My grandfather found it on the Internet.'

'When could you come and see me? I'm afraid it may be too complicated to discuss on the telephone.' The voice was precise, cultured, a little foreign. Betony fixed an appointment for the next day.

'Normally I wouldn't be able to see you so soon but the doors are closing. If you are going to make a claim it must be done quickly.'

Now she couldn't put off ringing Gran Bet any longer.

'I'm back, Gran.'

'Darling, where are you?'

'I'm at home, in the flat.'

'When did you get back?'

'Last night but it was too late to ring.' It was a white lie only. Gran Bet often went to bed early. 'Out of boredom,' she had once said. 'Then I just lie there.'

'How did you get on? Did you find anything, anyone?'

'There's lots to tell you but I'd rather not start on the phone. I'll come down and see you the day after tomorrow. Will you be there?'

'What day is that, darling?'

'Thursday?'

'I've got drinks in the evening. Some new people. The Arkwrights. They've bought Rose Cottage. Not quite my type but one has to be friendly. Can you come to lunch?'

'I'll take you to the Berks Arms.' She couldn't face the claustrophobia of the dining-room or Gran Bet's cooking. Better to be on neutral ground.

The offices of Whale and Whale were in the old legal quarter of the City, convenient for the Law Courts and the Inns of Court. Photographers clustered outside the Victorian railway station where judgement if not justice was handed down, ready to pin down the famous or notorious with the camera that cannot lie, in hope of a front-page scoop. Betony pushed her way past and turned up Chancery Lane. There was obviously a lot of money to be made from the law's delays. The Whale and Whale building was glossily modern, fronted by its canopied porch where a plaque recorded the bomb that had destroyed the original and its restoration twice since.

Inside, a girl smiled up from her marble desk housing the tools of her trade, computer screen and switchboard. Betony was directed to a panelled side room where she perched herself alone at a table that would have seated thirty people. The windows were in a ribbed glass that prevented her gazing out and diverting her thoughts with the doings of the world outside. She should have brought a magazine to read.

The door opened. 'Miss Falk.'

'Yes,' Betony stood up.

'Leonhard Kramer. I'm so sorry to have kept you waiting. Now, how may I help you?' The heavily built figure seated itself at the table and leant towards her, smiling encouragement. Betony began her story with the first visit to Anton van Falk.

'So, if I understand you well, until recently you had no idea of your history. You grew up in complete ignorance.'

'None at all. It still seems unreal, unbelievable.'

'You shouldn't think that. I am a databank of such stories. You are not in the least unusual.' He laughed. He looked, Betony thought, like a kempt Einstein. The high domed head, the smile behind the spectacles. But whereas Einstein in the famous photograph gave the impression of being sprinkled with ash and chalk dust, Leonhard Kramer's navy and white pinstripe and duck-egg blue shirt were immaculate. She could imagine him standing up before the judge and laying out his case meticulously, like Gran Bet's favourite television lawyer, Perry Mason, whose loss from the screen was still lamented.

'So you think I may be entitled to something?'

'Almost certainly. But you will need to go through a very lengthy bureaucratic process, provide a great many documents, fill in the correct forms . . .'

'My grandfather gave me these.' She passed over the envelope Anton von Falk had given her. The lawyer spread the papers on the table and began to examine them.

'These are an excellent beginning. You are so fortunate that he is still alive and can testify. So often there is no one left and then it is much more difficult. Sometimes I have to search in old telephone directories to identify people and properties. I was afraid that you would be too late. A limit is being set on claims. But that so much has been done already gives us a chance. You are also lucky that it is in East Berlin. The books were closed on the West in the seventies.'

'What would I need to do first?'

'You must register your claim with the local authority in order to obtain a certificate of inheritance. Are you sure you are the only person with a claim to this property? Often there are several claimants and then there is great difficulty in getting them to agree on a course of action. Some are elderly and living in a degree of poverty. They want to sell at once. Others younger, richer, want to wait and see if the price improves. May I ask what happened to the first inheritor, your father?'

'He found out in a rather cruel way when I was still a child. He couldn't cope with it.'

'I see. I am extremely sorry. It is often very difficult to face such unpleasant facts, the burden of survival, all that. The younger generation, like you, are stronger, more distant from it, as is right. You were the only child?'

'My mother died when I was born and my father wasn't the sort to keep a mistress.'

'Some people would say all men are "the sort".'

Betony considered this carefully. 'He had the opportunity. He lived alone in London all week. But if there had been someone to talk to then he wouldn't have killed himself, and even if he had I'm sure he would have left her or any child of theirs something in his will.'

'So you are the sole beneficiary. This greatly simplifies things.'

'Suppose I didn't want to sell. Suppose I wanted to live there?'

For a moment he looked disconcerted. 'That I have never heard of. Everyone wants to sell.'

'What happens if there are people living there?'

'You must provide alternative accommodation before you can sell. Now what are these properties?'

Betony described the house and the restaurant. Then she said, 'My grandfather also showed me a list on his computer screen of people who had money in Switzerland.'

His eyes lit up. He took off his glasses and polished them on a little piece of cloth that he drew from his spectacle case. 'Dormant accounts. How very interesting. And did you find anyone interesting on this list?'

'Both my grandmother and my father were there. Mr Kramer, will you help me with all this if I decide to go ahead?'

'With pleasure. There may be some difficulty with the restaurant because they will argue that its use has been changed, from a department store I think you said. But I enjoy a chase and a fight. First, if you will excuse me, I will make copies of these and then I will give you the necessary form. Some things no doubt you will need to ask your grandfather. Presumably he is rather elderly?'

'He's eighty-five or -six, I think.' She judged that Leonhard Kramer was probably seventy himself. He got up and left the room and came back with more papers.

'You will see there are a great many questions on twelve pages. Do give me a call if you have problems.'

'I haven't quite decided yet what I'm going to do. I might decide not to do anything.'

'Of course. I understand. It is a big decision and it could take many years before it is resolved. You may wish simply to get on with your life as you have been doing.'

'Can I ask you something else?'

'Please do.'

'I hope you don't think me cheeky but I've been very confused by all this. Sometimes I am not sure who I am.'

'How can I help?'

'I would like to ask about you.'

'I came over to England as a child on one of the kindertransports. I was lucky. You see, like you I had been brought up to think rather differently about myself, as a Christian. But under the racial laws I was still a Jew.'

'And how do you think of yourself now?'

'As a European. I can never feel quite British although some people who were younger than I was when they came manage it. How did your father get here?'

'He was brought by his mother as a baby. She left him and went back to be with her husband. He grew up believing the woman he was left with was his mother.'

'I understand his shock. He lost not one but two mothers and two countries. That takes time to assimilate and even then, years later, you may find yourself confused and depressed without understanding why. You mustn't blame him.'

'I did at first but I understand better now.'

'When, if, that is, you have filled in the form and assembled all the documents you will have to swear before a public notary. Get in touch with me then. I won't say anything more except I repeat that if you decide to act it must be soon. The Swiss accounts, of course, are a different matter. There we have time and a good chance of success because the banks are only now beginning to open their books.'

As she drove out of London through the western suburbs to the motorway the next morning, Betony noticed the bronze haze staining the roadside trees whose leaves were turning early under the deadly pall. She remembered Rayner's poisoned love affair with his car and wondered when she would hear from Gill again. The city seemed lacklustre under the sun. Those who could had fled to find fresh air and water. Perhaps England was tired after its long history. The figure of Gran Bet waiting on the steps behind the singed lawn, and beds drained of colour by August, seemed to have bowed and shrunk even more, although it was only a fortnight since Betony had seen her.

'Darling, so glad you could come. I thought if I was waiting out here we could go straight off to the Berks. You see what those new people have done to the cottage? They've put a straw cat and a peacock on the roof. We'll probably be offered Bristol Cream this evening.'

Betony parked on the tarmac beside the pub and guided her grandmother down the steps. She was relieved to find that she still felt the same exasperated affection for her. She had dreaded finding herself emptied of feeling by her recent access of knowledge.

'This is on me, Gran,' she said firmly. 'What will you have to start? A G and T?'

'Delicious, darling.'

The pub smelt of frying fat. It was unreconstructed fake traditional, beams, black panelling, horse brasses. Gran Bet waved to a racing crony in green wellingtons and ribbed green jumper above sandy cotton trousers, all from a country casual catalogue. 'That's Charlie Butts. He works for the Scarborough stable. Good for a tip from the horse's mouth. Now, tell me how you got on. Who did you see?'

'I saw someone called Anton von Falk.' Betony had rehearsed her words carefully.

'I never met him of course, only his wife. John knew him before we were married. After, I think they had dinner in London sometimes. I only met his wife once. He must be very old now, older than me. How does he look?'

'Oh much older than you, Gran. He's in a wheelchair. He has a manservant to push him about and a computer.'

'A computer. Why would he want that?'

'He uses it for research.'

'I suppose if you can't get out it would help to pass the time. What did you tell him about your father?'

'I told him as little as possible. I didn't want to hurt him. After all, the truth wouldn't do him any good or make him any happier.'

'And what did you say about me? Does he hate me?'

'Why should he?'

'Because I kept his son from him.'

'He doesn't know that and there's no reason why he should.'

'Don't you think the truth should come out after all this time?'

'What's truth, Gran? Aren't there lots of truths, versions I mean? Not just one. If you put it to a lawyer like the one I saw yesterday I'm sure that's what he'd say.'

'Why were you seeing a lawyer?'

'He specialises in recovering lost property. Now, what will you eat?'

'Oh, my usual: plaice'n'chips'n'peas.'

Betony went up to the bar to order, giving Gran Bet a chance to frame her next question. 'What sort of lost property?'

'Jewish property. Anton von Falk says I'm the heir to his wife's property through my father.'

'You won't be needing Glebe House then. It needs painting and repairing, old Harris says. I thought I'd sell some things to pay for it. The Thorpe Reprints for example. I never look at them. Maybe they'd fetch something. But perhaps I'd better just sell up and move into a bungalow.'

'Don't be daft, Gran. You'd hate it. Now, don't let the gin make you weepy or Charlie Butts will think I've just told you

I'm pregnant. I haven't decided yet what I'm going to do. The lawyer says it could take years to settle. You should see the form to fill in. Twelve pages of questions and so many documents you have to supply.'

'German thoroughness.'

'If I do go for it, it would mean there'd probably be enough money to look after Glebe House and make sure you never have to leave it unless you want to.'

Gill's voice on the answering machine brought her up to date. 'I'm coming back for a couple of days to collect some stuff and sort a few things out. Then I'll come back to Berlin. I don't know what will happen, how long this'll last, but I want to give it my best shot. I don't know what to do about my room but we can talk about that when I see you.'

## XXVI

'Do you have to go?' Ray says as he parks outside the glass revolving door at the airport.

'Just for a bit. I've got things to sort out. I'll be back very soon, so don't you be naughty while I'm away.'

'That call this morning while you were in the shower is from the gallery. They like my drawings of you. They want to show them. They say I am the Mapplethorpe of the pen. So I work on the others that are only sketches now while you are away. And when you come back I make some more. This way I am thinking of you all the time and be keusch.'

'Keusch?'

'Not doing anything, you say, "naughty". Only you don't be away too long.' He leans across and kisses me on the mouth as if he's imprinting himself there. Apparently it's cool for two guys to do this in Berlin. I get my bag from the boot, turn and wave and go in to look for the British Airways check-in down the row of airlines each with their jazzy logo and uniformed colour supplement girls. 'The departure gate is number nine,' mine tells me.

We're all nomads now, constantly on the move. If you could look down from space you ought to be able to see the waves washing from country to country. Nana never went anywhere in her life apart from day trips by coach to places that didn't impress her. 'Best off stopping at home. All this gallivanting about. Laura's bloke is taking her and the kids to Spain if you please. They'll all end up with the squits and sunstroke, I tell 'ee.' Your voice hasn't come back, Nana, not as my voice I mean. Having to talk so careful so Ray can understand seems to have seen it off for good. But I still have to reckon up with the past before I'm free to come back.

The note on the kitchen table from Bets welcomes me home and says she'll be in at seven. I head for the launderette with me bag of dirty clothes, drop others in at the cleaners. Gotta keep up appearances, keep the flag flying in little old Berlin even though Ray likes me best with clothes off. While the wash is going round I can collect a couple of bottles from the offo. It's almost as if I've never been away and yet everything's changed. I'm going to give it my best, I told Bets on the phone, and see how it goes. Strange to be back on streets of brown faces hearing the creole zapping out of their mouths. What would Ray make of it all? He's been to London of course, but it's different being a tourist. You have to live in London to know it. Maybe after a bit we'll come and stay here for a while. He says it'll be easy for me to get modelling work but he's not sure he wants me to. It's a gas him being jealous when if I took him into the King William here all eyes would swivel his way. Then there's the audition for that group, that wants me to choreograph for them if they like what they see. That'll be great, man, if that comes off. They're all in awe of our pop scene so for once there's an advantage in being a Brit, especially a black Brit. The washing goes round and round tra la la la and it comes out here.

They probably think I'm younger than I am and don't realise I'm nearly over the hill. So I've got to give that my best shot too, because it's what I've always wanted really, my own group to write for, dream up a dance and see it come to life. Dream on, Gill. No fucking harm in dreaming while you can. I stuff the washing in the dryer and give it another whirl, pick up a takeaway curry and leg it back to the flat with the bag of rough dried bumping over me shoulder. I settle down with the tinfoil dishes of hot pilau rice and vegetables and a plate to mix them on, a glass of lager and the phone. First I've got to deal with the agency, tell them I'm working abroad for a bit but not to take me off the books completely. Fuck it, I can't burn all the boats. Then I look up Laura's number. We haven't spoken for two years and I wonder if it's still the same.

'Laura. It's your little brother.'

'I know that. What do you want?'

'Nothing. Just a chat.'

'I'm busy.'

'I thought I might come over and see you all.'

'What for?'

'I'm going abroad for a bit. I thought I'd like to sort a few things out first.'

'Like what?'

This conversation is a real pain. She's so laid back she's practically invisible.

'Just family things. You know. Like blood's thicker than water, don't they say? Nana used to say so anyway.'

'I wouldn't know. She didn't talk to me, only to her favourite little black-eyed boy.'

'Laura, she's been dead nearly ten years. Can't you let it rest?'

'You let it rest then.'

'How are the kids? They must be getting quite big now.'

'They're all right. But that's why I don't want you coming here. I couldn't trust you. And Shaun wouldn't like it.'

226

'Why not?' It's my turn for the questions. I hear what she's saying of course, but I want her to spell it out.

'Well there's your hair and clothes for a start. Dreadlocks and all those poofy colours and styles. Blokes don't wear them things.'

'Those things.'

'You what?'

'It's "those things" if you want to talk proper. Anyway, even white guys wear dreads these days. And my clothes are part of my act. I'm a dancer, remember.'

'I thought you worked in an office, typing. Anyway, I don't want you near my kids. And neither does Shaun.'

'It isn't catching, you know.'

'I don't know. I don't know what you might have. I don't want you drinking out of our cups.'

'I thought you might offer me a glass. Or Shaun and me might go up the pub. Brothers-in-law ought to be able to have a jar together.'

'He wouldn't be seen dead in the pub with you. What would his mates think? They might think he was one too.'

I think of the only time I've seen Shaun. At their wedding. He's a lorry driver and looks it. All those hours sitting in the cab, eating junk food at pull-ins, have thickened his waist and his arse and his great hams of hairy arms hauling on the wheel.

'I don't think there's much danger of that. Maybe the kids should get to know their uncle. After all, they've only got one and I might be able to help them one day.'

'You couldn't help yourself let alone anyone else. I don't want you touching them.'

'I'm not a paedophile, Laura. I'm into grown-up guys. Kids aren't my scene.'

'What do you want to see them for then?'

'If they're growing up like you maybe I don't.' I know I shouldn't say this but she's got to me. 'All right then, I won't come. Next question. Where's our father?' Silence.

Then, 'What do you want him for?'

She's given herself away. She knows where he is. 'You kept in touch then?'

'I thought he should see his grandchildren.'

'So you can give me his address and telephone number.'

'You find out for yourself if you want them. I'm not telling you. He doesn't want you bothering him.'

'How do you know?'

'Because he never did, did he? You was the reason he went off in the first place.'

'People change, Laura. After all, here I am ringing you up, wanting to see you. I've changed. Maybe he has too.'

'I don't want you messing things up with Dad. We get on all right these days. He's married again with kids of his own. He wouldn't want you around them neither.'

'That's for him to decide. What's he doing now?'

'Find out for yourself.' The phone is slammed down. I tip the rest of the curry onto the plate. There's no way I'm letting her ruin me dinner but she's told me a coupla things without wanting to, such as that Ray Idbury can't be living too far away from her to get to and that he can't be doing badly or she wouldn't bother. And for the first time it strikes me, really gobsmacks me, that I've fallen for somebody with the same name or almost as my skiving old man and I hope it isn't a bad omen. That's weird man, really weird.

So how do I find out where he is? I reckon my best bet for a start is back to the public library where I took Bets. I can see the pile of books we got then, in another life, and that she's been looking through them because they're scattered on the table not in a neat stack any more and one has a torn strip of paper for a bookmark. If I go round there now I can be back before she gets home. I'm almost running down the road to Lavendar Hill where the blackened red building is and into that familiar hush.

They keep the telephone books in the reference section, one for every region. Front for business, back for residential. Three six three is the one to start with, that was Reading and Nana's village in it. I try business first and Eureka, as the man said, there's Idbury Motors. Hang about, Gill. It might not be the right one. So I try the residential section and this time it has to be true. R. Idbury and an address in Bracknell with a phone number. But I'm not going to make the mistake I made with Laura. This time I won't chance a refusal. I'll just go. I scuttle home with my information like a crazy autumn squirrel who's just found a nut.

When I open the door Bets has just come in. It's strange to be just the two of us, as if we'd never been away but with our life together on hold now. We sit with the bottle between us while she updates me. I've got less to tell. Just more of the same she knows already. She tells me about the old lawyer and how he thinks she should go for it. Then she opens a drawer and takes out a lot of papers. 'This is what I've got to fill in. Some of the certificates we got the first time we went to St Catherine's House will do but I'll need others. A lot of the German stuff they want, my grandfather had already copied for me. The lawyer said I was lucky. Compared to many people it should be easy. Except he said the restaurant would be a bit of a problem because of change of use.'

'Ray's lot would really like you to go for those bastards.'

'I hope it's all right, Gill. I hope I haven't got you into something . . .'

'Nothing I can't handle. Anyway, I got myself into it. No one can get someone into something they don't want. So are you going for it?'

'I still haven't decided. I'm going to fill in the form, do all that bit and see what happens. There must be a last minute when I can step back. When he said I was lucky he meant a lot of people had nothing to go on. Everything had been destroyed, as if the people, the places and things that belonged to them, had never existed. There's a picture I want to show you. I feel it could be me. But of course the person it could really be is my grandmother.'

I look at the picture she shows me and I can see what she means but I don't know what to say. I turn the page and there's living skeletons walking about in striped pyjamas, picking their way between piles of naked dead. I shut the book and pass it back. I don't want to think that Ray's father was caught up in that in any way, even though he's told me his dad was only a kid. And besides, what can we do about it, even now when it's still all going on somewhere in the world? We have to put it behind us and go on but the pictures don't go away, and if they do there are always new ones. Heavy, man, heavy.

'How long will you stay?' Bets asks, and I know she wants to get away from it too.

'Here or there?'

'Both.'

'I'll go back the day after tomorrow. I'm going to try to track down my father while I'm here. I feel it's time. I talked to my sister Laura today and when she wouldn't tell me his address, the cow, I went and looked him up in the telephone book and bingo. Then I'll go back and stay in Berlin as long as it works out. What will you do about the room? I'll pay till the end of the month, of course.'

'I'm not worried about the money. I shan't rush to look for someone else. After all I might be as rich as Al Fayed one day. And who knows, your luck might rub off on me and send me some dishy guy.'

'What about that Mark? I think you really liked him.'

'Yes, I did. But that's history. How will you manage for dosh?'

I tell her about the modelling Ray's getting me and the dance group that's interested. All of a sudden I'm very tired and I think Bets is too. 'I need to catch up on some sleep.'

'Don't complain. I expect I'll be away before you in the morning. I've got an early start. We're shooting an interior in the old studios in Ealing. All crap stuff. I'm quite pissed off with it really. I'll see you before you go.'

Alone in my old bed I sleep like a pig and I'm glad Ray's not there to get the snorts and curried farts I'm sure I'm letting off.

230

But I'm too tired to care. Bets has gone in the morning and I take me time working out how to get to Bracknell. Bus from Victoria? I ring the coach station. Every hour, couldn't be easier. Should I dress sober or smart? I try to pitch it between the two because of what Laura said. Then I think, why should I care? He's never cared about me. Let it all hang out.

Autumn's beginning to cut in seriously now. There's waxy red and yellow berries on the trees growing on the verges and in the central reservation between the cars, that look factory-made with collars of neat leaves. Some bigger trees have huge peeling patches of bark paler than the rest, as if a giant animal's been along stripping the trunks for fun. And back from the road are the little box houses with their tidy gardens with flowers that Nana tried to teach me the names of because she knew them all and wanted me to know them too, only most of the time I wasn't listening, but one or two stuck in me head from her own garden, like goldenrod and michaelmas daisy that I can see now through the dusty coach window, all blue and gold.

I get off the bus in what reckons itself the centre of Bracknell. The ring roads stretch in all directions. It's a new town dumped down on the countryside, with acres of estates run up by spec builders going away in all directions and signposts to jolly places like the crematorium and even an arts centre. I don't know which way to begin walking. When I ask a girl in the bus office she advises me to take a taxi. 'Idbury's run a taxi service,' she says.

I've been relying on Ray Idbury going home for his lunch. Now it looks as if I'll turn up in one of his own cars. The driver drops me at a chunk of raw brick, detached, with those frilly white curtains looped across the windows. There's kids' bikes parked round the one side and the closed eyelid of a garage on the other. My stomach's going up and round like on a Big Dipper. I unlatch the white iron gate and go up the crazy-paving path. I ring the bell and hear the chimes playing 'Ding, dong, Ding dong. Ding dong.' At least it isn't 'No place like home'. A girl opens the door and looks disappointed to see me. She's blonde and pretty, about eighteen, shortie T-shirt showing a brown midriff, pale blue jeans.

'I wanted to see Mr Idbury, please.'

'Okay. Hang on. I'll get him.' She turns away. I hear her calling through the house, 'Dad, it's for you.'

A man with grey hair and a trim waist, in shirt-sleeves and a quiet tie, appears at the door. 'Yes?'

'Hallo, Dad. It's Gill.'

He hesitates for a moment wondering whether to believe me and, if he does, what to do next. He could say, 'Sorry, I don't know anyone of that name,' but he doesn't. He doesn't fall on my neck either. He looks at me square, sizing up whether he's strong enough to take me if I go for him and whether to call the police. My clothes aren't outrageous, for me at least, just a tan suede jacket and trousers with a pale lemon shirt, brown leather string tie. Cool.

'You'd better come into the lounge.' He doesn't want me left on the doorstep where a neighbour might spot me. I guess Idbury Motors isn't some crap secondhand lot, but has pretensions to being a genuine respectable business. The taxi was clean and new-ish. We go into the lounge. He doesn't ask me to sit.

'Now, first, who exactly are you, and then what do you want? I haven't much time. I have to get back to the office.'

I decide to give the guy a break, play it straight. 'I'm Gill Idbury, yours and June's son. I thought it was time we met again.' He'll think I'm stoned of course at first, and wanting money for a habit. 'I don't want anything, not money I mean. This isn't a heist. Laura told me you were married again.'

'She gave you this address.'

'No she wouldn't. I found it out myself. You see, I'm going abroad for a bit. I don't know exactly how long. I just wanted to tidy up a few ends.'

The guy looks a bit less as if he's about to jump out of the window. 'I've done my best by Laura and her family. I fix them up with a cheap car from time to time, see to the servicing, that sort of thing. I suppose I could do the same for you.'

'No thanks, all the same. My partner's got all the car I need. I just wanted to gas a bit. That was my half-sister opened the door?'

'Gemma. She's off to uni in the autumn. Sussex, I think.' I wait, listening. 'Then there's Damien. He's in France doing his second year. Their mother's out at the moment.'

'Does she know about me?' There's a pause.

'She knows that I was married before, of course, and about Laura. She had to. She had to know why I was helping them out.'

'But not about me?'

'I wouldn't have known what to tell her. It was Laura got in touch with me when . . . I'm sorry about your mother. I was very gone on her once. She was very pretty, you know, as a girl.'

'I've seen some pictures that Nana showed me and anyway I remember how she used to be when we were little. Your going off made things very hard for her. She got hard.'

'You're saying it was my fault.'

'Laura always said it was mine. It was me you couldn't stand.'

'You were a bit of a shock, I'll admit. And June wouldn't come clean with me. I thought when I saw you she'd been, you know . . .'

'Having it off with someone else.'

'That's right. She'd never say, never explain. I might have forgiven her. Started again if she'd been straight with me.'

'She was afraid of what might happen if she told you the truth. See, I might not have been a one-off. It runs in the family.'

'What do you mean?'

'My grandmother, June's mother, had a baby by a black American during the Second World War.'

'What, that old crone?'

'Who do you mean?'

'What was her name? You called her Nana, you said.'

'She was our great-grandmother. Her name was Lily. Her

daughter, Margaret, had our mother June, with the black guy. Then she went away to Australia. No one's heard from her for years. June hadn't been with anyone else. I was a throwback but still your son. There was a time I'd have wanted to take after you but I'm used to being me now.'

'I don't know what to say.'

'I thought you ought to know, that's all. I'm your eldest son as much as Laura's your daughter.'

'How can I believe you when you look so different from either of us?'

'We could have a DNA test done if you're still not sure.' I watch him struggle with this idea.

'No, no, I believe you. After all, you wouldn't be offering if you weren't sure. Was it your Nana told you all this?'

'In the end. It took her a long time.'

'She was tough as old boots. She frightened the living daylight out of me.'

'She took us in and brought up me and Laura when you buggered off.' I make this rough to shake him up a bit. He was getting too cosy with it all.

'You said you were going abroad. I could let you have a hundred towards expenses.'

'No thanks. I don't need it. I've got me return ticket and somewhere to live.' The first is a lie. The second's a half-truth.

'Where's that?'

'Berlin. I've got a couple of jobs lined up.'

'Oh. What do you do?'

'I dance and model a bit. When that runs out I go back to computers.' Why am I trying to impress the guy?

'Computers? You could probably tell me how to run my business. I thought . . .'

'That I might be an HGV driver like Laura's Shaun.'

'You're not married, I take it?'

I chicken on this one. He's had enough to take in for now. 'No, not married.'

'Best thing really for a bloke. Get all the fun without the responsibility.'

'Will you tell your wife about me now?'

'It depends. You know, it's not easy after all this time. Now if you'd been in one of the adverts, Calvin Klein or on the telly . . .'

'I've only just started modelling since going to Germany. I'll let you know if I make Calvin Klein or even Rochas. I don't expect you to come and see me dance. That probably isn't your kind of thing.'

'I'm more into a round of golf.' He looks at his watch. 'I've got to get back, I'm afraid. You won't mind if I don't introduce you to Gemma. I'll have to pick my time to tell them about it. That's if you intend keeping in touch.'

'Oh I think so now we've met up again.'

'Well at least I can give you a lift somewhere.'

'I came down by coach from London.'

'Oh you don't live local then.' Great relief.

'Not since I was twenty, even before Nana died.'

He leaves me in the lounge perched on an arm of the velvet three piece and I hear an exchange of voices away in what's probably the kitchen or even out on the patio. There must be a patio.

'Shall we go then?' He's in a hurry now in case Gemma comes in and he might have to explain after all.

He opens a side door in the hall and presses a switch, a light goes on and there's a whirring noise as the garage door rises up like a portcullis on a castle. I get into the BMW, shut the door and fasten my seatbelt. 'Nice car.'

He's backing out carefully. 'Should be. It's my business.'

As we reach the end of the short drive a little car like in those French adverts draws up. Father Ray isn't pleased. He puts the handbrake on. 'Just a minute.'

At the same time as he gets out, the other car's door opens. A woman steps onto the road and waits for him. It really is just like the adverts, man. Any minute now they'll swap cars or drive off a cliff together. The woman looks towards me. I can't hear what they're saying. She's been to the hairdressers, I can tell by the manicured look. She's slim with high heels and an imitation Gucci suit bought in the local branch of Piccolos. I flash a smile and know from her response she's susceptible to toyboys, even, or especially, with a touch of colour.

Dad comes back to the car. 'Sorry about that. I hope you haven't got a bus to catch.'

'That's okay,' I tell him. 'Any time will do.'

At the bus station he insists on pushing a few notes on me from a wad he's carrying as if plastic hadn't been invented. I'll buy Ray a present with it before I leave England and I'll stop shortening his name. On the coach back I fall asleep exhausted. We've shaken hands and he's told me to keep in touch. Last thing he wishes me luck and I have the feeling he almost wants to kiss me because I haven't given him a really hard time. But guys don't do that if they're regular blokes, not even to their long lost sons.

Betony's waiting for me when I get in. 'Would you mind if I came back with you?' she asks. 'And could we take Gran Bet?'

XXVII

Our granddaughter is back. She telephoned me yesterday from her hotel, asking when she could visit me, and when I said as soon as she liked, she said she had someone with her she wanted me to meet. I asked if she had decided what to do yet. 'Not yet.' But she has seen the lawyer in London and has the necessary forms. Apparently he told her she hasn't long to make up her mind, so this morning she came to see me. I was waiting in my chair when Christoff answered the door. This time I was prepared for the mingled pain and pleasure of seeing her, seeing you, come towards me. I had expected the dark boy to come too. I'm not sure if they are lovers, or perhaps just friends and he is the lover

236

of the blond Berliner with the car. Instead, she had a little old woman, rather bent, with her. I knew at once who it was. What shocked me was the realisation that you might have appeared like that, whereas in my mind you still look like our granddaughter and I don't recognise the old man I see in the mirror, even though I know these hands whose skin's like plucked chicken necks, and these doddering legs, are mine.

'This is my grandmother Betony, and this is my grandfather Anton.' I wheeled myself forward to shake her hand.

'How do you do, Mrs Falk. Please sit down. Would you like tea or coffee?'

She took the chair I indicated. 'Coffee would be lovely thank you.'

'Christoff.'

I felt I should plunge in at once. 'I believe I have to thank you for taking care of my son. I was very sorry to hear that John was killed in the war but I guessed something of the kind had happened when there was no answer to my letters. Then I came and found the house at Blackheath had been destroyed, which explained everything. I thought that you might all have been killed by the bomb until Betony came to see me.'

'You came to London after the war?'

'Yes. I felt, for my wife's sake as well as mine, I should try to make contact, not to take Herman away from you but simply to know what had happened to him and ask perhaps that he might be told the whole story at the proper time. I understand he never knew who his natural parents were.' I saw she was collecting herself to speak.

'When your wife brought him to me I had just lost my own baby. I think I was a bit off my head for a time. I almost convinced myself that little Herman was my Henry given back to me. I was alone when your wife came. John didn't know that we had lost our baby. I'd told nobody. Only your wife knew. She understood. She didn't tell you?'

'She told me that if Hitler invaded Britain, conquered her, that

Herman would seem to be your baby and no one need know that he was Jewish according to the Nazi laws.'

'Surely they wouldn't have tried . . .'

'The lists of those to be imprisoned or exterminated were already drawn up. They would have applied the race laws as they did or tried to do in every country they occupied. Tell me something about him. What was he like?'

'He was a very good baby – John's old nanny came back to look after him and I think he was the favourite of all her children. He was sent to prep school, of course, and then to Ticehurst. Maths was his best subject. He was a quiet boy. Maths and music. They thought very highly of him at the merchant bank he was working for when he died. He might have become chairman in time.'

'And Betony's mother?'

'She was a fellow student at LSE. He decided to go there rather than Oxford or Cambridge. He didn't want the social life. We couldn't really afford it. I had John's pension and very little else. I should have moved out of Glebe House into something smaller but he didn't want me to. As soon as he was old enough he began to take an interest in it and the family. I suppose I should have told him then but it was always somehow too late. He would have felt such a sense of loss. Then when Betony was born and her mother died I was afraid it might all be too much for him. He liked to come home to us at weekends, especially when Betony had half term or other holidays. He loved her very much but in those days it was difficult for a man to bring up a child on his own.'

'It was very fortunate that you were there.' I felt that I wasn't being told the whole story, that English reticence, polite deviousness, was drawing a curtain over some part of it. I suspect that Herman/Henry took after me rather than you, Minna. That he hadn't your courage. It was a very English life in pastel shades, as mine has been since I lost your fire that could always warm my cold heart. 'Will you let me share a little of Betony with you now that we have met?'

'I'm not a piece of cake,' Betony said, 'to be divided up between you.'

'I'm sorry. I put that badly. Mrs Falk, has Betony told you about her grandmother's, I mean my wife's, family property?'

'I don't really understand it. At first, I admit, I was rather alarmed. She tells me it won't be easy to establish a claim.'

'I haven't made up my mind yet what I'll do. It's you two who keep shaking these things under my nose. I might just want to get on with my life.'

I could see she was a little angry and then she looked even more like you. She had put us both in our place.

'I feel I should entertain you while you are here. I can order a car to take us anywhere – a tour of the city, for example.'

'What Gran Bet likes is racing, the horses.'

'Then we shall go tomorrow.'

So I am going out into the world again, Minna, like a child on a school treat. Am I becoming absurd? I showed Mrs Falk what the computer could do, hoping, I suppose, to impress her. Betony is right, although she put it more kindly. We are like two dogs with a hare, in danger of tearing her apart.

'That's all very interesting but you should try to get out as much as you can, see people you know. I think it's horribly important as we get older not to let life get away from us.'

Oh the English common sense. She went on, 'I do hope you'll make the effort to come and see me now that I've been to see you. They tell me the airlines make it very easy for people in wheelchairs. I noticed a woman being driven to the gate on a sort of trolley at Heathrow. You and your companion would be most welcome to stay and you would be able to see where Henry, and of course Betony, grew up. I think you only visited the Blackheath house. That must have been before John and I were married.'

'His mother was still living there. I remember she showed me the family portraits.'

'Do you think there's any truth in the old story about the Falks who went to Germany? I've always thought it a little far-fetched.'

'Apparently, according to my mother, there was a tradition in my father's family that this was so.'

'I think it's time I took Gran Bet off for lunch,' our granddaughter said, standing up.

'Yes, yes. I mustn't keep you now, especially when we have the races to look forward to.'

We shook hands and Christoff showed them out. I have to admire the old lady for her continuing hold on life but it makes me wonder if she really loved John. Though I have to admit that, like me, she hasn't married again. If you put our two ages together we should be contemporary with Goethe or Napoleon. Shall I go to England? Would that complete the circle and leave me nothing left to do except to die? I want our Betony, yours and mine, Minna, to claim her inheritance. That way she will continue to keep in touch with me. I am a little afraid of that country which preserved but swallowed her father, of its ability to assimilate.

I shall make a new will and I shall give her the back-up copy on disk of all I have been writing to you over the years so that perhaps she, and in time her children, may read it. I don't quite know why I didn't tell her about the second note I found in our hiding place behind the stove, which simply said, 'I will always love you. Minna. October 21st 1944.' You must have risked coming back, in spite of the Remers, to let me know you were still alive. A dangerous act that was so much you and may have led the Gestapo to you. Perhaps the children of the Remers still live there. I can't believe they themselves are alive.

By the time of your note we prisoners were starving in that camp to the north of Moscow, where the Russians had held us for nearly two years. Rain fell incessantly and the camp was deep in mud that would turn to cold steel when the first frosts came. We had taught ourselves the craft of survival that you must have tried to learn. I don't know what to wish you, this or that your ordeal was short. I've never been able to follow you on that journey because what we suffered was different in kind from what

I know you must have felt. We were starved, neglected and beaten. Every attempt was made to humiliate us, but there were no orders for our extermination, no gas chambers. If we died, it was from hunger and exhaustion or from forced labour. When we complained, the Russians simply pointed to our own atrocities. But at least we were still soldiers.

We stayed alive by stealing food or by barter if we had anything left or could steal anything to exchange for food. We organised scavenging platoons that would slip away or hang behind when we were marched out to work. As we worked in the fields we would try to pocket grains or even ears of wheat, rye or barley, half-rotten potatoes that something could be saved from, or which could be boiled for a thin soup with sometimes a cabbage leaf or a beet. Occasionally a peasant would take pity on us and give us half a soda loaf or a piece of meat fat or bone to add to our pot, then to be sucked until all the goodness had gone out of it, and lastly hammered to a powder to be boiled again. Once, a woman gave us a slice of pig's ear and a whole tail. When we found a bird that had died of cold we would pluck and add its shrivelled body and sharp bones to the mix.

That dark autumn evening in 1944 it was my turn to forage. The guards were often lax at night. They knew that deep in a hostile country we had little chance of escape. With few exceptions the people hated us unrelentingly and would have been only too pleased to let a stray pitchfork run us through. Later, when returning Russian prisoners who had managed to escape ahead of their advance brought back stories of their treatment by us, their soldiers had to protect us from the peasants when we marched out of camp, and in the fields. Any small gifts they might have made us before stopped completely.

The one whose turn it was to go on the nightly scavenge had to creep out of his hut when it was judged that the vodka had gone round enough in the guard house, and head for the place in the fence where we had managed to loosen a couple of boards at the bottom so that they could be swung to one side and then back again. I crawled through the gap, replaced the timbers, waited for my eyes to become adjusted to pick up what little light there was, then set off across the perimeter clearing into the shadowy countryside. Already the nights were bitterly cold for those whose coverings of both flesh and cloth were so meagre. I reached the edge of the field where they had begun to cut the cabbages, globes the size of a man's head. The edges of the leaves glistened with freezing dew under the clouded moon. I took out the knife I had honed from a piece of shrapnel by rubbing it on a stone, and cut two icy spheres. I wouldn't be able to carry any more. I slipped them into the poacher's pockets on either side of my coat and retraced my steps to the fence.

The two hard globes pressed into my bones through the thin cloth like cannonballs. The planks made a little scraping sound as I pushed them aside. I began to try to wriggle through on my stomach but the cabbages made my body too thick for the space. I reversed into the clearing and turned on my back. Now I could manipulate the cabbages and planks as I wormed my way back into the camp. I had been so absorbed in the tactics of my enterprise that I had forgotten the long-term strategy of caution.

The guard let me get through, draw in my feet and replace the planks before he switched on the torch, blinding me. I lay there on my back, completely helpless, prodded by the barrel of a rifle from above. I knew if I made the wrong move it would blast my face away. I held my hands above my head as I lay there. A boot thudded into me and there was a barked command in Russian. I turned onto all fours, presenting my back to him, hoping not to feel the splintering pain of a bullet in the spine. Carefully, I stood up. The guard barked at me again, prodding me with the rifle. Then he must have reversed it because I felt the flat of the butt smash into my shoulder driving me forward. I stumbled towards the guard house, trying to think what I should do and say to survive. Could I try the one about needing to shit and not wanting to use the bucket? The door was opened and I was pushed sprawling on the wooden floor. A good stove kept the other two guards warm while they played cards. They broke into loud exclamations and laughter when they saw me lying there.

The one who had caught me knocked on the far door and opened it. He was obviously explaining his catch to the officer in charge. Then he came back into the room and booted me to my feet, gesturing me with his rifle towards the door while the others laughed again. He announced me to the officer and stood back, blocking my retreat. I focused on his commander. I had seen him before, about the camp and sometimes at roll-call. I even knew his name: Karminsky. He spoke to me in German.

'Well, what have you got there?'

I opened my coat, took the two cabbages out of the pockets and placed them on his desk. The warmth of my body had thawed them a little and they were dripping mud that threatened to dirty his papers.

'Take those stinking things off my desk at once.'

I picked them up and held their freezing weight, like two green boules, in either hand. 'You know the penalty for looting?'

'Yes, sir.'

'It seems a little ridiculous to lose your life for a cabbage or even two. But those are the camp rules. You will be shot when it is light enough. I don't shoot prisoners in the dark.'

I decided to try my shaky Russian. 'Could I speak to you alone for a moment, Herr Leutnant?' He looked at me coldly. 'Why should I grant you that privilege of speaking privately to a Russian officer?'

'I too am an officer. I know that Russia doesn't adhere to the Geneva Convention on the treatment of prisoners but you take the trouble to speak to us in our own language. You are clearly an educated man. I think from what I have seen that you are not inhuman.'

'What is your name and rank?'

I saluted by clicking my heels and bowing since my hands were taken up with the cabbages. 'Anton von Falk, Major.'

243

He looked at me closely. 'I will hear what you have to say, Major.' He spoke to the guard, who saluted and left the room. 'Now speak.'

'Herr Leutnant, we are starving. It is as simple as that. There is no chance of our escaping, as you know. Germany is losing the war. Soon it will all be over. Surely it is time for a little compassion.'

'What compassion have you fascists ever shown? We have heard the stories of the concentration camps from returning prisoners and of the murder of thousands, possibly millions, of men, women and children in Poland, in the Warsaw ghetto.'

'I have never been a member of the Fascist Party.' And then, not knowing why, I said: 'I am a Jew too.'

'What makes you think I am a Jew? I don't believe you. This is some trick. I know that, unlike the Russian army where we are all comrades, there are no Jews in the German Wehrmacht. Show me your penis. Drop your trousers.'

I stood quite still. 'I am a Jew by marriage.'

'What do you mean? There is no such thing.'

'In Germany, under the race laws, we have Aryans by marriage, Jews, that is, who have Aryan marriage partners. By the same laws I believe I can in justice claim a privileged marriage. My wife is Jewish. If laws can be made to work one way they must work the other. If it isn't blood or religion that governs what a person is, then they can choose what to be. And I choose to be a Jew.'

# XXVIII

Now I've left them all – Grandfather Anton, Gill, Gran Bet – and I'm truly on my own. I'm sure it was right, as Gran Bet and I had agreed, not to say anything about how my father died. It would only have given Grandfather Anton unnecessary pain and perhaps turned him against Gran Bet. After all, what could he do with that kind of knowledge except let it sour the rest of his life. When we were doing English 'A' levels I quoted that bit about 'beauty is truth, truth beauty' in an essay on Keats. 'What do you think he meant?' Old Haggers wrote in the margin. Now I think he must have meant that beauty is more important than just facts and that all sorts of things can be beautiful, even a lie. And it gave Gran Bet a glow of superiority to think she was stronger than him, that she knew what he didn't. Her feelings of guilt were very short-lived. Soon she probably won't remember it was her carelessness, if that's the word, that destroyed my father. And I can't punish her. I was cruel to Mark, after all, and if he was cruel to me I understand why now. My cruelty was mainly ignorance. I must have driven him crazy I was so naive. When I think back on it I feel such an idiot. I could blame my upbringing, of course, that taught me so little about the real world of other people, the yuppie years when nothing seemed to matter except making money and spending it. Maybe that had something to do with all of us not wanting to think about the past any more, not wanting to feel guilty ourselves for any of it, encouraging the belief that most things are beyond our control and nothing we can do or say really changes anything.

I suppose that's why I've become a stylist. It doesn't need you to think except about the surface of things, where to place something, a shoe, a flower, a trowel, what angle of shot to choose that'll show the best side of everything. Well, I can say it cheers people up, it presents life as desirable, beautiful and accessible. 'You can have it if you really want it', as the song says. Mark's pictures were different. He'd deliberately choose a subject that was harsh, that made you question, and yet because of the angle, the composition, it was beautiful too in its rough way.

I don't know if I can go on with what I'm doing but then I don't know what else I can do. I am different. I have been changed. But how long will that last if I go on doing the same things I did before, and I don't mean just the job? I suppose it's rather like a religious conversion, Paul on the road to somewhere, as they taught us in RI. The sudden stroke, the blinding light. Well there wasn't anything like that. My mind goes round and round it all, a fly buzzing at a window, buzz, buzz, as I remember them doing when I was a kid at Gran Bet's in the school holidays, great lazy bluebottles. I'd sit up in the window seat trying to read, bored, so bored, longing for the boy to leave the harpsichord and step down out of the picture, and then the buzz would become frantic, not lazy any more, and I'd know, even without looking, that one of them had blundered into the strands of web in the corners of the panes and was trying to tear itself free before a little black spider came with its paralysing bite and bound it up in a shroud and sucked it dry. The empty cases used to lie on the windowsill like burnt currants until they were swept up. I never made any attempt to save one in case the spider caught me. I just watched.

I have to decide what I'm going to do. They all keep putting the pressure on but it's my decision in the end. None of them can make me do anything I don't want to, except maybe Minna herself. She's someone who's suddenly stepped out of her frame, more real in a way than people like Sadie that I see every day. Yet until I knew about her she didn't exist for me, wasn't part of me. And now I can never forget her. But if I don't do as Anton says she would want me to do, it will be as if I'm denying that part of me.

Would she have loved me if everything had been different, if there'd been no Hitler, no war? There's no guarantee. I would have grown up in Germany. But I can't say that because there's my own mother I know so little about, who has just as much right to be remembered. I have to find out more about her. There must be people who were at school with her, relatives even, fellow university students of both my parents.

And if I can't find anything more, if the trail ends with just her name? Then I'm left with me. The trouble is we're defined by the outside world, by how we are seen, who we think we are. The Jews must have got into the transports because they'd lost a sense of themselves. Not Minna, of course. So not 'the Jews' but some of them. I'd have done that. Accepted what I was told, how I was defined and climbed on board. That's what civilised people do. Then what I'm saying is that there has to be a point when in order to say yes you have to stand up and say no. Is that it? Heavy, man, Gill would say but he'd understand.

And where do I go from here? The church is up for sale, the Falk monuments all gone, that past my father was so proud of. Perhaps I should buy it, use the flat as collateral. Even if I never get Minna's money I could still buy it, save it from being knocked down at least. I could turn it into a gallery or a studio theatre, build it up gradually. Gill could come and dance there and Rayner show his pictures. Maybe Mark? No, that's history. I can't go back. But I won't forget either, because that's my own history, part of me, and I'll carry it with me always. I won't let it weigh me down though. I won't be caught and paralysed by what I know or what's happened to me. I'll ring those estate agents tomorrow. I hope I can still find their number.

I'll call it Minna's Place.